A VERY FRENCH SCANDAL

ANYA LONDON

Chapter 1

Evie Campbell felt his presence before she saw him. *Guess he still has that effect.* Taking a breath against the panic pounding in her veins, she braced to face the enemy.

The din of the crowded café, the savor of just-ground coffee and fresh pastries, the expansive view of the Avenue des Champs-Élysées through the wood-framed windows all disappeared. She only saw him.

He looked good, even ten years later. His shoulders had broadened, his biceps widened. The sleeves of his button-down contoured the swell of muscle beneath. A tan heightened the azure of his eyes, which glinted angrily as he prowled toward her. She had claimed a round table in the corner, but jumped to her feet at his approach. She intended to meet him toe-to-toe. He was too tall for eye-to-eye.

"You violated our agreement. France is my territory." His words vibrated with fury. He stopped close enough for her to smell his cologne. The familiar scent of wintry spruce enveloped her. Overwhelmed her. Sent a jolt of recognition through her nerve endings. He shouldn't inspire this kind of reaction in her anymore. They'd been through too much together.

Her body disagreed.

He glared down at her. "We split up regions for a reason. What the hell are you doing here?"

He had every right to be angry. Ten years ago, they had pulled up the map and divided the world to ensure that they'd never overlap again. He took France, she took Italy. He had New York in winter, she got spring and fall. He wasn't allowed to set foot anywhere west of Colorado. She was forbidden from all the southern states. The lawyers had gone country by country, and divided accordingly.

"My parents invited me to join them for vacation— I couldn't think of a reason not to go."

"We had a fucking contract. We signed on the dotted lines."

She couldn't argue. He was right—they had. She remembered every detail of that day, even if she never allowed herself to think about her time with Jackson Auclair.

"You need to be on the next flight out."

Evie crossed her arms. His eyes zeroed in on her breasts as the move shifted them higher. Uncomfortable with the heat his look generated, Evie forced her arms to drop to her sides. "You're kicking me out of all of France?"

"I'll drag you to the airport if I have to."

She tried for negotiation. "How about a compromise? You can go to Italy while I'm here."

"You took Italy to spite me."

He wasn't wrong. She had been so angry. So heartbroken. She would have taken anything he held precious.

The hurtful things they had said to each another.

The insults they'd hurled.

The accusations.

Having him so near her again brought it all back— the anger, the bone-wrenching sadness, the guilt. The guilt had been the strongest feeling of all. The physical pain from the accident hadn't even come close.

"I did," Evie agreed. "I claimed it to hurt you."

He hadn't anticipated her words, that was clear. Surprise flashed in his blue eyes. He shoved his fingers through his too-long dark tresses, as though unsure how to reply. She used to love to sink her hands in his hair, to run her fingers through his silky locks. *Whoa, Evie, now is not the time for those kinds of memories.*

"I've kept my business out of half the world because of you. You don't get to traipse in with your boyfriend now and enjoy my town."

He knew she was here with David. How had he learned that? Did he know—

As if reading the thoughts racing through her brain, his eyes dove for her hand. She hated the sudden pull to hide her ring.

"You're engaged to him." He spat out the words like an accusation. She must have imagined the hurt that flashed in his gaze.

She glanced down at her ring. It sparkled in the light streaming in through the café windows. "I am. We are going to tell my parents tonight."

He tensed as though she'd lashed him. She felt the jolt in every cell of her own body. They'd always had a strong physical connection—from the moment they had met in Nice ten years ago, they'd burned for each other. That fire had proved deadly. Something they could never repeat. Yet, the embers kindled now, came to life…

She fought hard to douse them.

She was an engaged woman. She had no business feeling anything for another man—especially for one demanding she leave an entire country.

"I'm not going anywhere," she said, though she knew that she should. She needed to take the first flight back to America. The pull that he still had on her felt too strong, like a rip current pulling her under.

He cocked his head. Dangerous calculation gleamed in his eyes. "To clarify, you are nullifying our contract."

She refused to back down. "I just want to have two weeks in France with my family and David. Aren't we ready to move on from what happened?"

His gaze narrowed. "If you choose to stay, our contract is null and void."

"What do you mean?" She desperately wished she could take a step back, but retreat wasn't an option.

"You're here, despite our deal. That means I can now go anywhere in the world."

"Where would you want to go?"

"None of your concern."

Evie thought about the repercussions. She lived in California, from which he was banned, vacationed in areas she knew would be free of him. Now, he would be able to go anywhere. *I would have no escape from the possibility of running into him.*

She must have hesitated too long because he pulled out the wooden chair and sank into it, waiting. She came around the table and sat, too. Her hands reached for the miniature cup of espresso she had been too nervous to drink earlier.

She took a sip. The espresso had long gone cold and bitter. She finished it anyway. "All right. We can remove all of the boundaries."

Triumph flashed briefly in his blue eyes, but he banked the emotion quickly. "Welcome to Paris, Mrs. Auclair."

"Don't call me that. It's soon-to-be Mrs. Barnsley now."

He didn't like that, she could tell.

"How'd you know it was me texting you to meet me here?" he asked, changing the subject.

"Who else would it have been?" She had broken their treaty, and she knew he intended to make her pay.

He watched the movement of her hand as she set down the now-empty espresso cup. "One more thing."

Her heart sped up as he scrutinized her with cold calculation. "What now?"

"Since the contract is voided, so is the NDA."

Evie closed her eyes against the panic rising through her. No one had known about their quick wedding—and quicker divorce—because his father, the French actor Valentin Auclair, had insisted on the non-disclosure agreement. She had readily signed it, not wanting any news of her very brief marriage and divorce to reach her parents. She'd been grateful for that NDA ever since.

Her new book's release date hadn't been announced yet, but he could mess with her sales if he started to run his mouth. No young adult book author should be tangled up with Jackson Auclair, owner of Zohra—the biggest sex club chain in the world.

What did he intend to do?

"You want to nullify the NDA."

"You just did, by coming to the country that belongs to me."

She tried for reason. "Can't we just take a pause? A time-out for two weeks? I haven't been on a vacation in years. David barely knows my parents. We need this trip."

Wrong thing to say. His eyes flashed. "You want me to void our agreement so that your new fiancé can get closer to your family?"

When he put it that way, it sounded absolutely illogical. She pressed on anyway. "I'm just asking for two weeks."

He appeared to consider it as his eyes zeroed in on her lips. She knew she shouldn't feel the dangerous thrill that zinged up her spine at the look. And her nipples shouldn't tighten at the small gesture.

"Fine. That will work for me. On one condition."

Her eyes narrowed. "What condition?"

"You owe me one favor. For me to call in at any point in the future."

"What kind of favor?"

"Carte blanche."

"No! What if you want something"—she dropped her voice to a whisper—"sexual?"

His gaze darkened and his voice flowed like dark honey. "I always want something sexual. But, in this case, it will be nothing of the sort."

"One non-sexual favor for my being allowed to stay in France for two weeks? And you keep the NDA in place?"

"Yes. Deal?" He extended his hand. She forgot how massive he was—his fingers engulfed hers as she let them close over her hand. She hadn't touched him in a decade, and the sheer power and heat of him scorched her. She yanked her hand out of his grip, cradling it as if burned.

Jackson Auclair had her where he wanted her. On his turf. She had agreed to the boundary removal. Played right into his hands. She hadn't even been on French soil for an hour—and he had already won. He should be satisfied with his accomplishment.

Yet as his gaze settled on his estranged ex-wife, he

knew that it wasn't enough. He wanted her, and he always got what he wanted.

He had thought he'd be immune after all these years. Had thought he'd outgrown her. One look at her proved him wrong. His dick reacted. He had to flex every muscle in his body to not reach for her and let the familiar feel of her wash over him.

His gaze raked hungrily over her features. How did she look this perfect coming off an eleven-hour flight? She had grown out her blonde hair, which cascaded over one shoulder and down to her waist in thick waves. Not a strand out of place. She looked regal and untouchable. It made him want to tangle his fingers in the silky locks and pull her close. To make her look as muddled as he felt.

He remembered how tanned she had been from their outdoor adventures across Europe. Evie appeared to prefer the indoors now. Her lashes, impossibly dark and long as always, framed her chocolate-brown eyes. She watched him warily, refusing to retreat.

He let his gaze trail lower—to the swell of her high breasts under the modest cut of her thin sweater. He remembered how responsive they were to his fingers, his mouth. He wanted to feel their weight in his palms again. He craved to taste the distended peaks.

"Are we done here?" she asked, her voice cool even as his body heated. The angry flush that overtook her pale cheeks belied her detachment.

He wouldn't let her off this easily. No other woman had ever affected him like this, had ever caused this illimitable hunger. Even ten years later, his body still wanted her.

Jackson made a decision. Her fiancé didn't matter, her feelings didn't matter. He was a selfish bastard. He flexed and unflexed his fingers as anticipation unfurled deep within him. He wanted Evie Campbell, and Evie Campbell he would have.

Her wide innocent eyes, which had once looked at him with trust and adoration, nervously darted to the café exit.

Good, let her think she could escape his presence.

He wanted his new demand to be a surprise.

Evelyn Campbell would soon be open and willing in his bed. He wouldn't settle for anything else. He'd make her regret the day she thought of herself as anyone else's but his.

Evie stumbled back to her hotel on Rue de la Paix, barely noticing the buildings around her. The crisp May air seemed too icy. The midday sun too bright. She needed the indoors. She needed quiet. She needed to think.

Reaching her hotel, Evie hurried past the lobby and into the small elevator that took her to the third floor. She could hear David's snore before she even approached their room. The long-haul flight had been too bumpy and uncomfortable for David, a light sleeper by nature. His catnap had allowed her to sneak away.

Sneak away.

I don't sneak around. That's not me. Yet, today, that was exactly what she did.

Maneuvering quietly around the bed, she made her way through the curtain-darkened room to the bathroom. Splashing cool water on her face from the cold tap didn't help. She still felt like the worst kind of human being.

She should change, come out of the bathroom, and cuddle up next to her fiancé. That would be the right thing to do. Yet her blood buzzed with guilt and anxiety and caffeine. She couldn't bring herself to lie down next to David in this state.

She could meet up with her parents, but they had arrived a day early and booked a bus tour of the city today. They wouldn't be back in the hotel until dinnertime. She wished she could call her sister, Joy, but it was four in the morning in California.

Restless, she pulled her laptop out of her bag and headed down to the lobby. She'd do what she did best when emotions and thoughts and feelings overwhelmed her—she'd write. She wouldn't think of the man who had ripped out her heart and tore her life into disposable shreds a decade ago.

With luck, she'd never lay eyes on him again.

Chapter 2

It couldn't be him.

Not here, in the middle of the crowded Parisian restaurant. Not sitting at the very same table as her parents. Evie froze mid-step. David glanced at her. His hand tightened on hers as he paused too.

His brows drew together. "Everything okay?"

No. Nothing was okay.

She couldn't breathe. Did the air suddenly get thicker? Her lungs struggled to inhale. Why had the room become sweltering-hot? The restaurant had squeezed too many people inside. Evie needed air. She needed to breathe. What the hell was he doing here? She had thought their conversation from earlier that morning had been enough.

"Evelyn?" prodded David. "You look a little pale."

"I need… I need…"

She needed to leave. She couldn't be here. She couldn't walk up to that table and pretend like he wasn't there. Like she didn't know him. As though they were strangers. What was he thinking? How was he here? He didn't know her parents. Why was he at the same table as them?

Maybe she was having a nightmare. She had never gotten around to a nap. Did jet lag cause fever dreams?

No. Oh no.

Jackson, who had been chatting amiably with her

parents, suddenly paused as if he sensed the weight of her gaze. He turned his head—glanced up—

His eyes collided with hers.

He smiled. The grin of a predator who had his prey exactly where he wanted.

She couldn't make a run for it now. It would look too pathetic—too cowardly. She'd never let him have that kind of upper hand.

Evie sank her teeth into her lip, letting the sharp pain ground her. She needed to walk up to that table, to pretend like Jackson hadn't caused the worst memories of her life, to act like nothing was wrong, to… to…

"Evelyn? Babe?" David prodded.

She dragged her gaze from Jackson to David. Sweet, reliable David. Her fiancé. He looked both confused and concerned as he stared at her, anticipating an answer.

Evie cleared her throat. "I'm fine. Just a little tired."

"You need some food in your stomach. That airplane meal wasn't much."

Evie feigned a smile. She knew that she wouldn't be able to eat a bite.

Each step that carried her closer to the table echoed in her ears and throat. She barely noticed the buzz of the restaurant. She only catalogued Jackson's clear blue eyes as he watched her approach. His cocky smirk rankled.

Her parents, following the direction of his gaze, jumped up in excitement.

No, no, no. She couldn't sit at the same table as him, couldn't pretend like her insides weren't disintegrating. The words came out of her mouth before she thought them through. "I need to wash my hands." Tugging her hand away from David, she dashed toward the back of the restaurant. David stayed to greet her parents alone.

She heard her mom's excited voice address David. "You guys made it! How was the flight? Did you settle in at the hotel okay?"

Evie hurried to seek refuge in the water closet.

Once in the small bathroom, Evie stared at her reflection in the antique mirror.

I won't let Jackson have this kind of effect on me.

I'm a grown woman now.

He means nothing to me.

Taking a few deep breaths, she stepped away from the sink. *I can't hide in the restroom forever.*

Evie moved to exit the small space. Reluctantly, she snicked the lock, opened the door.

Strong hands wrapped around her upper arms. Jackson pushed her back into the bathroom, away from prying eyes. The door swung closed, trapping them inside.

"What the hell are you doing here?" she demanded.

"Figured I'd come see why you're hiding."

"Not in the bathroom. Out there. With my parents."

"Oh. Are those your parents?" His eyes twinkled.

"You know very well that they are. What are you doing, Jackson?"

"I'm not doing anything. Your parents invited me to join them for dinner."

"They did not. They don't even know you."

"I got to know them pretty well while we were waiting for you guys. You weren't ever the type of person to be late before."

"Well, I've changed."

"You've become tardy?"

She didn't take the bait. "How did you meet my parents?"

"Funny story," he said. "Your parents just happen to know my parents."

"They know Valentin?" she asked. His dad had been so helpful after the accident—during the divorce—for them both. She'd always be grateful to him for that. He hadn't taken just his son's side. He had made sure they were both all right.

"No, they know my mother and Leonard."

His mother and stepfather. The couple who had barely acknowledged him as a child. The ones that had sent him away to boarding school in the UK. The boarding school he had begged Valentin to rescue him from, the one he had hated.

"How?" she asked. Lisa and Leonard lived nowhere near her parents.

"They moved to Coronado, imagine that. Right next to your parents."

"No, they didn't."

"A year ago."

"My parents would have told me."

"About their neighbors?"

"How do you know all this?"

He shrugged. "I make it my business to know."

"That still doesn't explain how you're here with them."

"*Surprisingly*," he said, making a mockery of the word, "Lisa and Leonard are also in France for the next two weeks. Paris and the French Riviera. They happened to be on the same flight as your parents. My parents were supposed to have dinner with me, but you know them. They can't stand me. So they invited your parents as a buffer. And here we all are."

Evie's mind reeled as she tried to process. "What are you saying? Your parents are also coming to dinner?"

"Indeed. What a coincidence."

His tone let her know that it was nothing of the sort.

Evie knew he had dipped his hand into this. She didn't know how or why, but she'd get to the bottom of it.

She and Jackson couldn't stay in the bathroom forever. At some point, someone would notice. She didn't want to explain their reason for hiding in the water closet to anyone. She wouldn't even know where to begin.

"We should go. We've been here too long."

His eyes challenged her. "I recall you used to like being locked in restaurant bathrooms with me."

A blush heated her face. She yanked open the door with more force than it necessitated. "When I was twenty-two and stupid." Not waiting for him to follow, she headed for the table.

Jackson slowed his steps as he observed her return to her family.

Evie's mother—her blonde hair and dark eyes so similar to Evie's—rushed to embrace her daughter. Her father's lanky body enveloped her slight form in a hug as well. Although he hadn't met Evie's family ten years ago, he knew that they were close. Today made that clear. The two wouldn't stop talking about their daughter, the author.

He'd been following her career. She had recently become one of the most sought-after young adult novelists with her debut series, but he never read her books. He didn't trust himself to hear the sound of her voice in his brain.

"There you are, Jackson," said Michael Campbell, gesturing to him. "Come meet our kids. Evie, David, this is Jackson Auclair… Jackson, our daughter Evie and her boyfriend, David Barnsley."

When Evie's gaze velcroed to his, her father paused, frowning. "Do you two know each other?"

"No!" Evie shook her head so vigorously he worried that her brain would bruise against her skull. "We don't."

Jackson's teeth clenched. Who was he to say otherwise? He barely knew the woman she'd become.

Her father pulled out her chair. Not David, he noted. "Jackson is a son of our good friends," Michael explained. "We realized that we're all in France at the same time and figured we could have dinner together tonight. Their son happened to be in Paris too."

David walked around the table to shake his hand. A slip of a guy. Weak grip. Sweaty temples. Not Evie's type. What the hell was she doing engaged to him?

Jackson watched David settle himself in the chair next to Evie, the seat that once belonged to him.

Her father lifted the bottle of wine he'd ordered for the table while they waited for everyone to arrive. "Wine?"

"Please." David slid his glass toward Michael, placing his hand on Evie's as he did. Jackson curled his fingers into his palms to prevent himself from leaping across the table and yanking their hands apart. *Evie is mine. She belongs to me.* The thought, one he hadn't allowed in a decade, jolted him. Evie was no longer his. Either way, she shouldn't be engaged to some asshole, another man's engagement ring sparkling on her hand.

Evie's mom, Rose, caught the direction of his gaze. Her eyes settled on David's hand clasped over Evie's. It took a moment for her to process the ring on her daughter's finger. She squealed. "Oh my God! Evie! When were you guys going to tell us?"

Evie looked confused at her mother's statement. David preened. Of course he did. Evie was way out of his league. He raised her hand to his mouth and lay a kiss across her knuckles. Jackson almost punched him square in the face. He knew he had no claim on her anymore. But she was his wife, dammit.

It pleased him to see Evie tug her hand away. She showed her left hand to her parents, the ring brilliant under the glow from the restaurant chandeliers.

Jackson gulped down his wine. He wasn't supposed to see this. His ex-wife announcing her engagement to another man. He shouldn't be there that evening, celebrating the damn thing. He refused to leave.

"What a beautiful ring! Good job, David," Rose cooed.

"Come on," Michael piped in. "Tell us how you did it."

Jackson's curiosity made his ears prick up. He didn't want to hear the story, yet he couldn't make himself walk away.

As David launched into the details of his Manhattan Beach restaurant proposal, Jackson's blood sizzled and boiled. David had planned out every step of his proposal, a far cry from his own proposal to Evie. It had been a brash decision, a quick demand. She had agreed instantly.

Gripped by a red anger he couldn't explain, Jackson pushed back his chair. He needed air. He couldn't listen to another moment of this celebratory conversation, which made his blood run like black sludge in his veins. Evie's parents peppered her and David with questions.

As he stood, Evie glanced up.

Jackson opened his mouth to make a quick escape.

No such luck.

"Baby, how do I look?"

Shit.

Chapter 3

Tilly Harvey's breathy voice cut through his plans. She must have finished her hair appointment early. He turned at the sound of her voice. She looked perfect as always, with her lustrous hair and golden tan.

Her appearance interrupted David mid-sentence, and he gave his full attention to the newcomer.

Jackson's gaze flew to Evie. Saw her zero in on the hand that Tilly laid across his bicep.

Flashing her perfect white teeth at the group, Tilly gave a small wave before tucking her hand in the crook of his arm. "Hi, I'm Tilly. Jackson's girlfriend."

"Oh, how lovely to meet you. Join us," Rose insisted.

"Would you like some wine?" Michael raised the bottle.

"I'd love some," Tilly murmured, sliding into the chair next to Jackson. When he sat back down, she settled her hand on his thigh.

Accepting the glass of wine from Michael, she took a sip. "So, how do y'all know Jackson?"

"We should have started with that!" Rose made the quick introductions, running through everyone at the table.

"It's very nice to meet y'all." Her eyes lifted to his. "Are your parents on their way?"

His jaw tensed at the question. The last people he needed at this over-crowded table were Lisa and Leonard Icefall. "Not yet."

Tilly's shiny red nails curved into the denim of his jeans. "I can't wait to meet them," she murmured low into his ear.

He wanted to shove her hand away, to tell her to stop. Her touch was all wrong. As Evie's gaze danced over Tilly, Jackson felt like a cheater. Regardless of the fact that he and Evie had finalized their divorce years ago.

Tilly was a beautiful girl, but the feelings she stirred in him were a cheap replica of the connection he had shared with Evie. Not that it mattered. He brought Tilly to be a pleasant distraction, one he'd desperately need even more once his mother and stepfather joined the dinner.

Rose smiled widely at the newcomer. "Tell us how you two met."

Evie wanted to scratch the woman's eyes out. Tilly, with her hair extensions and fake tan and too-white veneers, cuddled up close to Jackson as she shared details of their first encounter.

Evie knew her reaction was unjustified. Her fiancé sat next to her, held her hand in his. The weight of her engagement ring stung like freezer-burn on her finger. Evie felt like the scum of the earth. How could she be jealous of Jackson when her handsome, kind, reliable fiancé sat at her side?

What am I doing?

This isn't me.

She leaned closer to David. Maybe the familiar feel of him would stop these wild reactions clawing through her, would remind her that she was an engaged woman and loved her fiancé.

Evie didn't allow her brain to compare the two men, who looked so physically different. David was the opposite of Jackson. That's why she chose to commit to him, had agreed to marry him. Comparing her ex-husband to him now would be deeply unfair. She refused to do it.

Her gaze slid back to Tilly. If that's who Jackson now went for, that was his business. He was free to date anyone he wished.

Something behind Evie captured Jackson's attention. His face lost all trace of emotion. Evie turned.

The couple walking toward their table must be his parents. The ones who had wanted nothing to do with him as a child.

He looked remarkably like his mom, with her brilliant blue eyes and dark hair. His stepfather followed close behind, speaking into his phone. As they stopped at their table, he ended the conversation but didn't tuck away the cell.

"Glad you're all here. Sorry we're late," said Leonard, flashing a bright smile at everyone but Jackson.

Neither parent much acknowledged Jackson, Evie noted. They introduced themselves to her and to David, made a mild attempt at a hello to Tilly, and settled in to talk about their day. Neither one had greeted their son. They seemed to disregard him completely.

Against her own volition, her eyes met Jackson's familiar gaze. Her heart began to pound against her rib cage. How did he always have this effect?

Looking away, she took a generous sip of wine.

She knew he watched her as she swallowed.

His determined focus unnerved her.

***

A sense of resolute calm entered Jackson's body as he observed Evie anxiously set down her glass. Good. She should be nervous. Because he was about to turn her life upside down.

Seeing her with David, seeing David kiss her hand, had cemented his decision.

She'd hate him forever.

He was okay with that.

He didn't need her love. He had no love to give. It had burned away in the crash a decade ago. He would never let himself be that defenseless again.

He wanted Evelyn Campbell's body, and that's what he would have. He would work the unanticipated itch for her from his system, and never set eyes on her again.

Chapter 4

Evie barely tasted the food. She couldn't even recall what she'd ordered. Everything tasted as bland and dry as cornstarch. Sitting across from Jackson and Tilly blistered her veins. She couldn't focus on anything else but the caustic acid in her bloodstream.

Her parents and their new neighbors chattered excitedly about France, making plans for tomorrow. Lisa and Leonard had checked into the Ritz just across the street from the hotel she and her parents had booked, but Tilly and Jackson had reserved a room in their exact hotel. Evie knew enough about Jackson to recognize that it wasn't a coincidence. The man left nothing to chance.

Cheese and dessert followed dinner, but she didn't have the strength to stay and face her ex-husband and his new lover.

"I'm exhausted," she finally offered. "I'm going to head back to the hotel."

David, a homebody and introvert, looked relieved to follow. Meeting new people was never his idea of a good time.

As they reached their hotel room, he held open the door for her. "Want to shower first?"

Her phone pinged in her purse, distracting her from his question. She tried to focus. "You go ahead. I'll shower after you."

Heart hammering, she pulled out the device and looked at the screen. *Please be anyone but Jackson.*

No such luck.

The unknown number she knew to be Jackson taunted her. She refused to save it into her phone.

Opening her messages, she read his missive.

Meet me at the lobby bar.

Fat chance. He didn't get to order her around. She and her fiancé were about to put on their pjs and slide into bed.

She didn't reply.

Two minutes later, as she heard David sing off-key in the shower, her phone pinged again.

You come down here. Or I come to you.

Well, that wasn't an option.

We'll talk tomorrow.

His response was instant.

Downstairs bar. Now.

He had never been this demanding before. She remembered the playful Jackson from a decade ago. She'd have never married this intense Jackson. He had no right telling her what to do. She typed out a reply.

I will see you tomorrow.

It took two minutes for the knock to sound.

The insistent rapping echoed through the European-sized hotel room.

She had no doubt that Jackson stood on the other side. What was his problem?

Evie listened to see if David heard the visitor. When she didn't hear the water in the shower pause, she assumed he hadn't. Good. Evie needed to get rid of Jackson as quickly as possible.

She opened the door a few inches. There he stood, imposing and handsome and irritated.

His jaw twitched. "I gave you a choice."

"This isn't a choice. What do you want?"

He tried to glance beyond her shoulder. "Let me in."

She refused to budge. "No. Why are you here?"

"You and I need to talk."

"I don't have anything to say to you. Haven't had anything to say to you in a decade. Go away."

"I have something to say to you, and you'll want to hear it."

She let out an exhausted sigh. "What do you want from me?"

"It's not something you'll want your fiancé to hear."

Evie glanced behind her. She still heard the water running. David loved a luxuriously long shower.

"Fine." She grabbed the key and joined him in the hall. "Tell me out here."

He glanced at the door to her right.

She followed his eyes. "I'm not hiding in a stairwell with you."

"You never minded before."

She crossed her arms over her chest in frustration. "Just fucking tell me."

"Tsk, tsk. Not seemly for a pastor's daughter to swear."

"I don't have time for this, Jackson."

"I suggest you make time." He swung open the door to the back stairs, waiting for her to precede him.

She huffed in frustration, but marched into the secluded space. "Now can you tell me why you're bothering me in the middle of my evening?"

"You are breaking up with David tonight."

Evie laughed. He hadn't expected that. She threw back her head and roared. "Are you high? That's not going to happen. Now if you'll excuse me." She tried to move past him.

He blocked her.

He wasn't done with her yet.

She raised a brow.

He didn't budge.

"Did you have your fun yet? Can I get back to my fiancé?"

"Ex-fiancé."

"Why don't you stop focusing on David and me and focus on you and your girlfriend instead. What's her name? Tilly? Where'd you pick her up anyway? A soap opera audition?"

He grinned. She wasn't wrong. She had been one of the performers auditioning for one of his evening shows at Zohra Charleston. She had been flexible. He had been impressed.

"She's taking a bath."

"Go bathe with her. I need to get back."

He knew it was time to tell her. He wouldn't have her undivided attention otherwise. He needed her fully at his mercy.

"I haven't made myself clear. I'm not here to argue over this with you. You need to end it now."

"Why?"

"Because I'm going to fuck you and I don't share."

Chapter 5

The statement shocked Evie, he could tell. Her eyes widened. Her skin flushed. Her brows jumped, then furrowed. Suddenly, she looked ready to scratch out his eyeballs. "You're never touching me again. Are you delusional?"

"I want you. You still want me too."

"I don't want you at all."

Liar.

He took a step toward her. She hopped away like a frightened parakeet. He didn't pause, taking another step until he had her where he wanted her. Backed into a corner. The wall stopped her retreat.

He reached out his hand, intending to cup her cheek, to prove to her that she wanted him too. She blocked his progress with her hand. "Stop it."

She ducked under him and beelined for the exit, her hand reaching for the handle. He countered her attempt by pressing his palm to the door, holding it closed. The position placed him dangerously near Evie.

His body tightened at the heady scent of her tropical perfume. She had twisted her hair up in an intricate bun for the evening, but a few tendrils had escaped and tickled the nape of her neck. He wanted to put his mouth there and feel her warm heat against his lips.

Careful not to touch her, he leaned in closer.

"Do you remember that video we made?" he drawled against her ear.

She froze. Her hand dropped away from the door handle.

He watched her inhale sharply at his reminder. Slowly, she turned. Her accusing eyes met his. "You said you had deleted that almost instantly."

"I lied."

"Where is it?"

"In a safe place. You don't want it getting out, do you?"

"Are you blackmailing me?" Her voice rose with the question.

"Shh. You don't want David to come looking for you here. How would you explain this?"

"As blackmail." She crossed her arms again, a protective gesture. "What do you want from me, Jackson?"

He couldn't help but let his gaze drop to her breasts. "I want to fuck you."

"Out of the question. I'm engaged."

"I know. And you're not a cheater. That's why you're going to march back into your room and break it off with Barnsley."

"I will do no such thing. He and I have dated for six months. He just proposed. I'm not going to do that to him."

"You and I both know you'd never do it behind his back, so what's the alternative?"

"Give me the recording."

He shrugged. "No can do."

He saw the panic in her eyes. He knew to sting exactly where it hurt. She'd always been concerned about appearances. The pastor's daughter, she cared about what people thought. He never did. The disparity had been the source of their loudest arguments. Even if she had learned to disregard her concern about people's opinions, her latest book would soon be released and she'd never allow the bad publicity. He knew that he had her where he wanted her. And she knew it too.

Anger radiated from her body. He could see her shake with it. If she had been prone to violence, she'd have attacked him by now. But she had been raised the perfect young lady—the perfect young lady he had once enjoyed corrupting—and she didn't lash out. She just stood there, her chest rising and falling in desperate heaves, her eyes glued to the ground. Like she couldn't bring herself to look at him.

"I want that tape destroyed."

"It will be. As soon as you agree to dump Barnsley. And join me in my bed."

"What about Tilly?"

"What about her?" he asked. Satisfaction began to unfurl within him. She had asked a legitimate question. It indicated she was considering his proposition.

"You have a girlfriend. You're not a cheater either."

"You don't know anything about me anymore."

"You'd expect to fuck me and to fuck her in the same day?"

"Unless you'd let me do it at the same time."

The sudden sting surprised him. She had slapped him. Sweet, proper Evie had lashed him across the face. He deserved it.

"Let me out of here," she said, face so red it was almost purple. "You were a decent guy once. You're disgusting to me now."

"I meant what I said. I will release the video if you keep saying no. How would that look? Pastor Michael

Campbell's daughter, the young adult novelist Evie Campbell, making a sex tape with a sex club owner."

"I hate you."

"I don't need you to feel anything else for me. I need you to agree."

She was breathing so hard that he was afraid she was going to hyperventilate.

"Show me the tape," she demanded.

"Fine. Come to my room."

"You really never deleted it, did you? I can't believe I trusted you."

"Never trust anyone—life's safer that way."

"So let me get this straight. You want me to break it off with my fiancé and have sex with you once, and you'll make the tape disappear? Delete it for good?"

He shook his head. "No, not once. For as long as I want you."

He let the statement sink in.

Tears gathered in her beautiful eyes. "Why are you doing this to me?"

Seeing her cry cut him to the bone. She'd spent days sobbing in the hospital bed ten years ago. It had broken him inside. Seeing her cry now brought back that memory. He hated himself. He didn't back down.

"Come on," he coaxed. "I'm not asking for that much. You're not even in love with your fiancé."

"I am in love."

"No, you're not. You two haven't even slept together."

"How do you know that?"

"I have my ways. You two have been dating for six months. He just proposed—probably trying to get you into bed. I know you. You don't love him."

"You don't know me at all."

He didn't offer anything more. Waited for her to speak.

After a tense minute, she swallowed. Her gaze never met his. "I'm not saying yes. I want the full picture of what you expect though so that we're on the same page."

He tamped down the exultation at her words, tried to keep his voice steady. "That sounds reasonable."

"You want me to dump my fiancé and have sex with you for however long you want while you still have your girlfriend."

"Tilly can go. She and I met a few weeks ago. I'm not set on keeping her."

His callousness surprised her, he could tell. Her eyes slammed to his, searching. He let her look. She'd never see through the impenetrable shield he had learned long ago to enact around himself.

Her tongue slid across her lips. A nervous gesture. "I'm not saying yes, but were I to agree, I'd have some stipulations."

He leaned back against the doorframe. "Go ahead. Let's hear them."

"There has to be an end date."

"A month."

"A week."

"Two."

"Fine."

"You leave France in two weeks anyway."

"But I go to Nice with my parents in a few days. I guess I can stay in Paris until the two weeks are up."

"I've already made arrangements to join you. Showing my parents around the French Riviera and all."

She processed the statement, but didn't question it. "No one can know," she said instead.

He mimicked her earlier response. "Fine."

"You'll destroy the recording and any copies immediately."

"Done."

"And you can't sleep with anyone else if I were to agree."

"Trust me, I plan on fucking you morning, noon, and night. I won't have the time or the energy for anyone else."

Her eyes glazed over, as though she was picturing what that morning, noon, and night would look like. She caught herself quickly. Shook her head, as if dislodging the images from her mind. "Is there anything else you want instead? Money? I'll transfer my house to you. I'll move every penny in my savings account to you. I'll do anything but what you're asking me to do."

"I don't need your money. All I want is your full surrender for the two weeks you're in France. You. Willing. And the tape is destroyed."

The tears came then. Big, round ones rolling down her cheeks. They soaked the top of her shirt. Her shoulders shook with the effort to contain her weeping.

He hated this. He hated seeing her cry. Her tears ripped through him. He had to curl his hands into fists to prevent himself from taking a step toward her, from reaching for her.

He wished he were a better man. A man who'd back away. Apologize. Soothe her.

He wasn't that man.

He wanted her in his bed, and he always got what he wanted.

She wiped at her eyes. "I need time to think."

Triumph rolled through him. He knew he had her. He knew she'd say yes.

"Go ahead," he allowed. "You can take the rest of the evening. I want an answer first thing tomorrow, or the tape goes live on every streaming platform imaginable."

"Tomorrow morning is too soon. The day after tomorrow."

"Tomorrow night then. Final offer."

She gave him a brief nod. "Okay. Tomorrow night."

Chapter 6

When Jackson left, Evie sank to the cold stone step of the empty stairwell and cried into the palms of her hands. She wished she were crying because she didn't want to do this. She was crying because she did. But how could she want him after everything that had happened between them? It was absolutely preposterous. They were both mad—him for insisting, her for considering. No good would come of it.

When she had exhausted her tears, she wiped her nose with the sleeve of her sweater, since she had nothing else at hand.

She couldn't appear back in her room in this state. How would she explain it to David?

Wiping at the fresh tears that welled, she headed down to the lobby. She'd take a walk to calm down.

She strolled blindly down the streets of Paris. How stupid had she been to let him record them? How dumb had she been to trust him? She had been twenty-two—old enough to know better.

Now he had her pinned to a crossroads, and she didn't know which way to go.

On the one hand, she couldn't let that tape go public. It would destroy her fledgling career as an author. Her first two books had been wildly successful, allowing her to fully pay off her parents' mortgage, cover her aunt's knee surgery, and pay for Joy's medical school tuition. Were sales to stop or slow, she wouldn't have money to cover her own mortgage, much less Joy's school bills.

Were the tape to go public, her father's career would be destroyed too. Her dad was head pastor at the Coronado Reformed Church. Who would allow him to keep that job once they heard about his daughter's exploits? She couldn't let his world fall apart because of her. Her mom wouldn't be able to face her friends, to ever show her face in their community again. They'd want to leave the state. Maybe even the country. It had been her mistake to make that tape. She couldn't let it destroy her parents' world.

Yet, on the other hand, how could she break it off with David? Sweet, solid David. When she had told him that she wanted to wait to sleep with him, he hadn't argued or pressured her. Instead, had ungrudgingly agreed. Even proposed some six months later.

She may not love David with the same all-consuming passion that she had once felt for Jackson, but she cared for him in a different way. She loved that he made her feel safe, that he never caused any strong feelings in her. He had always been a steady influence. How could she betray him like this?

Never caused any strong feelings…

Evie stopped walking.

None at all.

Realization dawned. She had agreed to marry David because she loved that he inspired no emotions in her.

How was that fair to him?

Even if she blew up her life and let Jackson release that video, she still couldn't be with David. She couldn't do that to someone as loving and gentle as him. She had lost her ability to love in the car crash that awful summer, and David deserved to find someone who loved him as much as Evie had once loved Jackson. As much as Jackson had once loved her.

Evie glanced around. Where had she walked to? Night had fallen like an inky blanket, the air cold and fresh against her skin. She hadn't brought a jacket, and the wind nipped at her exposed skin. She had barely noticed the temperature drop until then.

No matter what she decided to do about Jackson's blackmail, she couldn't snare David into a loveless marriage. She owed it to David to break it off.

But now? In the middle of Paris? *Better to do it now than to pretend for two more weeks, and then blindside him back in the States.*

She'd refund his flight, of course. Give back the ring. Hating herself for what she had to do, she set a determined path back to the hotel.

And she cried all the way there.

When she returned to their room, David had the television on, some French show, as he read a book under the covers. Seeing her tear-streaked face, he sat straight up. "Evie, honey, are you okay?"

She shook her head. "No. Not really. Can we talk?"

A hint of wariness entered his face. "What about?"

Evie hesitated. Taking a deep breath, she strode toward the bed and sat on the edge. "Do you remember when we talked about first loves?"

His voice sounded cautious as he replied. "I do."

"And I told you about mine? The boy I met in Europe?"

"That was him today, huh? I knew there was something between you. Could see it instantly."

There's nothing between us, she wanted to argue, yet now wasn't the time or the place. Needing to explain, she reached out her hand, placing it on his thigh over the blanket. "David—"

He covered her hand with his. "Do you want to be with him?"

"No, of course not."

"I saw how he looked at you at dinner. He still wants to be with you."

"He doesn't. He definitely doesn't."

"Do you want us to leave? Was that too much today? I can change our flights back to the States."

The ring lay too heavy and too cold against her finger. It didn't belong there.

She twisted it off.

Understanding dawned in David's kind eyes.

"I'm so sorry," she said. "David, you deserve so much more. You deserve everything, David. I—"

He kicked off the blanket, crawling from under the covers to sit right next to her, hip to hip, on the edge of the bed.

"Evie, it's okay." He wrapped his arm around her shoulders. "I also felt like something was missing. I just… I guess I didn't have the guts to bring it up myself."

Hot tears leaked from her eyes. He pulled her close, kissing the top of her head. "You deserve everything too, you know."

She smiled into his shoulder. "I had it once. Don't think I want that kind of love ever again." Reaching for his hand, she dropped the ring into his palm.

He closed his fingers over the diamond. "I better go."

She glanced at the night outside the window. "No, don't leave. It's so late. Stay the night."

He mulled the decision over before agreeing. "Fine. First thing tomorrow, though, I find a hotel, turn this trip into a solo one." He moved back to his original spot on the bed. "Want to watch something?"

Evie nodded, wiping the tears from her eyes.

"They're showing a *Friends* rerun in French on another channel. I can put that on."

She reached over and kissed his cheek. "You know me well."

David made room for her next to him. Tucking herself into the crook of his shoulder, she settled against David as he flipped the channel to their favorite show.

She didn't know if she'd agree to Jackson's deal.

She still had a whole night and day to consider it.

Either way, she'd wait until the last second to share her decision.

Let him dangle. Let him squirm.

Whatever she decided to do, she swore that she'd make Jackson Auclair pay for betraying her like that. She'd find a way to ensure that he regretted the very day he decided to blackmail her.

Chapter 7

"You animal! I hate you! How dare you do this to me! And in Paris?! In the middle of our vacation? After you introduced me to your parents?!"

The screeching didn't stop.

"Is that… Tilly?" asked Evie, though she recognized the voice. Her parents and the Icefalls, who'd made the short walk from the Ritz that morning, were already seated for breakfast when she and David joined them in the glassed-in atrium that housed the hotel restaurant. White tablecloth-covered tables lined the black-and-white-checkered floor. Despite the early morning, every table was full. The chatter of voices, all speaking a plethora of languages, and the clinking of silverware filled the space, but didn't drown out Tilly's yelling.

The waiter, an older gentleman with salt-and-pepper hair, handed them their menus. He enunciated over the loud fighting in the lobby as he took David's and her drink orders. They both asked for coffee.

As the waiter stepped away, her mom leaned across the table. "They've been going at it all night."

"Yelling, screaming, throwing stuff," added her dad. "Their room isn't even that close to ours, but they raised such a raucous, the entire hallway shook."

Leonard frowned. "That's going to cost a pretty penny."

"You heard them all the way in your room?" Lisa asked.

"Yes!" Her mom took a sip of her cappuccino. "Especially when she started to toss what sounded like furniture."

Lisa tsked, and reached for her latte. "Must have been really bad." She turned to Evie and David. "Did you hear any of it?"

Evie shook her head.

"We were waiting for you all to get here to order food," said her dad. "But now I don't think we should wait for Jackson or his girl."

The phrase stabbed Evie straight into her stomach.

"I hate you!"

Every single diner turned toward the lobby at Tilly's screech. That decibel must be universal.

Jackson and Tilly had moved their fight closer to the restaurant doorway. Evie craned her neck to catch a glimpse of them through the large entryway. Jackson, still in last night's clothes, looked annoyed and utterly exhausted even from a distance. He rolled what appeared to be Tilly's two very large suitcases.

"Did you hear what I said? I hate you!" Tilly repeated, tottering behind him in her high heels. She grabbed a stack of magazines from a side table in the lobby and hurled it straight at him.

The air resistance didn't let them go far. They fluttered to the ground, not quite reaching Jackson. Not satisfied, Tilly reached for an ornate vase next. Evie didn't know much about pottery, but it looked old and expensive. She hurled it straight at Jackson. He dodged the hit, and it crashed to the floor, breaking apart with a cacophonous clatter.

Jackson, leaving the suitcases, stormed toward her. He loomed over Tilly, but didn't touch her. "Get yourself together." The growled command reached every diner in the restaurant.

"Get away from me!" shrieked Tilly, shoving at Jackson.

Scintillated, everyone from the breakfast room stretched their necks to see. The hotel manager, a statuesque blonde woman in maybe her mid-fifties, quickly clicked her way toward them in her heeled pumps from somewhere beyond Evie's eyesight.

"May I help you?" she asked in English.

"Yes!" Tilly demanded instantly. "Tell this asshole he's a moron."

The woman glanced between her and Jackson. "May I ask you to please keep your voices down? Or I'm going to have to ask you to leave the premises."

The security guard approached next.

"Everyone just leave me alone!" screamed Tilly. She turned to Jackson. "I hate you!" She walked around him, grabbed her two suitcases, and jerked them angrily toward her. "You'll regret this, Jackson. I swear to you! You'll come crawling back to me, begging for forgiveness. I can't wait for that day. You jackass."

With that final word, Tilly left, rolling her gigantic suitcases through the glass hotel doors.

"Apologies, everyone," said Jackson to the lobby and restaurant at large.

A few guests had taken out their phones to record the interaction.

Evie settled back in her seat. She and David exchanged a glance. His gaze seemed too insightful. It implied things. Evie didn't like it.

"He broke up with his girlfriend," observed David in a mild tone close to Evie's ear.

"It's not what you think," she whispered back.

Nevertheless, her heart raced. Jackson had broken up with Tilly before she gave him her answer. Was he that confident that she'd agree to his proposition? She hadn't agreed to his terms. Wasn't even sure if she would. So why the hurried breakup?

The entire dining room seemed to hush as Jackson made his way toward their table. He pulled out a chair.

"Always making an entrance," grumbled Leonard, his eyes scanning the menu, before Jackson could sit.

"Was that necessary?" Lisa stage-whispered at her son. "You made a scene in front of all these people. In front of our friends."

Evie chewed her lip. Jackson and his mother and stepfather had always had a tense relationship, from what Jackson had shared with her. Seemed like not much had changed.

Ice glittered in Jackson's eyes. He didn't offer an explanation, nor did he sit. Just shoved the chair back under the table. "I'll let you have your breakfast in peace."

Evie found it impossible not to peek at him. He looked gaunt in the morning light, like he'd been up the entire night. Dark circles shadowed his bloodshot eyes. A small part of her wanted to reach out and smooth the hair from his brow, but she squashed the impulse. That reflex didn't belong in her brain. She shouldn't be thinking about Jackson at all.

She tucked her left hand under her thigh. She didn't need him noticing her lack of engagement ring. Just because she and David broke up didn't mean she'd leap straight into Jackson's bed.

"Have a nice day, Jackson," Evie said, dismissing him.

His face remained impassive. He stepped away from their table, leaving a hollow silence in his wake.

After Lisa and Leonard Icefall left to get ready for the river cruise they had booked, Evie and David broke the news of their breakup to her parents. Rose and Michael had been disappointed but understanding. David packed up and departed the hotel a half hour later, leaving Evie in the room by herself.

The ping of her phone interrupted the silence.

T-12 hours. Tape gets released at midnight.

She threw the phone to the bed. She couldn't believe she had loved him once. She didn't recognize this ruthless blackmailer.

Could she let him release that recording? Could she let her parents' entire life be flipped upside down? Their congregation would shun them. Her mother would lose all her friends. Joy would have to take on hundreds of thousands in student loans. All because of her and her stupid, stupid mistake.

If she said yes to his extortion, could she live with herself? Giving her body away for two weeks to a man she hated? One who was responsible for the thick callous that had formed around her heart, making it impossible for her to love anyone again?

Did she have any other alternative?

Her parents' and sister's lives as they knew it were on the line. Her own career and reputation as well.

Evie grabbed her purse and headed out the door. She and her parents had tickets to the Louvre. She'd tell Jackson her decision that evening—and not a moment sooner.

Let him squirm.

He found her in the Louvre.

Her phone vibrated with the text message in her purse.

Meet me at the Venus de Milo.

Her parents, still glued to the Mona Lisa on the second floor of the Denon Wing, didn't even notice her breaking off and finding her way to the quieter Sully Wing of the museum.

A few tourists ambled by as she approached the statue.

"Where's Barnsley?" Jackson asked. He came up behind her, only stopping when he was close enough for her to feel the heat radiating from his body. She turned to face him.

Might as well tell him. "David and I broke up."

He didn't show surprise. Not that she could read him well anymore. She had trouble reading him even years ago. Since then, he'd learned to completely school his features. His gaze appeared impenetrable.

His voice sounded low and dangerous in the cavernous room. "Are you agreeing to my proposal?"

"To your blackmail you mean?"

"Call it whatever you want. I need your answer."

"I am still thinking about it… I have until this evening. We had a deal."

"I'm an impatient son of a bitch."

Evie refused to budge. "I'm on a family vacation. My parents are in Paris with me. What would you have me do? Ditch them so I can go…" *Screw you*, she wanted to say. The words wouldn't leave her mouth.

He considered her. "Let's talk this out. What are your hesitations?"

As a group of visitors milled closer to them, she moved away from the sculpture. Seeking privacy, she headed to the adjacent gallery, one devoid of visitors. Jackson followed. She kept her voice low. "My hesitation is that you want me to prostitute myself to save my reputation."

He leaned close, his minty breath washing over her face. "It's not like we haven't fucked before."

"That was different."

"Yes. It was."

Evie glanced around, making sure no one eavesdropped. "If I were to do this, I want some ground rules."

"Name them."

"No kissing."

His reply came instantly. "Denied."

"Excuse me?"

"Denied. I need you willing. If I can't kiss you… it makes it seem… transactional. Like I'm forcing you."

"It is transactional. You're making me exchange my body for your deleting the video."

"Think of it as a… reunion. A way for us to screw each other out of our systems."

"We can discuss the kissing later. No doing it in… bed."

He offered a small nod. "No bed. That's fine. I can be creative."

"The geographic boundaries you and I had worked out ten years ago resume back after these two weeks. You stay out of all the places you had to stay out of before."

He puffed out his broad chest. "No. You voided our contract with your visit. Now I can go anywhere I want."

Dammit. She couldn't live in fear of running into him on a random Tuesday afternoon. "At least keep out of California. I can't go about my life worried I'll run into you."

"California can remain yours. But the kissing stays."

"No. No beds. No California. No kissing. Those are my stipulations. Tape is destroyed before our deal begins."

He appeared to consider it. "Fine."

She met his eyes in the filtered light of the museum. She'd be lying if a frisson of excitement didn't run through her. *What am I doing? I shouldn't be aroused by this. I should be angry.*

He stepped close to her. The familiar scent of him surrounded her. She had forgotten how overwhelming his sheer presence could be. Her heart thumped in her ears as his intent gaze settled on her face, skimmed to her lips, focused there. Her tongue moistened the anxiety-parched surface of her lower lip. His eyes darkened as he followed its trail.

"I'll see you tonight. Remember my stipulation. Willing and ready."

I'll find a way to make you pay.

Chapter 8

Evie tried to put Jackson out of her mind as she and her parents explored the city, strolling from the Louvre to the Place de la Concorde and the Arc de Triomphe. Her body refused to listen. She barely noticed the Tuileries Gardens, her once-favorite place in Paris. Her brain didn't take in the kaleidoscope of the blooming flower beds and the neatly lined green chairs around Vivier Sud. As she and her parents left the Gardens to walk along the Seine, she didn't absorb the sights and sounds of their walk nor the taste of the crepes that they bought and ate along the bank.

Evie and her parents returned to the hotel soon after dinner. Shutting the door to her room, she video called Joy. Her sister answered on the first ring, headphones in place. Evie recognized the coffee shop she was in.

"Are you busy?"

"Just grabbing a snack before class. What's up? How's Paris?" Joy said the last word with an exaggerated French accent. "Are Mom and Dad bonding with David?"

"Guess who's here."

Joy understood immediately. "No! Jackson? What are the odds? I thought he lived in Charleston now. I figured you'd be okay for your trip."

"He texted me as soon as I landed."

"You talked to him?"

"I saw him. In person."

"How was it? Are you okay?"

"I don't think I'm okay. I broke up with David."

"Good."

"What?" Evie frowned, confused by Joy's response.

"David is a nice guy, but I would've given your marriage a year. You two just don't seem that excited to be in each other's company. Did you break it off because of Jackson? Are you two back together?"

"No! Of course we're not back together."

"So you didn't break up with David because you saw Jackson and realized you're still madly in love with him?"

Evie raised a brow. "You should cut down on the rom-coms you read."

"But I'm in med school. They're the only joy I have in life."

"David and I broke up, but Jackson's mom and stepdad are apparently friends with Mom and Dad."

"Since when?"

"Recently, I think. They're here too."

"Sooo… you're in Paris with Mom and Dad, your ex-husband, and his parents?"

"Yes."

Joy sank into a nearby seat. "How did this happen?"

"I don't know! I think Jackson had something to do with it."

"Awwww. He wants you back." Joy placed a hand over her heart.

"He doesn't want me back. But he does want to sleep with me."

Her sister gasped in sheer delight. "He told you that?"

"He's made it very clear."

"Are you gonna do it?"

"It's complicated."

Joy rolled her eyes. "Sure, sure. Soooo complicated." She stood. "I have to go. I have ten minutes before class starts. I'm going to need a play-by-play later."

"You're not getting one."

"Oh, come on!"

"Bye, Joy."

"Tell Jackson I said hi!"

Evie would do no such thing. She wished she had never introduced Joy to Jackson that long ago summer. The impression he'd made on her sister had never wavered.

She glanced at the time on her phone. Crap. She had an errand to run, and time was running out. She grabbed her purse and headed to the French lingerie shop she had spotted on the corner earlier that day.

Stepping out of the store less than ten minutes later, branded store bag in hand, Evie felt better about the upcoming encounter. She didn't rush out to buy the short silk nightie to please Jackson. She bought it to armor herself. She needed to take back the power he was so intent on keeping. What better offense could she have against Zohra sex club chain owner Jackson Auclair than French lingerie in his favorite color?

She took a quick shower and slid on the outfit. She glanced at herself in the mirror. Not bad at all.

The knock on her hotel door that evening startled her, but didn't surprise her. They'd made a deal and he was here to collect.

Evie was grateful that her parents' room was in the other side of the building. She had a feeling Jackson had had a hand in that too.

She couldn't believe she had agreed to this. Even

worse, she couldn't believe the anticipation that started to thrum in her veins back in the Louvre.

Evie blew out a breath in an attempt to calm her jangling nerves. She managed the trek to the door on unsteady knees. Her clammy hand reached for the knob. The door seemed heavier than usual as she opened it.

Jackson stood on the other side. Evie hated how good he looked. She hated how much he had grown into his body—the biceps straining against his long-sleeved shirt.

His gaze went from cocky to shocked in an instant. His eyes darkened, raking over her like a parched traveler finally finding an artesian spring. The deep blue nightie lifted her modest breasts up obscenely high. He stared.

Satisfaction unfurled within her. She could do this. She could have sex with her ex-husband while keeping herself fully closed off from feeling anything for him ever again. She may not have his experience, but she had her resolution. She'd make him want her like he had wanted no one else, while keeping her heart safely locked away. She would remain detached. She had to protect herself.

"What are you wearing?" he asked in a strangled voice. His gaze never left her breasts.

Evie attempted to sound blasé. "My nightgown. Why?"

"This is what you sleep in?"

Worth every penny. "Do you want to come in?"

His eyes met hers then. He looked like he had lost track of where they were. He stepped inside, closing the door and withdrawing a bouquet of bright pink tulips from behind his back.

Now it was her turn to be shocked. She hadn't expected flowers. Her eyes narrowed. "What is this?"

"A peace offering."

"Did you destroy the recording?"

"Recording's gone."

"If I find out you're lying, I will slice off your dick with a very, very dull saw."

"Noted," he said, shoving the flowers at her. "Here."

She took the bright blooms. They looked dewy-fresh and brightened the dark-toned room. She didn't have a vase to put them in, but she improvised with her large travel mug, striding to the bathroom to pour water into the forty-ounce traveler.

When she returned to the room, the fire in his gaze had been banked. He looked rigid and professional—and he held a folder.

"What's that?"

"Our new contract."

Evie extended her hand. "Let's see it."

It was a short one. It laid out the points that they had negotiated earlier—no kissing, no bed, all copies of the tape destroyed. It also listed the new lineup of the states, including all forty-nine states accessible to him, and California off limits. Why would he need a signed contract? Why would he take the time to write out all the states?

Making a mental note to investigate further later, she took the pen he offered her. The heavy ballpoint said Zohra in gold lettering across the front.

"From your club?"

"Yep."

She signed quickly, then handed him back the contract and pen. "I want to see it."

His brow furrowed, as though he misheard. "The club?"

"Yes."

"No."

"Why not?" she pressed. Not that she wished to tour a sex club, but curiosity about Jackson Auclair's new life had eaten at her all day. She wanted to learn his secrets. She wanted to learn them and use them, to hurt him as much as he had hurt her.

"That's not the kind of place you'd enjoy frequenting."

"I don't want to frequent it. I just want to tour it. Is it all padlocks and chains and whips and… ball gags?"

He didn't say anything. His Adam's apple bobbed.

Maybe she was in over her head. "Oh God, is it?"

He cleared his throat. "A room or two. For those interested. Not the entire club."

"I want a tour," she insisted. "Not tonight. But sometime when it's closed. I don't want to run into any of your… guests."

"I'll think about it."

"I insist."

"Fine. Later this week. But our deal's still on, whether you like what you see or not."

"I just signed the new contract, didn't I?"

His fingers curled tighter around the signed documents, and he didn't offer anything more.

Against her better judgment, Evie glanced at the bed. She had insisted beds were off limits—beds were too intimate, too… comfortable. She didn't need the closeness, couldn't allow it. But what did they do now?

Holy fuck, she wasn't wearing underwear. He'd have noticed them through the gossamer fabric. Evelyn Campbell stood in front of him in nothing but a scrap of dark blue silk. His favorite color. She had known that. She wasn't playing fair. He had to give it to her. He never played fair either. She wanted to keep him off balance? He could do the same to her.

She stood there, watching him with wide, chocolate eyes. A nervous pulse beat a staccato against the delicate skin of her neck. He wanted to put his mouth there and soothe it.

A blush began to spread from her chest to her neck and chin, crawling up higher. A dead giveaway. She was nervous, as much as she didn't want to appear it.

Good.

He wanted her off kilter.

He wanted her tumbling so hard she didn't know which way was up.

He'd take what he wanted, satisfy his craving, and leave. Two weeks should be plenty of time. Enough to work her out of his system once and for all.

When he took a step forward, he expected her to skitter away, but she stood her ground. He'd always admired her backbone.

As he planted himself square in front of her, the urge to kiss her pounded through him. It would be so easy to lean down and brush her lips with his, to claim her mouth with his tongue. But rules were rules. She had set them. He'd listen.

Instead, he reached out his hand, let his fingers trail along the curve of her shoulder, tracing the thin strap of her negligee.

Her breathing caught. She didn't retreat.

He let his hand skim down her waist along the silky material, to the high curve of her ass. She had been rail-thin when they had met ten years ago. Now toned muscles greeted him. He wanted to strip her of the gown and look his fill.

Her entire body looked flushed now. He wanted to follow the trail of her blush with his tongue. He let his hand rest on her ass, her muscles flexing beneath his fingers.

Slowly, he lowered his lips to her ear, reveled in the shiver that raced through her body.

"Get on the table."

Her unfocused gaze blinked up at him, as though she couldn't quite process the words.

The antique-looking console behind her looked like it could hold her slender frame. She glanced at it. Her gaze found his again, uncertain.

"I said, get on the table."

He could so easily lift her to it, but he held off. He needed her to move on her own, needed her there of her own free will. If she said no and turned him away that very second, he'd leave. He knew that she knew that. She wouldn't be here, dressed in that, if she didn't trust him.

Despite his certainty, he had to hear the words. "You want this?"

She swallowed. He waited, holding still as she searched his face. "Yes," she answered on a frustrated breath.

"Then get on the table."

She backed up the five steps, her gaze never leaving his. Placed her pink-manicured nails on the edge of the table.

She no longer wore the ring that David had gotten her. Good. He hated to see the reminder that another man had staked his claim on her.

She was his.

Once she wore his ring. It hadn't been as flashy as David's. He had no money back then. They had picked out her ring together in a small antique shop in Antibes. It would be different now. He could buy her the largest diamond out there, to make it clear that she was his to anyone who dared look at her.

Except she wasn't.

He had two weeks to work her out of his system. He better start now.

She pulled herself up on the table. It barely shifted under her weight. Good. It had been built to last.

He didn't move closer. "Spread your legs."

Her fingers tightened against the edge.

Her chin tilted up. But she did as she was told. The nightie rode up her thighs.

"Drop the shoulder straps."

He barely recognized his own voice.

Red-faced but determined, she flicked the shoulder straps off, letting the blue silk fall around her waist, releasing her high breasts. Bright pink nipples, the color of the tulips he had brought her, puckered at him. He had once loved to lave and lick them, to feel her writhe against his mouth as he did.

Every ounce of him wanted to move closer. His dick pushed to escape the confines of his jeans. Jackson wanted to sink deep inside of her, to feel her around him.

He wanted to fuck her until she screamed.

Not yet.

He needed her to want him as much as he wanted her.

He took a step forward.

"Lift your breasts up."

She didn't hesitate this time. Her hands moved up

her body, skimming up the silk. She knew the effect that she had on him. She lifted her breasts.

"Come taste them." A gauntlet dropped.

He didn't have to be told twice. He stalked forward. Her nipples had always been sensitive. She didn't like too much pressure. He remembered that even all these years later. He leaned down—

Tap, tap, tap.

He froze.

Fuck. Someone was at the door.

Before he had time to process, Evie scrambled away from him, readjusting the nightie around her as she slid off the table. She crossed the room to the robe she had left on the bed.

"Who is it?" she called, tugging on the hotel bathrobe. It satisfied him to hear the breathiness in her voice.

"Evie, it's Mom and Dad. Can we come in?"

Evie belted the robe. Crap! What do they do now? Her parents could not catch Jackson in the same room as her when she wore this outfit. She was a grown woman, but her parents would judge. She had just broken off her engagement with one man, and now she was in her room, semi-naked, entertaining another.

"One second!" She turned to Jackson. "Hide!"

His expression radiated confusion. "Hide where? I can't fit in the armoire. Just open the door. You're in your thirties. Your parents can handle you having a guy in your room."

"Not like this," she whispered. "Go into the bathroom!"

"I can't believe this," he grumbled. "Ten years later, and you're still scared of them."

"I'm not scared of them."

"Then let them in."

She considered him.

"Evie?" her mother called through the door.

"One minute." Her eyes pleaded with Jackson.

He stood his ground.

Fine. If he wanted her parents to know she had him in her room, so be it. With one final glance at Jackson, who resolutely refused to move, Evie knotted her belt one more time and went to unlatch the door.

"Oh!" Her mother's wide eyes reflected the shock both of her parents must have felt.

Her father turned beet red. "We're interrupting."

"No!" Evie rushed to reassure them. "No, not at all. You remember Jackson from dinner… and this morning."

"Yes." Her father cleared his throat. "We remember."

"Jackson just came by… to, um…" Evie's brain struggled to find the words.

"I stopped by to share that I've secured Versailles tomorrow. I've reserved us rooms at Le Grand Contrôle for tomorrow night. It's a hotel right next to Chateau Versailles. We'll have a private tour of the palace after the visitors leave, and tour the surrounding areas. I dropped by to tell Evie so she could share the news with you."

"You did!?" her mom exclaimed.

"That's very generous of you to invite us."

Jackson's lips twitched. "Anything for my parents' friends." Giving Evie a brief glance, he turned for the door. "I should go. I'll see you all downstairs tomorrow morning. A private car service is picking us up."

The buzz of Jackson's phone broke through the silence that had descended over his hotel room. *What time is it?* Now that the phone cut into his focus, the sharp twinge of cramped muscles in his back and neck made him wince.

He leaned away from his laptop and stretched. He had been hunched over the document for hours, and his eyes burned as much as his muscles. Evie's presence in France—and their new contract—had catapulted Arlo into reality, and he had a lot to do to take it to the finish line. He wouldn't let anything derail his plans. Jackson reached for his phone, answering the video call from his brother.

"You got her to sign off?" Hayes asked immediately. Like Jackson, he had invested a lot in their fledgling venture. If Evie hadn't allowed Jackson to operate in Nevada, Arlo Las Vegas would be DOA.

"Yep. We can't open up a club in California any time soon, but the Vegas deal can now go through."

He expected Hayes to grin or fist pump. Instead, his brother's lips thinned. "You should have talked to her. She's a reasonable person."

Great. A guilt trip was the last thing he needed. Jackson refused to feel bad about the blackmail. "She's not reasonable when it comes to me. She hates my guts."

"Well, this won't help. When she finds out that you're the reason she's in France in the first place, she'll rip your balls right off."

"She can do whatever she wants to my balls. A nightclub in Vegas in a once-in-a-lifetime opportunity. I wasn't about to let it slip through my fingers because of some stupid map she and I drew up when we were kids."

"You sure you know what you're doing?"

"Positive."

Hayes looked dubious as he hung up. Jackson didn't

care. Hayes couldn't understand. Hayes and his two other half brothers, Nate and Oliver, grew up loved and supported by his mother and Leonard. He never had that luxury.

He had always felt like someone's darkest secret. Lisa and Leonard had never wanted him around as a child, a reminder of Lisa's first husband, Valentin. Even as an adult, he had never been welcomed to spend a single holiday with them. Evie had hidden their relationship and then had abandoned him too. He hadn't been good enough for her either.

That would change. Arlo would provide him with the legitimacy he had craved from birth. He wouldn't let anything get in his way. Now that he had access to Vegas, anything was possible.

Chapter 9

When Evie and Jackson had visited Paris a decade ago, they had taken the train from Paris to Versailles. It had carried them along the Seine while she and Jackson had made out in their seats. Evie would have liked to take that train again. Instead, she waited for the car service to scoop them up the following morning.

Evie suspected that Jackson had reserved the private car service to impress his parents. In fact, Jackson had designed the entire Versailles trip to thoroughly stun the people who had shunned him in childhood. Of that, she had no doubt.

She, Jackson, and her parents piled into one private car while the Icefalls caravanned behind them in the other. Evie knew that Jackson had arranged it that way on purpose. The less time he spent in his parents' company, the happier he seemed.

The driver, Jean-Charles, drove past the main entrance to the Chateau de Versailles and pulled up to the upscale hotel that Jackson had reserved for them for the night.

Jean-Charles had shared that Le Grand Contrôle, built in 1681, had once been a private residence. Fully restored, it was now the first and only hotel on the grounds of Chateau Versailles.

Walking into the five-star hotel felt like moving back

in time or stepping onto a set of Sofia Coppola's *Marie Antoinette*. Evie was mesmerized.

Jackson had reserved rooms for them all, no doubt intent on demonstrating to his parents that he was as successful as his brothers. She felt uncomfortable with Jackson paying for such opulent rooms for her and her parents, but she also knew how much each membership at Zohra cost. He could afford it. She'd enjoy this once-in-a-lifetime experience.

Evie strolled into the beautifully restored room assigned to her. Bright light streamed in through the windows that overlooked the gardens. She drank in the intricate wallpaper that matched the curtains and bed canopy, the polished herringbone parquet floor, the gold accents. The bathroom held the claw-footed bathtub of her dreams. She checked the time on her phone. No time for a bath quite yet.

The hotel had arranged a private tour of the Domaine de Trianon for the group, and she refused to miss it. Evie had never gotten to see the Grand Trianon, the Petite Trianon, or the Queen's Hamlet when she had visited Versailles with Jackson. Anticipation at the opportunity thrummed through her.

As the tour began, Jackson's presence incrementally drove away her urge to see the Trianon estate. He had glued himself to her during the excursion and refused to budge. Sometimes, he'd let his hand rest on the small of her back as the guide directed them in a certain direction. The warmth of his touch seared her even in the breezy May day. She knew she needed to step away, to put some distance between them. But when he'd drop his hand, tracing the curve of her hip as he did so, she missed his touch. She hated herself for the feelings he stirred in her.

Jackson Auclair had been the center of her world once. She'd never let that happen again. They were both too stubborn, too independent. Together, they had been a firestorm. She still heard the sound of the rescue saw in her nightmares as it cut through their car's frame.

His hand grazed her hip again. "Stop it," she hissed.

His deceptively innocent eyes met hers. "Stop what?"

Two could play that game. He thought he was immune?

As the tour guide shared tidbits of Marie Antoinette's life at Petite Trianon, the group focused on Marie Antoinette's former bedchamber in front of them. She and Jackson found themselves at the back of the group, not a single eyeball directed their way. Evie's gaze leapfrogged from one back of the head to another. Perfect timing.

She let her hand find Jackson's thigh, felt his sharply indrawn breath. He glanced down at her, but she didn't dare make eye contact. She'd lose all courage otherwise. Pretending to pay attention to the guide, she slowly caressed the powerful muscle. His entire body froze under her hand, as if in anticipation of where she'd direct her touch next.

The tour guide turned away from the bedchamber.

Evie removed her hand.

She didn't need to look at Jackson to feel his labored breathing.

Good. She wasn't the only one affected when they touched each other. This went both ways. She could make him beg and plead and forget his own name with just a touch. He was playing with fire, and she'd ensure it burned him.

They moved on to the king's bedchamber.

"People were much smaller then! Look at the size of that bed!" exclaimed Lisa, raising her phone camera. "Here, Rose, stand just there. Look this way. Hold it like that." Jackson's mother proceeded to take several dozen photos in quick succession as Evie's mom smiled into the camera.

"I'm going to make you pay for that stunt," Jackson murmured into her ear.

She met his gaze. "I'd like to see you try."

The hotel set out lunch for them on the Grand Canal lawn. As soon as they finished eating, her mom insisted that they tour the Gardens of Versailles. The hotel had arranged a private tour of the palace for later that evening, so it didn't make sense to fight through the crushing crowds to see it sooner.

The Icefalls chatted amicably with her parents as they set out to explore the gardens. Evie let them walk on, slowing her pace to take in the sounds. The rustle of the trees, the buzz of the insects, and the distinctive trickle of the water fountain sparked instant memories of her time there with Jackson.

Jackson's footsteps advanced behind her. He had a distinctive walk. Hurried. Like he knew where he was going and he wouldn't let anyone get in his way.

He caught up to her quickly. His warm hand engulfed hers. "Come with me."

The whispered command sent Evie's pulse pounding. How did he have this effect on her even so many years later? The scent of him made her want to bury her nose in his chest and inhale. She didn't like it. It was an unnecessary complication.

He tugged her behind a grouping of trees. Evie didn't argue as he weaved in among the trunks until he had them in a fully private copse. Only the chirping of birds and the flutter of leaves surrounded them now. They were alone in the little patch of forest, and Evie's blood hummed with anticipation of what he intended to do.

His eyes looked stormy, intent, as they settled on her face. He knew exactly what he planned on doing next, she could tell. He had mapped this out long ago. His large, warm hands settled on her shoulders, kneading the tense tissue.

Suddenly, he turned her, so that her back pressed against his hard chest. His familiar scent intensified as his lips trailed along her neck to the sensitive hollow just below her ear. When his teeth sank into the tender flesh of her earlobe, Evie basked in the pleasurable shiver.

While his mouth distracted her, his palm stole under her sweater, found her breast, and cupped her over the lace of her bra. His fingers tightened. Her head fell back against his shoulder as he kneaded.

"God, you smell good," he murmured as his hand moved to her other breast. His fingers found the erect bud of her nipple through the fabric, squeezed the sensitive flesh. Of their own accord, her hips moved back against the hard ridge of his erection. *I should step away.* He groaned as she pressed closer.

"We can't do this here," she murmured while she still had room for sanity in her brain.

"We can do anything we want," he growled, and his hand moved under her bra. The heat of his palm on her breast branded her. She needed more. Urgently, she covered his hand with hers over her clothes and pressed him closer.

His other hand flexed on her stomach, holding her immobile as he teased her. The warmth of his lips against her neck and the sandpapery rasp of his stubble sent goosebumps to rise along her skin.

She craved to turn in the circle of his arms and kiss him, to regain the connection they had once shared, but she knew that would lead to calamity. Their connection had been severed in the crash outside of Monaco ten years ago, and she couldn't let them reweave it. Instead, she stayed where she was, and let the exquisite feel of his touch overtake her, pressing closer to him as the sensations scaled.

A cry, like that of a child or a puppy, cut through the haze of yearning Jackson drew from her.

"Wait," she gasped, stepping out of his reach on wobbly legs. She tried to get her erratic breathing under control as she readjusted her clothing. "Do you hear that?"

Jackson cocked his head. He heard it too. His gaze sharpened on something in the distance.

"It's coming from over there."

She followed close behind him as he strode toward the sound. They had to navigate around a thicket of trees to find the source.

"Oh my God, are you okay?" Evie gasped, seeing a small child, all of three or four. No parent in sight.

Jackson glanced around. "Think she walked off and no one noticed?"

Evie dropped to her knees in front of the little girl, switching to French. "Do you know where your mom or dad is?"

The child cried harder.

She laid a gentle hand on the child's back. The little girl immediately fell into her arms, her tiny body hiccupping with tears.

Evie attempted to soothe her, rubbing gentle circles

along her back. She glanced up at Jackson. "We have to find her parents."

Jackson knelt next to the child, making himself eye level with her. His French was better than Evie's. "Can we help you find your family?"

The child didn't react, just cried harder against Evie's chest.

Jackson repeated the same phrase in English. The child paused mid-cry. She lifted her head and looked at Jackson with big, sad eyes. She understood his English better than she had understood their French.

"Progress," said Jackson to Evie. He turned back to the child. "It's okay. How about we go look for your parents together? Do you know where they were? Were they over there?" he pointed to his north. "Over there?" His east. "Over there?" West. "Or over there?"

The child appeared to think about it. After a watery pause, she pointed west.

"All right, let's go look for them. Is that okay?"

The child considered Jackson. Then Evie. She nodded.

Evie lifted her up in her arms. She felt light in her grasp. Her little fingers curled into Evie's sweater, holding tight.

Jackson set the direction. "Let's take her to visitor information. Maybe they can make an announcement."

The child's tears stopped as they strode toward the milling groups of tourists. She made herself comfortable in Evie's arms, looking around as they walked with her.

"I have a feeling that's the parents," said Jackson. Evie followed the direction of his gaze.

Several guards had gathered around a tearful, trembling woman and her pale, panicked husband as passersby stopped to gawk at the scene.

"Mommy!" yelled the child, recognizing her parents instantly. "Daddy!"

The parents, preoccupied in explaining the situation to the guards, did not hear her cry of recognition.

"Lose something?" asked Jackson, his deep voice carrying over the buzz of the surrounding voices.

The couple turned at the question. Unmistakable relief made both of their bodies sag. They rushed to pull their baby out of Evie's arms.

Evie stood back, not wishing to interrupt the teary reunion. Her body grazed Jackson's. Feeling a jolt of pleasure at the contact, she stepped away immediately. Dangerous road, pleasure. Never led anywhere smart.

"Thank you!" said the relieved father. "Where was she? We looked away for a second, and she was gone."

The teary-eyed mom, balancing her child on her hip with one hand, clasped Evie to her with the other. "Thank you so much for bringing her to us. I can't even think about the alternative."

"We heard her crying in the trees over there."

"You must have been terrified, Harper!" exclaimed her mom, pressing her baby close.

"I'm glad you were easy to find," said Evie.

The child and her parents moved away, walking toward the palace.

A familiar sadness bubbled up inside of her. She didn't do well around small children. The old wound had never closed, it continued to fester. She couldn't face Jackson. "I think I want to head to my room now."

"I'll go with you."

"No. I… I'd rather go alone."

The tears came before she reached the hotel.

Chapter 10

Evie spent a good half hour wallowing in bed, trying to chase away the memories and the guilt. Even ten years later, the crash, subsequent hospitalization, and the horrible things she had thrown in Jackson's face remained embroidered in vivid detail into the calloused tissue of her broken heart.

Reluctantly, Evie made herself count to three, and got up to work on her book. The writing helped chase the gloom like wind scattering fog. She was grateful for the distraction.

Her parents stopped by to invite her to join them and the Icefalls for afternoon tea in the hotel, but Evie declined. The claw-footed tub beckoned instead. She'd been dreaming of it ever since she'd stepped foot into the beautifully appointed room. Closing the door behind her parents, she headed straight to the bathroom.

Evie twisted the white-tipped nobs and watched the stream fill the tub with steaming water. The bubble bath that was provided foamed gently, releasing the scent of citrus and mint into the air.

Evie tied up her hair in a knot on top of her head, stripped out of her clothes, and sank into the water.

Her tub at home wasn't nearly this deep, and she loved this height that allowed her to rest her neck against the rounded edge. She closed her eyes and let the hot water permeate her tight muscles. Her continuous interactions with Jackson had formed hard knots under her skin.

She didn't hear the snick of the door, or the footsteps. When his familiar voice groaned, "Fuck," she sprung open her lids.

"How the heck did you get in my room?" she demanded, setting both hands on the rim of the tub to glare at him.

The hunger in his eyes was unmistakable. He held up a room key. "Got an extra one downstairs."

Her jaw dropped. "That's illegal!"

"All of these rooms are in my name—I can get any key I want."

"Go away," she said. "I want a nice, quiet bath alone."

"I recall we had a lot of fun taking baths together."

She let out a dramatic sigh. He couldn't leave the past alone. She settled back against the tub.

His gaze zeroed in on her body, barely concealed by the suds. She liked how his eyes darkened, how his jaw instantly tensed. Slowly, he began to roll up the sleeves of his shirt, exposing his strong forearms.

"What are you doing? I'm not letting you join me."

"You don't need my help scrubbing your back?"

"I don't need any help from you ever. Can you go back to your room, please?" She waved him off with a soapy hand. If only he were that easily dismissed.

He approached her slowly. Why did he have such sexy forearms? Her thighs pressed together as she thought about all the things he could do to her with his hands while she was in the bath.

He must have had similar thoughts. He sank to his

knees in front of the tub, and sent one hand to skim the surface of the water. Not touching her, but dangerously close.

"Let me help you relax." His deep, decadent voice washed over her, made the intimate place between her legs throb at the wicked suggestion.

"How would you do that?" Her voice came out much too needy, but the sight of his fingers playing in the soapy bubbles constricted her breathing.

She wanted him to touch her, to skim the pads of his fingers along her sensitized flesh. Her nipples puckered at his closeness. That didn't escape his attention. She wished she could blame the cool air, but they both knew she'd be lying.

"I have a few proven methods," he drawled. His hand skimmed from her knee to her thigh, paused where thigh met hip, explored the ultra-sensitive skin on her hipbone. So close, yet so far. She wanted him where moisture began to pool. Instead, he rubbed slow circles along the sensitive flesh, dipped into her hip crease, but didn't venture further. "Want me to try a few out?"

She needed to say no.

It was imperative she decline.

Yet as his fingers traced along her inner thigh, all thoughts evaporated with the steam rising off the surface of the water.

She succumbed with a nod.

It wasn't good enough.

Satisfaction glinted in his eyes. He continued to draw patterns across her skin, sending frissons of restless need through every nerve ending. "Is that a yes?"

"Yes, damn you!"

She expected him to move his hand then, to finally

settle his fingers where she craved to feel them, yet he didn't do any such thing.

"Put my hand where you want it," he demanded in a low voice.

He asked too much of her.

He wanted her complete surrender.

She couldn't give it to him. He'd eviscerate the last of her self-control. Yet her body had already started to give up sovereignty. Her hand moved. She laid it on top of his, and slid his fingers between her legs.

Jackson's blood pounded, his dick strained against the thick denim of his jeans. He wanted to free himself and sink into her welcoming heat.

Her lashes fluttered closed as she leaned her head back against the lip of the tub. The steam rising from the water made her skin dewy, her cheeks bright pink. He craved to trail his tongue along her skin and taste the blush forming there.

His fingers found the center of her. She was soaked for him, her desire unmistakable. Triumph surged through him. Her body still desired him, yes, but her mind wanted him too. She wouldn't have let her knees drop open wider if doubts rang in her head.

He let his fingers stroke through her heat, grazing her sensitive peak with every glide. She released a low breath, but kept her lids tightly shut.

He wanted her to know that it was him touching her. To know that she was allowing it. "Open your eyes," he demanded. "Look at me."

For a brief moment, she squeezed her lids tighter. When she opened them and her chocolate eyes met his, he felt all-powerful, like the kings staying in Versailles in centuries past. Her lips parted as he continued stroking her. He remembered everything about their time together. Knew exactly how much pressure she liked, how to wind her up tighter until she'd beg and writhe for more.

His own hand trembled.

Only she had ever caused that reaction in him.

He hadn't realized how much he needed her. How much his body sought hers. Now that she was within arm's reach, every nerve ending in his body screamed for more.

Slowly, he worked two fingers inside of her. Her tight channel gripped him, and she closed her eyes.

"Keep your eyes open," he growled.

To his satisfaction, she complied. Her chest heaved as she tried to catch her breath. He wanted to seal his mouth to hers, but rules were rules. Instead, he pressed his lips to her glistening cheek.

The familiar scent of her, mixed with the bubble bath, sent his senses reeling. Her honeyed need coated his fingers. He concentrated his attention, wanting— needing—her to come for him.

She closed her eyes.

He stopped his ministrations.

Her lids lifted, confusion and desperate need reflected in her gaze.

"I said. Keep your eyes on me."

"I hate you," she groaned, but she didn't let her lashes flutter shut.

He quickened his movements, touching her exactly as he knew she liked. Her body began to tighten, her movements against him jerky. Her fingers curled into the tub's rim, and she arched into his hand, coming apart under his fingers.

Trembling, she sank deeper into the water. The wild heaving of her chest echoed the frenzied beating of his blood.

He couldn't help himself. He leaned down and pressed another kiss to her cheek. The salty taste of tears froze him.

Pulling back, he saw the diamond droplets streak down her face.

Alert, he withdrew his hand. "What's wrong? Did I hurt you?"

She shook her head, covering her face with her hands.

Panic gripped him.

He didn't mean to make her cry.

She flicked the tears away with her fingers. "No. It's fine. I'm okay," she said after a moment, wiping at the last of the drops.

"Evie?" he asked. Uncertainty tore through him.

He'd made her cry hundreds of times during their incessant arguments before, but she had never cried after an orgasm with him ever. He didn't like it.

"Tell me what's wrong," he demanded.

She shook her head. Tears dry, her expression turned resolute. "Jet lag?" The weak excuse fell flat, but he didn't press her.

"The tape is destroyed," he said, drying his hands on the nearby towel. "We can end it here. I want you willing or not at all. We can call it. I have nothing else hanging over you. You can walk away."

The idea that she would call it quits caused panic to zing through him. He wanted to fuck her. He didn't know why he had just given her an out.

She shook her head. "We had a deal. I'm not crying because of that."

The relief that rushed through him almost brought him to his knees.

She stood up, soap bubbles clinging to her skin. As she climbed out, he unwrapped the towel. She let him enfold her in the cotton, but stepped as far away from him as the bathroom allowed.

"I don't want to want you," she finally offered.

"I don't fucking want to want you either."

"Two weeks should be enough to end this… madness."

"Agree. Then you go back to California. We never have to see each other again."

She watched his face with an unnerving intensity. Whatever she read in his features relaxed her. "Okay. Two weeks and then we never lay eyes on each other again."

She took a slow step toward him.

Then another.

She stood an arm's reach away. His dick needed her closer.

Without giving him any warning, she dropped the towel.

He pounced.

His lips found the sensitive hollow under her ear as his hand closed around her breast.

His phone buzzed in his pants.

Evie pulled back. "You need to get that?"

"Ignore it," he said against her skin. "They'll go away."

The vibration didn't stop.

He reached into his pocket. Without looking, he tossed the phone into the main room. It hit the parquet with a thud. Ducking his head, he lifted her breast to his mouth.

The room phone rang next.

Evie glanced toward the ringing. "Could be urgent."

"Don't care. Let them wait."

She extricated herself regardless and hurried to the antique-looking phone next to her bed.

"Hello?" She listened to the voice on the other end of the line. "One second." She extended the phone toward him. "It's for you."

He reached for the receiver, and raised it to his ear. "This is Jackson." He didn't expect to hear Noémie Fournier's voice. He had hired her five years ago to run Zohra Paris, and she'd been pretty self-sufficient ever since. He expected the news she shared even less.

Chapter 11

Jackson's face looked grim when he hung up the call. "Someone tried to set my club in Paris on fire. I need to go."

Evie's heart dropped. She hadn't expected to hear that. "Was anyone hurt?"

"No, thank God. The damage is minimal, but I want to go see in person."

"I'll go with you." She didn't know what had spurred her to volunteer to accompany him, but as soon as the words left her mouth, she knew she meant them.

Surprise flitted across his face. "To my club?"

"Yes."

"Evie—"

"You think seeing it will frighten me out of our deal?"

He seemed to weigh the options. Maybe he did think that. Finally, he grabbed his cell off the floor and thrust it into his pocket. "All right. Let's go to Zohra."

They made good time and reached Zohra just forty-five minutes later. She had imagined a secret door leading to a shadowy basement, but the club stood proudly on one of the quieter streets of Paris. A discreet hedge enclosed the space. Jean-Charles navigated through the gated entrance and stopped right in front of the main door.

Even though it had been her idea to accompany Jackson, apprehension prickled her skin. What if someone recognized her? Her career as a young adult book author had taken off a few years ago, her book series selling speedily across multiple continents. Would her presence at a sex club halt their sales? She hadn't even thought of that when she had insisted Jackson bring her with him. Reality dawned now, and her body glued itself to the leather seats. She didn't want to leave the safe confines of the car.

Jackson must have sensed her hesitation. "You don't have to come in if you don't want to. Jean-Charles can take you straight to the hotel."

"Are any of your clients here?"

"No. We closed down until we fix the fire damage. You nervous you'll be recognized?"

"A little."

"You won't run into any members today. But you don't have to go inside if you don't feel comfortable."

Hopefully the club being empty would keep the chance of recognition very low. She had come this far. No use backing out now. "No. I'll go with you."

Jackson offered his hand to help her out of the vehicle. She didn't want to take it, but he hadn't touched her since Le Grand Contrôle and she craved the contact. He'd had that effect on her a decade ago too.

Stay immune. Stay strong. Don't… just don't.

Pep talk complete, she tugged her hand free of his. His fingers flexed after he released her.

Striding ahead of her to the gigantic front doors, he swung them open. Evie expected a dark space that reeked of sex and shame.

Instead, a bright room greeted her. Although the

emerald-green window curtains had been drawn shut for the evening, a mammoth crystal chandelier lit up the room as brightly as daytime, its light bouncing off the gleaming white marble floor. Emerald velvet furniture clustered around a massive stone fireplace on one side. A check-in desk stood on the other.

Jackson's face looked wary as he turned to her. "You want a tour?"

Curiosity got the better of her. "Most certainly."

The distinctive clicking of high heels interrupted their tour before it even began. A svelte redhead came out of a door tucked away behind the front desk.

"That was fast," she said in French-accented English. "The fire brigade and investigators just left. They have the suspect in custody."

"What was he attempting to do?" asked Jackson.

"He's claiming he was trying to impress a girl. He poured gasoline at the back door and set it ablaze. The fire fighters put it out quickly, but there was some damage to the outside of the structure. We'll have to close down to repaint."

Jackson didn't care about the painting details. "Make sure it's done swiftly," he told her.

"I'm on it."

The woman's curious gaze moved to Evie.

"Noémie Fournier, this is Evelyn," Jackson said as an introduction. "Evelyn, Noémie is the manager here."

Looking at the perfectly coiffed Noémie unfurled green jealousy in Evie again. The French woman's hair was twisted into the perfect updo, her bright red lipstick immaculate. Her clothes looked expensive and tailored to emphasize her figure.

Evie felt like a ragamuffin in comparison. Her hair

had frizzed up from the steam of the bath and long car ride back to Paris. She had hurriedly tugged on her joggers and a white sweater to accompany Jackson, but had failed to put on any makeup in her haste.

Evie threw a rueful glance at Jackson. Even in his simple button-down and jeans, with his hair too long, the man looked like he'd stepped off the pages of a luxury watch ad. Noémie must be wondering from under which rock he had found her.

"Let's see the footage."

"I have it up in the control room."

Noémie led them back to the room from which she came. Eight huge monitors were mounted on the wall, and two more took up the only table. Each one displayed a different angle of the building. One showed a paused recording.

"I gave the original to the investigators. This is our copy." Noémie pressed a key and the recording began to play across the wall-mounted screen.

The video showed the arsonist clearly. He didn't look to be older than twenty-four or twenty-five. He had somehow snuck past security at the gate, threw gasoline quickly on the back entrance, and tossed the match. Security officers tackled and restrained him, but the fire spread quickly. More guards ran out with fire extinguishers, but the flame raged sudden and strong. The fire fighters arrived a few minutes later, putting out the fire. The curling smoke could be clearly seen in the video.

"I'm so glad no one was hurt," breathed Evie.

"The team worked quickly. They saved a lot of lives today," said Noémie.

"Do you get incidents like this often?" Evie asked. "I know this guy was trying to impress someone, but from protestors and such?"

"Never arson. Never even a protest in the European clubs," Jackson said. "Local conservative groups tried to shut down Zohra Charleston once or twice, but not recently. Zohra New York has a group of elderly protestors who swing by every other Thursday. The Manhattan clients like it, though. It gives the club a taboo feel they enjoy. And I like to think it gives the protestors a reason to get out of the house. Win-win, in a way."

Evie acknowledged his response with a nod. "I hope they prosecute the arsonist to the fullest extent of the law."

Jackson turned to Noémie. "How many members were here when the fire started?"

"A few… I gave them complimentary tickets to the Cannes event. Georgia and Sebastian Carlton had already registered for the event, so I credited their account—" Noémie spun to Evie. Recognition flashed in her eyes. "You're Evelyn Campbell. The author."

Uh oh. Evie's worst nightmare.

"I am," she hesitantly admitted.

"My kids love your books. We even went to your book signing a few years ago in New York. You had been so nice and friendly—they still talk about meeting you."

Relief suffused her. "That's so nice to know. Thank you for telling me that. Ummm…" Evie hesitated. "I just… I worry that, given my fanbase, I shouldn't be seen in…"

"Say no more," Noémie assured her. "We're very discreet at Zohra. Besides the security officers, it's just me here right now. And I'm about to head out." Noémie hesitated. "I know this might be too much to ask… but if you're in Paris much longer… do you think you'd like to come to my house for dinner? The kids would be so excited."

"I'd love that!" Evie readily agreed. She loved meeting her young fans. Their questions always charmed her. "Maybe not dinner, but I'll swing by and say hello. Tomorrow is our last day in Paris. We go to Nice the day after."

"How about tomorrow at four? We'll have champagne."

"Sounds great," Evie said.

"We'll be there," added Jackson, laying a possessive hand low on Evie's back.

Noémie walked around the desk to reach for her purse. "Okay, I leave you to it. I must get home." She headed for the door. "I'll see you both tomorrow."

She clicked her way out of the office.

Jackson dropped his hand. "You still want a tour?"

She considered his question. This part of Jackson's life had been fully closed off to her. Yet it was a significant part of the person he was today. Despite her better judgment, she yearned to learn every facet of the man he had become. *It's morbid curiosity, nothing more*, she told herself. "Yes. I've never been inside a sex club before. Show me your lair."

Something flashed behind his eyes. An emotion she couldn't name. Frustration? It evaporated quickly as his blue eyes swept hotly down her body.

He reached out his hand, palm up, to her. "Let the tour commence."

Resolute, Evie placed her hand in his.

He took her back to the main entrance.

"Members check in here, and leave their phones in one of the secured lockers on the other side of that wall. No devices are allowed on the premises."

He walked her further into the club.

"The restaurant and one of the bars are through there. I dare you to find any place in Paris that serves better food—or cocktails. This place is smaller, but Zohra Barcelona has an actual theater as the focal point, and we host various performances."

"Like strip shows?"

"Depends. Differs month to month. I like to keep the members titillated. The lounge is through there. That's a favorite for group sex, for people who like to be watched, and for people who like to watch."

He pointed up the expansive stone stairwell that led to the second level. "Private rooms are upstairs. Some are themed."

"Can I go into one?"

"Not tonight."

"Why not?"

"It's been a hectic day. I'm not sure the cleaning team has gone through yet."

Evie nodded. "Good call."

"Each private room comes with certain items and others are available upon request—vibrators, dildos, you name it."

"I hope they're tossed upon use."

"They are. We take health and safety very seriously here. Every member goes through an extensive background check and a rigorous vetting process. Condoms must be used at all times for any penetrative sex. And we limit the amount of alcohol one can consume to two drinks maximum. If anyone breaks any of our rules, they are banned for life, no matter how much they'd paid for membership."

Evie saw that the stairwell led down a level as well.

"What's downstairs?"

"What about downstairs?" His voice sounded evasive.

"What's down there?"

He studied her, as if trying to decide whether or not to extend the tour. "You really want to see everything tonight. Fine. Come on."

Taking her hand, he led her down the steps to the lower level. A Zen-like oasis greeted them. She felt like she was walking into a fancy spa.

"Oh my God, you have a pool!"

"Yep. Pool, three hot tubs, and another bar down here. No sex is allowed in the pools or hot tubs. Several private rooms through there."

She walked further into the space. "Where do you host your orgies?"

"You think I host orgies?"

"I know you do! Come on. I still stay in touch with your brothers. Your orgies go for… what $250K a ticket? There's one you have coming up in Cannes."

He looked uncomfortable. "This space turns into one large room. The pool is covered. We bring in comfy furniture. It's really something. Our designer goes wild every year. But let me clarify. The event at Zohra Cannes isn't an orgy. It's our biggest event of the year. Members fly in from all over the world to rub elbows—and other parts— with celebrities already in town for the Film Festival."

"Have you ever participated?"

His gaze was earnest. "I've never partaken in any of the activities here or at any other club. Don't shit where you eat."

"Not even once?"

"A few months ago, one of the members—buck

naked—found me in my office at Zohra Amsterdam. I escorted her right out of there. I have only made one exception in ten years. That's Tilly."

"You met her at your sex club?"

"She auditioned to be one of our theatrical performers in Charleston. She can do insane stunts on the trapeze."

Jealousy burned through Evie's blood, even as she told herself she shouldn't feel anything. Jackson didn't belong to her, after all. He could date any acrobat he wanted.

Jackson watched emotions flit across Evie's face. Even ten years later, she hadn't mastered her poker face. Mention of Tilly sparked a reaction in her. He knew he shouldn't enjoy her irritation, but it unfurled a tendril of satisfaction deep within him. She wasn't as unaffected by him as she pretended to be. He liked that.

He didn't tell her that he'd only gone for Tilly to drown out the loneliness that never seemed to leave him, the loneliness that gaped wider when he'd learned that Evie was in a serious relationship. He'd used Tilly for his own selfish needs.

"Did you and Tilly ever… in any of your clubs?"

"No."

She looked like she didn't believe him. "Not even once?"

"I told you. I draw the line."

Evie looked around. "I have to admit, it is a really beautiful space. If I didn't know it was a sex club, I'd assume it's some fancy private club. I love the green touches."

He refused to divulge that the color scheme had been inspired by the decorations in the room where they'd first made love. The image of naked Evie across the emerald-green bedspread in the Nice hotel had burned itself into his memory. He had gravitated toward that color ever since.

"Can we go into your office?"

Evie had always been a curious little cat.

"Sure. Noémie and I share it, since I'm never in town."

"Where do you spend most of your time?"

"Lately, in Charleston. Zohra there is relatively new, so needs more attention. I have a handful of politicians fly in from DC almost weekly. And Amsterdam."

"I remember how you've always wanted to live in Europe."

He did too. He'd shared so many dreams and hopes with Evie as a silly young kid desperately in love.

As they returned to the main level, he opened the door to the office, and motioned for her to precede him. Evie took a cautious step inside. Her gaze quickly scanned over the room: two hunter-green leather arm chairs, a desk in front of the expansive, curtain-draped windows, built-in bookshelves lined with antique-looking tomes. Jackson shut the door behind himself, enclosing them in the space.

Evie walked over and plopped herself into one of the armchairs. "This is a nice club. It's definitely not how I imagined."

"What did you imagine?"

"A dungeon. Whips, chains."

"Well, to be fair, the whips and chains are upstairs."

He expected a reaction at his comment, but she surprised him with her question. "Is the door locked?"

"No. But I can lock it. Why?"

Evie leaned back, looking slight and vulnerable in the oversized chair. "Because I want to finish what we started earlier."

Shock crashed through him. "Here?"

As though reconsidering, she glanced around. "You don't have cameras in here, do you?"

"No. No cameras inside the premises."

She stood from the chair and approached him. He could tell she was nervous. The pulse beat rapidly in her throat, and a flush had worked its way up her neck.

She stood close enough for him to see the flecks of amber and gold in her brown eyes.

"The sooner I work you out of my system, the better."

"Sexy," he drawled, sardonic.

Her hand reached for the ridge straining against his jeans, stroked him. "You always find me sexy."

He fucking did.

No one had ever compared to Evelyn Campbell.

He snagged her wrist. "Not here." He didn't want to fuck her here, in his sex club. The lifetime membership may go for $1M, but fucking Evie in the club felt cheap, and he didn't like it.

They'd made love in every possible location once. But it didn't sit well with him to screw her at Zohra.

"Why not?" she asked, pulling her hand away.

She stepped out of reach. He wanted to haul her back.

He didn't know why he was angry. The feeling was irrational. He knew it, but he couldn't shake it. He kept his tone matter of fact. "You want me to fuck you at the sex club? Which room? Want me to tie you down in one of the BDSM rooms upstairs? Strap you down and spank your pussy? Is that what you want? Or should we go to the lounge? I can get the security guards to watch, if that's your thing now."

Her face paled. She observed him from beneath her lashes. Anger steamed from every labored breath. "I want to go home."

He continued to taunt her, unsure of why her request had irritated him so much. "You wanted to see my club. Pick a room. I'll fuck you in any room of your choosing."

She reached for her bag. "I'm heading back to the hotel. Goodnight. I'd reconsider joining us in Nice if I were you. I don't want you there."

"I don't give a fuck what you want. We have a deal. I'm coming to collect."

"You'll be coming on your own," she bit out, heading for the door.

He reached her in two strides. "You don't get to walk away from me like this. Though it is what you do best."

"What does that mean?"

"You know exactly what it means."

"I don't run away."

"Yeah, like you didn't run back to the States at the first opportunity last time."

"I didn't run. I went home. I couldn't stand—I couldn't be in France anymore."

"You couldn't be with me anymore."

The words hung in the room like fireworks suspended midair.

"I couldn't even look at you."

He strode to the door, swinging it open. "Go then. Go wherever the hell you want to go. Go to hell, for all I care."

"You are my hell."

With that, she set a direct beeline for the exit. He didn't follow. She knew Paris like the back of her hand. She could find her own way back to the hotel.

Chapter 12

The private car service delivered Evie's parents back to the Paris hotel at just past noon the next day. The sleepless night dragged at her as she met them downstairs for a late lunch.

"Where did you go yesterday?" asked her mom. "We were so confused when Jean-Charles said he took you back last evening."

"I caught a ride with Jackson," she offered, but didn't elaborate. "How was the drive back?"

Her parents chattered happily, her mother pulling up her phone to show Evie the photos that Lisa and she took.

"We had the fanciest dinner at the hotel! The waiters were in period costumes, and we dined under candlelight. It was spectacular."

"And we took a private tour of the palace. Did you know…" Her dad launched into recounting several historical facts.

Evie reached for her cup of coffee and took a sip. Maybe she should have stayed in Versailles last night. She at least would have gotten a good night's sleep.

Her parents had made plans to go to Montmartre and the Basilique du Sacré-Coeur with the Icefalls later that day. As much as Evie loved the views from the basilica, she bowed out of joining them. Her interaction with Jackson had left her too raw. She needed time alone to think, to figure out how to handle Jackson—and their deal.

Evie returned to her room after lunch to change out of her dress and boots into something more comfortable. She'd go explore Paris by herself—visit all her old, favorite places. The fresh air would do her good.

She had just grabbed her purse when she heard the familiar knock on her door. Jackson. Her instinct screamed for her to pretend she had already left, and that the room was vacant. Yet his second knock implied that he knew she was there and he wouldn't give up that easily.

With a resigned sigh, she set down her bag and headed to open the door. He looked exhausted, like he hadn't slept a wink. He still wore last night's clothes, and they looked rumpled on his large frame. That sting of jealousy from earlier bounced through her once more. Where had he spent the night?

His eyes glittered dangerously as they skimmed down her body. She had dressed simply in jeans and a cable-knit sweater, but his gaze burned like she wore the most revealing of lingerie.

"You and I have a deal," he ground out. "I've come to collect."

"Screw our deal." Irritation and scintillation thrummed equally through her. She didn't know whether to kick him out or pull him inside the room.

"You going to break our contract again? Your word means shit nowadays."

"I don't need you coming here to insult me. I was ready to act on our deal yesterday. You refused."

"I'm not refusing now." He didn't ask for permission, just strolled inside like he owned the place. The door shut quietly behind him.

He stalked toward her slowly, as though he wanted her to feel every step of his approach. Evie did. She felt it in every pulse point in her body. Her blood heated at his hungry gaze. He stopped when the wall impeded her retreat further.

"Strip."

The command in his voice sizzled through her, setting her nerve endings on fire. She could bring him to his knees with one look, one stroke. Unfortunately, he could also do the same to her.

When she didn't move, he leaned closer. "You know what happens when I have to repeat myself."

A decade ago, she'd loved his whispered demands. He liked to be in control in the bedroom, and she'd let him play-act in exchange for her taking charge once in a while. They'd made love through half the country, not leaving their room for days at a time. That was a long time ago.

He still had that same effect on her.

"Do I have to repeat myself, Evie?"

She lifted her chin. "I'm late for a day of sight-seeing."

His lips quirked up. Humor glinted in his eyes before he banked it. He took another step forward.

"Have places to be, do you?"

She glanced up at him, her gaze challenging. "What are you going to do about it?"

He reached for his shirt. Her eyes glued to his fingers as he undid the buttons… one… at… a… time.

His broad chest was all muscle. *The man must work out a lot.*

He had been fit a decade ago, but he had a man's body now. His muscles rippled as he divested himself of his shirt completely. His fingers went to the button of his jeans next.

Evie couldn't inhale enough air.

He dropped the jeans—the boxers went with them.

His cock stood hard and ready. She hated to admit how much she'd missed it. The lust that overwhelmed her scared her. She shouldn't feel this sort of powerful attraction for this man. She had felt it before, and it had nearly destroyed her.

Did she dare play with fire again?

She was still recovering the pieces of her life from the last time.

"Your turn."

Evie fought against the faint tremor in her fingers as she tugged the sweater over her head. She wore a silk and lace camisole underneath. She thanked the stars that she'd always had a passion for French lingerie. The hunger in his eyes overwhelmed her as he zeroed in on her breasts rising above the low neckline.

He reached for her.

She stepped out of the way, shaking her finger at him. "Not done yet."

Grasping the lace hem, she pulled off the camisole. The lace bra she wore didn't do much to conceal her breasts. Her fingers felt thick and clumsy as they undid the button of her jeans and slid down the zipper. She shimmied out of them, revealing the thong that matched the bra. White lace with tiny blue rosettes.

"On the bed," he commanded.

She shook her head. "No beds. Remember?"

"Ah. Yes. I appreciate the challenge."

He closed the distance between them. Reaching for her bra, he tugged down the cups and released her breasts.

His mouth fastened on her sensitized flesh, the heat of him burning her. She threaded her fingers through his hair, urging him closer, her head falling back at the riot of sensations his lips drew from her.

Undoing the clasp with one hand, he sent her bra fluttering to the ground, and tugged off her thong. His hands wrapped around her ribcage, pressed her against the wall. She barely felt the hard surface. He sank to his knees in front of her, and settled his mouth on her. With one flex of his powerful arm, he lifted her leg, setting it over his shoulder. Suddenly off balance, she tightened her calf against his back and pressed herself closer to the wall even as his fingers tightened on her ass to steady her.

The position left her open, her center spread for him. With a satisfied groan, he brought his mouth against her. His tongue licked her once, teasing. Her hips canted toward him. The move—and her unsteady position—sent her tilting sideways. Yelping, she pushed every inch of her arms and back tighter to the wall for support, managing to right herself.

He glanced up at her. "Okay?"

Her fingers curled into the hard surface behind her, trying to find any semblance of steadiness. "Yes."

She watched satisfaction suffuse his face. He had her just where he wanted her—off balance. Sparklers danced along her skin as he returned his mouth to her and feasted. He found her pulsing center and focused, the single-minded attention causing a moan to escape her throat. The pleasure built quickly, overwhelming her. She struggled to escape the onslaught, but he held steady, winding her up higher and higher with exultant pleasure.

Every stroke of his tongue, every move of his mouth and lips, drove her wild. Stars danced behind her eyelids.

The pleasure exploded. She came against his mouth, desperately gasping for air as her entire body shook and shuddered. She would have fallen to the ground if his strong hands weren't holding her up, his fingers digging into the flesh of her ass.

He lowered her leg from his shoulder to the ground. Evie forgot how to stand. The floor felt foreign under her bare feet.

Jackson rose slowly, kissing his way along her body. His lips grazed the delicate skin along her hip bone, traced her stomach, the tops of her breasts. "Don't move."

And he was gone. She lifted her heavy lashes to watch him stride back to her, condom in hand.

"Turn around."

Fresh need thrummed through her at his low growl. She twisted herself against the wall, her back now to him. His hands ran desperately over her breasts, tested their weight, thumbed her nipples, slid lower. He pulled her hips toward him and entered her from behind in one inexorable thrust.

They both groaned with pleasure. She was grateful to face the wall. She couldn't let him see the frantic need etched into her features. His arm encircled her, his hand wrapping around her breast, holding her in place as he began to move. His other hand slid down to her clit, rocking against the delicate nub. His teeth sank into her earlobe, scraped the nape of her neck. He bit at her skin, soothing the bites with his tongue before sinking deeper. She went wild, clawing the wall, heedless of the sounds that fell from her lips. She came apart even as he kept going, anchoring her hips with his hands, guiding her to bend deeper, powering into her.

Her next orgasm built. When it rolled through her, she almost blacked out.

He pulled out, still rock-hard, flipped her to face him. The hunger in his set features scalded her. He entered her again, lifting her up his body until her legs wrapped around his hips. He never lost his rhythm, moving in a frenzy that echoed in her.

She sobbed at the feelings he wrung out of her, at the exquisite pleasure only he could draw. Her nails sank into his back in a frenzied attempt to pull him closer. His eyes didn't leave her face. He watched her with an all-consuming desire as she gasped and moaned, lost to sensation. Watched her as she came again, her body covered in their sweat, marked with the scent of him.

The intensity in his face unnerved her. He sought to read every one of her secrets, the hopes and fears she never shared with anyone. He continued to move, branding her. Her inner muscles quivered and fluttered once more. Her orgasm washed over her in a tidal wave. She sank her teeth into his shoulder to keep herself from screaming.

He came with a guttural cry that must have echoed across every Paris rooftop.

Chapter 13

Evie felt like she had just survived a tornado that came out of nowhere, tumbled her around and around, and disappeared just as quickly. Her brain had been wiped blank. She didn't know what she was feeling or thinking, just that the two-week agreement had been a terrible mistake. They were bad for one another—they demanded and inspired too much in each other. The result would be total annihilation again. She wouldn't be able to survive it this time. She wouldn't be able to survive him.

He had left quickly after they'd finished, dressing hurriedly with not a single word to her. Before she could utter a syllable, he was gone.

Evie headed to the shower. She didn't want an ounce of his scent on her; otherwise, the reminder would consume her every thought. She set the water to scalding and stepped under the stream.

I'm a grown woman. I won't let him have this much power over me. Never again.

Scrubbing her skin with too much soap, she made herself a promise. She would let him pleasure her body but keep her heart and her mind strictly off-limits.

Jackson stumbled back to his hotel room, shaken to his core. He still held the taste of her on his tongue, remembered the feel of her tightening around him as she came again and again on his cock.

She was always so responsive to him. Their bodies were made for one another. He could never get enough. Would never get enough.

He wanted more.

He wanted all of her all over again—

The realization left him reeling.

Wanting to fuck her was fine. Human. She made him so hot, his brain melted. But wanting more? That was unacceptable. Out of the question. Especially after what had happened.

She'd never let them get close again anyway. He shouldn't want to reconcile either. They were reactive together. Dangerous. A Category 5 hurricane neither one could control.

He had engineered her trip to France for a reason. So far, she'd played perfectly into his hands. His joint venture with Hayes was finally within his grasp—a legacy his family could proudly support. *Arlo Las Vegas is the prize. Don't lose sight of that.* The sex was simply the cherry on top of his cake. He needed to keep it purely physical. There could be nothing more.

Evie had a few hours to herself before she had to meet Noémie. She wished she had never agreed to go. Seeing Jackson again today would be too soon for her jangled nerves. How could she possibly face him after… that?

She wanted to text Noémie and cancel, but she didn't have a number for her. Or an address. She'd have to ask Jackson for both, and she was not ready to face him yet.

Desperate for a jolt of fresh air, she strolled along the streets of Paris, from the Arc de Triomphe to the Seine, then walked along the bank to the pont d'Iéna. She and Jackson had made out on that very bridge one hot summer long ago. She pushed the memory from her mind as she made her way toward the Eiffel Tower.

Although the cool air nipped, the sun shone brightly. Evie found an empty bench on the Champ de Mars with a clear view of the Eiffel Tower. She perched there, and tried to map out her plan.

She couldn't let Jackson make her lose her mind like that. She'd never recover once the two weeks were over. She had to steel her emotions—*Think like a man, Evie. Be physical. No emotions. Physical. No feelings.* She could do it. She knew she could. She had to.

She also had to find a way to apologize for the awful things she had thrown in his face ten years ago. Terrible things she had never meant. The guilt from their last day together all those years ago still ate at her. She owed him an apology. She'd brave up and do it before the two weeks were done. Then she and Jackson would part forever, and not even her guilt would tie him to her from then on.

A clean break.

She returned to her hotel later than she had intended, and hurriedly changed into a cashmere dress. Refusing to wait for Jackson to come to her room, she texted him to meet her in the lobby. She pulled on her heeled leather boots and headed for the—

What in the world?

Her eye caught a small mint envelope that someone had slipped under her door.

How long had that been there? Was it a hotel bill of some sort?

Evie reached down. The envelope felt heavy in her hand. Quality paper.

Her eyes traced her name, written in black ink across the front in an unfamiliar hand.

She snapped open the wax seal. Had she ever received an envelope sealed like that before? Never.

She pulled out the thick white card from the envelope.

Her brain took a moment to process the words:

STAY AWAY FROM HIM.

Unease shot through her. "This can't be good." She flipped over the card. Nothing on the back. *It has to be Tilly.*

She shoved the card back into its glossy envelope with unsteady hands and headed toward the elevator bank. *How unnerving. Who sends handwritten threats on fancy cardstock nowadays?*

She exited the elevator, searching for Jackson. He was easy to find in the lobby, looking unfairly sexy in a crew neck sweater. She stormed toward him.

She looked good enough to eat.

His heart lurched as soon as she entered the lobby, jaw-dropping in her red dress and boots. He wanted to peel up the fabric of the skirt and explore how far the boots went up her thighs.

She honed in on him like a missile, face angry.

He had it coming.

He shouldn't have left her like that in her hotel room, but he had been fighting a hurricane of emotions he couldn't reel in—he had to get out of there before they exploded and forever changed the course he'd intended for his life.

Finally in front of him, she shoved something into his chest. *An envelope?* He took it from her, confused. Opening the flap, he pulled out the card.

"Is this from Tilly?" she demanded.

He read the words. Then re-read them.

"What the fuck? Where'd you get this?"

"Someone slipped it under my door. I don't know who did it, but I'm thinking it's your ex-girlfriend. Is this her handwriting?"

He hesitated.

"What?"

"I don't know what her handwriting looks like," he admitted, feeling sheepish.

She rolled her eyes. "Well, tell her to stop. That's creepy."

"The fuck is wrong with her." He reached for his phone, dialing Tilly. Straight to voicemail.

He sent a quick text for her to call him. The text message didn't go through.

"Maybe she blocked you," said Evie, reaching for the envelope.

Before she could take it back, he slid it into his pants pocket. "I'm keeping this until I figure out who it's from."

"You got more than one upset ex roaming the streets of Paris?"

He didn't think so, but his gut churned. Someone had taken their time to write out the threat and knew Evie's exact room number to leave it there. Tilly was the only answer. He'd find a way to reach her. Threatening Evie was unacceptable.

"We should head out," said Evie, turning to go. "I don't want us to be late."

He couldn't help but admire the sway of her hips as

she walked in front of him to the exit. How far did those boots go up her thigh?

Noémie's Le Marais apartment was bright and airy, with exposed wood beams in the high ceilings and large windows. She had set out champagne and a beautiful display of soft cheeses and fruits.

Her two twin boys rushed up to Evie as soon as she crossed the threshold, speaking in enthusiastic French. Evie could catch every third word. Jackson had shared that they had just turned thirteen and had an Alvin Alby-themed birthday party. They peppered her with questions about her book series that Noémie's husband, Henri—a tall, slightly older gentleman—helped translate.

Noémie marshalled the group to the table. The two boys flanked Evie, pressing their chairs as close to hers as they could, and continued their exuberant questions. Evie, charmed by their vivid imagination, spoke to them in a mixture of English and her basic French.

"We are all big fans of your work," said Henri.

"I'm delighted to hear it!" She looked at the kids. "I will personally ship you both the next installment in the series as soon as it's released."

The twins rejoiced at the news. They begged her to see their playroom. Evie barely had time to set down her glass before they dragged her away. Henri, the steadfast translator, followed.

Jackson watched Noémie's children pull Evie away from the table. She had always been good with kids, had always wanted kids. It was one of the first things they had talked about when they'd met—the brood of babies she wanted to have. He had half-expected her to be married with a gaggle of them by now. When he'd sought her out, started looking into her life and found her unmarried, exultation had rung through him. Misplaced exultation. There couldn't be a future for the two of them.

He pulled out the note from his pocket and handed it to Noémie, lowering his voice. "She found this in her room today. Think it's from Tilly?"

As Noémie read the note, her eyes rounded. "A disturbing sentiment. Is it Tilly's handwriting?"

"That's what I'm trying to find out. Her phone is off." He saw Noémie hesitate. "What?"

"She came looking for you at the club yesterday. We had just opened for the day."

"*Merde.* You talk to her?"

"Told her you were out of town. She stormed off."

"She's still in Paris then."

Noémie shrugged. "I'd assume so. I knew she was crazy from the moment you introduced us."

Chapter 14

The kids insisted that Evie stay longer, and Jackson had to cajole them into letting her leave for the evening. She enjoyed watching him interact with the two rambunctious boys, even as a pang of melancholy sliced through her abdomen. Their own child would have been just a few years younger than the twins if the wreck hadn't changed their lives forever.

A wave of sadness and guilt threatened to tug her under. She fought it with all her might. She couldn't rewrite her past, but she could apologize to Jackson… and she would. Just not right now. Her emotions roiled, and she refused to cry in front of him again.

Jackson had booked an early dinner on the second floor of the Eiffel Tower for their last day in Paris. Evie had never dined at Jules Verne herself, but her parents had been delighted by the surprise, however extravagant, when he had shared the news with them that morning. Now that dinner was a half hour away, Evie dreaded it.

She didn't want to sit across from Jackson and act as though nothing had happened between them. She didn't want to tolerate the Icefalls' cool treatment of their son. She had met Jackson's three half brothers a decade ago, and stayed in touch with them still. Hayes, Nate, and Oliver were kindhearted and delightful. Clearly, they hadn't inherited those traits from either of their parents. Lisa and Leonard seemed resentful of Jackson, and Evie didn't know why.

Determined to skip the fancy meal, she headed to her parents' room to break the news to them.

Her mom opened the door in a bright pink gown.

"Lisa insists that she and I color-coordinate for the photos! How does this look? Is it too bright?"

"You look beautiful."

"I just bought it today. I don't know if I'll ever have the guts to wear it when I'm back home, but Lisa insisted it's Instagrammable." *When did her mom learn that word? She barely used her social media account.* "The restaurant tonight sounds so fancy. I want to fit in."

"She bought me a whole new ensemble too," grumbled her dad. "Said I'll be kicked out if I wear my regular clothes."

"I'm sure you'll both look great."

"Oh, Evie!" Rose's excited face turned to her. "You should color-coordinate with us. Do you have something pink?"

"Ummm…" Evie hesitated. "I'm not joining for the dinner."

"What do you mean you're not joining?" her mom asked. "It's our last day in Paris. The reservations Jackson made must have been hard to come by."

"I have to catch up on my writing. You all go ahead. I know you'll have a great time."

"Are you sure, honey?"

"Positive. And I'll see you guys tomorrow morning for our flight."

"Flight leaves at eight," her dad reminded her. "We should leave early. Never know what the traffic is like here in the mornings."

"Meet at six?" asked Evie.

"Better make it five," said Michael.

Evie knew they'd be knocking on her door before 4:30 a.m.

Evie curled up in her bed with her laptop, letting Alvin Alby's next adventure sweep her away. Her phone pinged an hour later. She ignored the zing of excitement at seeing Jackson's number.

You didn't join our parents for dinner?

She typed out a hurried reply.

Had to write. Hope you guys enjoy!

The familiar knock on her door told her more than she needed to know. Jackson hadn't joined them for dinner either.

She climbed out of her bed and padded over to the door to let him in.

His hot gaze swept over her, sending her heart skittering. She had changed into simple loungewear, but the thin material clearly outlined her bra beneath.

His dancing eyes met hers. "Jules Verne not up to your standards?"

Evie could never resist his teasing. "It would have ruined me for all other restaurants," she said, smiling.

She backed up a few steps to let him in. He strode inside with decisive steps. "You hungry?"

"A little. I was going to eat here. Why didn't you go?"

"And sit through Leonard's grumbling? No, thanks. What about grabbing a bite down the street? There's a new place that's supposed to have good roast chicken."

She was a sucker for roast chicken, and he knew that.

"Give me two minutes to change."

Jackson reached for the hem of her shirt. "Need a

hand? I can think of a few ways to get you off… and ready for dinner," he murmured.

Evie's body responded to his touch. She had been powerless to fight their attraction at twenty-two. She barely could fight it now. Before she could talk herself out of it, she pulled off her shirt.

Jackson's large hands wrapped around her waist, hauling her to him as his mouth found the sensitive hollow where neck met shoulder.

The hotel room shook with a sudden thunderous pounding on her door.

"Jackson! I know you are in there!"

Evie glanced at the door. "Is that… Tilly?" She reached for her shirt, put it back on as the pounding continued.

Face grim, Jackson strode for the door. When he opened it, a furious tornado leapt into the room.

"*You cheater!*" Tilly screamed. "I knew I'd find you here. With *her*!"

"Lower your voice," Jackson ground out. "I told you that you and I are over."

"*I don't care!* You brought me to Paris. I met your family. And now you're here… in her room… with her! Who *are* you anyway?" demanded Tilly. Her gaze dismissively scanned Evie from head to toe. "You're not his type anyway. What are you doing with her, Jackson?"

Jackson took a step toward her. "Tilly. I'll walk you out."

"Don't touch me!" Tilly screeched.

"Why don't we all just talk?" suggested Evie. "Tilly, you're obviously upset."

"I *am* upset. At myself. For falling in love with an *asshole*."

"We barely know each other," Jackson ground out.

The slap rang out in the room.

Evie gasped. Tilly had socked Jackson.

"*I hate you!*" she screamed. Turning on her heel, she marched out of Evie's hotel room.

Jackson's palm rubbed at his cheek. "I'm going to go talk to her downstairs."

"I'll go with you."

"I don't think that's a good idea."

"Why? It's not me she's mad at." Evie grabbed her room key. "Let's go."

Tilly had taken one of the elevators before Jackson and Evie reached the elevator bank. Jackson pressed the button to call the other. A few seconds later, the doors opened with a ping.

They rode down in silence, Evie's thoughts gathering like a dark storm cloud. Apparently, Jackson had a powerful effect on all women. No one was immune to his charms.

"She's not in love with me." The quiet words broke the heavy silence in the elevator. It felt as though he'd read her mind.

"She thinks she is. It's not your place to convince her otherwise."

"We met weeks ago. It's not like that—"

The elevator doors opened. They caught a glimpse of Tilly as she reached the exit and slipped out.

"You don't have to explain anything to me. Just… go talk to her. Hurry, before she gets in a cab."

Jackson sped up his stride, disappearing out the door as he followed Tilly's path. Evie lingered in the lobby. The two needed time to talk.

A hollow *thunk*, the screech of tires, and surprised gasps from the outside froze Evie's blood. She ran.

Exiting the hotel, she saw a group of people gather

around someone on the street. She hurried toward the cluster. Rapid French phrases flew like pinballs.

"She jumped out of nowhere!"

"Where'd the driver go?"

"Someone call the police!"

Evie shoved her way through the crowd. Tilly lay sprawled on the road; Jackson knelt next to her. She sank down next to Tilly.

"I hate you!" Tilly continued her tirade.

"What happened?" Evie looked at Jackson and the faces around them.

Someone hurried to explain in English. "She jumped into the road—the scooterist couldn't stop in time. He dashed away. The police are on their way."

Jackson's hands ran over Tilly's body. "Where are you hurt?"

"Don't touch me, you bastard!" Tilly hissed.

Evie leaned over her. "Tilly, can you move? Is anything broken?"

"My leg hurts."

The first responders arrived quickly. The medics lifted Tilly into the ambulance and sped away. The police stayed to take witness statements.

"I'm going to go to the hospital," said Jackson. "She doesn't want to see me, but I don't want her to be there alone."

Evie nodded even as ice prickled her limbs. She knew she should go with Jackson, make sure Tilly was okay, but the idea of being inside another French hospital, with its sounds and smells—her body rejected the idea. She couldn't bring herself to do it. She couldn't relive that.

Evie bit her lip, fighting the panic that threatened to engulf her. "I can't go with you."

The press of Jackson's lips to her forehead soothed her erratic heartbeat. "I know. I'll find you afterwards."

Hours later, Jackson still hadn't returned. Evie couldn't sit still. She paced her room, unsure if she should text him or give him space to handle Tilly and the hospital.

When she heard his footsteps down the corridor, she ran to her door and swung it open, meeting him in the hallway.

"Tilly twisted her ankle, but she's perfectly fine otherwise. They want to keep her overnight just in case, but it should be an easy recovery."

"Oh good! That's a relief."

He didn't enter her room, hovering in the hall instead. "I'm going to pack up my stuff, bring it with me, and then meet you at the airport for our flight tomorrow."

"Good idea. She shouldn't be in a foreign hospital all alone."

He hesitated.

"You okay?" Evie asked.

"I want to clarify something." A muscle ticked in his jaw. "Tilly and I knew each other for less than a handful of weeks. I only brought her as a distraction, because I knew you were with David. It wasn't fair to her. I know that. But I can't have you thinking there's more to it than that."

She tried not to overthink his statement. "I know… I got that. Either way, she shouldn't be all alone tonight in that hospital."

"As long as we're clear."

"We're clear."

"I'll see you tomorrow at the airport," he said, turning to go.

She watched him until he turned toward the elevator bank and disappeared from sight.

Jackson brought his hastily packed bag with him to the hospital. Visiting hours had ended, but when he explained the situation to the nurse, she took him up to Tilly's room.

Tilly's empty room.

The bed lay empty.

Her clothes were gone.

"Where did she go?" Jackson asked in French.

The nurse shrugged. "I'm not sure. She's supposed to be here."

Jackson reached for his phone and dialed Tilly. Straight to voicemail. He sent a text. The message bounced back to him.

He asked around the floor. None of the medical staff knew where she could have possibly gone.

Frustrated, Jackson called Evie.

She picked up on the first ring. "What happened?"

"Tilly left the hospital. I don't know where she went."

"Do you know where she might be staying?"

"No. And I don't want to be running all over Paris looking for her. She knew I'd be back. She chose to leave before I returned."

"She probably needs space. Maybe the accident served as a wakeup call of sorts to her."

"Maybe. I'm heading back to the hotel."

He swallowed, body coiling with anticipation. *Ask me to your room. Tell me you want to see me tonight.* He waited for her to say the words.

"I'll see you tomorrow morning in the lobby."

Disappointment crashed through him. He took one

final glance around the hospital, and headed for the door. The scent of the space stirred up nightmares he had fought for years to forget.

Chapter 15

A car service picked them up from the Nice Côte d'Azur Airport. Another Jackson surprise. Evie understood why he continued to try and impress his parents. His mother and stepfather had treated him terribly in his childhood—sending him away to boarding school while smothering their three other sons with attention and love. It was a sheer miracle that Jackson and his half brothers remained close. They had barely known each other in childhood.

His ambition and hard work had paid off. He'd built a world-famous business from the ground up, and continued to expand it. Even if his business involved sex clubs, it made her proud to see the things he'd accomplished since they'd met. No competitor even came close to Zohra's fame or reach. Evie remembered reading that Jackson owned twelve clubs across seven countries. An insane accomplishment for someone told by his own mother and stepfather that he'd never succeed.

Alain, their driver for the duration of their stay on the French Riviera, brought the spacious vehicle to a stop in front of a stunning white-stone hotel along the Bay of Angels. As Evie stepped out of the car, warm Nice air enveloped her, a pleasant change from the cooler weather of Paris. She glanced across the palm-lined Promenade des Anglais to the expansive Mediterranean just beyond.

The shimmering blue of the sea brought back bittersweet memories.

Evie had met Jackson in Nice, just a few blocks from this very beachside. She had signed up for an exchange program during her last semester of college, which sent her to the UK for fourteen weeks. When the study abroad program concluded, Evie and her roommate bought discount tickets to Nice to explore France before they had to return home to California.

They had met Jackson and his three half brothers at a local bar during their first night there. The four siblings were celebrating Nate's impending college graduation by exploring Europe, and Nice was their first stop. The connection between her and Jackson had been instant. Evie ended up extending her trip, missing commencement and staying in France with him for three months—the entirety of her summer. She spent every penny of her meager savings account, but she was in love and didn't care. Until that love crashed in an accident outside Monaco.

She returned home broke, heartbroken, and in a cast. Her parents never knew about the wedding, or about Jackson. They had always cared about appearances. Their roles in the community depended on it. Not telling her parents about the wedding and baby still tore at her—they had always been close, but she had been so ashamed. They only knew the bare details of the car accident. Evie worked hard to lock every memory away, and to never talk about it to anyone. Only Joy knew the truth, and she never brought it up.

Now Evie returned, with Jackson and their parents in tow. Maybe if she hadn't resisted Jackson's insistence on sharing their rushed marriage with their families, things would be different. She had never felt as free as she had with him, but he had wanted to tell the world, and she couldn't, and then it was all over. Their ball bounced the way it had.

"Evie? You coming?" asked her mom.

She tore her gaze away from the Mediterranean and followed the group into the spacious lobby.

The two sets of parents checked in first. After they retrieved their keys, they moved to the side of the check-in counter, chattering cheerfully as they waited for Jackson and Evie.

Jackson waved her ahead of him. "Your turn."

She slid over the required documents to the receptionist, a serious young man who reviewed them without a word and started to type into the computer in front of him.

White hydrangeas lined the dark wood check-in desk. Evie couldn't resist the urge to touch the delicate blooms.

The receptionist watched her for a beat too long as she studied the flowers. He flipped over a digital screen for her to sign. "My nephew is a big fan of your books," he said with a neutral expression.

Evie wanted to offer an autograph, but she didn't know if that would be too presumptuous. She didn't want him to think that she was full of herself, so she opted for thanking him instead. She took her keys from him and moved out of the way, joining their parents while Jackson checked in next.

The receptionist handed Jackson his keys and regathered their group in front of him to give them a quick rundown of the hotel amenities before calling the porter to help with their luggage.

Jackson's and Evie's rooms ended up on the same floor and right next to each another. Surprise, surprise.

Her parents' and the Icefalls' rooms were located several floors up and in the straight-opposite wing. She knew Jackson had had something to do with that too.

Walking into her room, Evie glanced around the space, with its pale blue walls and gold-fringed curtains. The view of the Mediterranean drew her attention, and she slid open the glass balcony door. As she stepped onto the balcony, sounds of traffic from the busy Promenade des Anglais below became more pronounced. She didn't mind, she'd missed this place. Every breath of Nice reminded her of her time here with Jackson. The shifting azure of the Bay mimicked the color of his eyes—

Stop it, Evie. He lied to you about the sex tape. He used that sex tape to blackmail you.

She needed to focus on those facts.

Not on how good his tongue and fingers and body made her feel.

How did he get the hotel to put the two of them next to each other? She had booked this hotel herself for David and her parents—she hadn't even known the Icefalls would be accompanying them then. She certainly hadn't anticipated Jackson to join.

Had he planned this…?

No.

He wasn't that diabolical.

Was he?

Had he machinated their entire trip from the start? What would be the odds of his parents and her parents going to Europe like this together? She didn't believe in this odd, and constant, set of coincidences.

She had questions for Jackson to answer. She'd ask them now, before her imagination got the better of her. Evie exited her hotel room and crossed the short hall distance to his door—

A door that had been left ajar. Was he expecting her? She pushed it open wider and stepped inside.

The floor fell from beneath her feet.

Two naked women stood in his room—and faced a very unclothed Jackson Auclair.

Her eyes catalogued the scene even as her brain told her to run. Jackson's hair dripped wet, the water beading across his nude body. Clearly, he had just walked out of the shower.

The two stark-naked women faced him, his large bed at their back. Three heads turned at her entry.

Evie had no words.

She backed up quickly and hurried out of the room.

"Evie!" she heard Jackson call her through the blood rushing in her ears.

The thud of his footsteps shook the hallway.

She hurried to get back into her own room. She couldn't face him right now.

The keycard didn't work on the first try. Evie struggled for the chip to allow her entry. When the light turned green, she shoved at the door, but it was too late. Jackson had reached her. He had managed to throw a towel over his hips, but water still beaded his naked chest.

His hand wrapped around her upper arm, an attempt to stop her.

She shook him off.

She needed to enter the safety of her room and to slam that door in his face, but he held the door wide open, even as she struggled to close it.

"Evie. It's not what you think. Come with me. I have as many questions for them as you do."

"I have nothing to say to them. Or to you." She released her hold on the door. "Please leave."

"I was in the shower—I thought it was you in the room! I don't know where they came from. Evie, nothing happened. You have to believe me."

"Why would I believe you?" she asked. "I don't even know you anymore."

Blood pounded behind his eyeballs. All he had wanted was a fucking shower. Hearing rustling in his room, his first thought had been Evie. Expecting to see her, he had walked out of the shower stall. Instead of Evie, two buck-naked women had faced him.

He had no idea who they were.

When Evie had entered right there and then—before he even had time to ask a question—it was obvious where her mind had gone. He didn't blame her. It looked bad. Even he knew that.

He couldn't let it end like this.

Wouldn't have her believing the worst of him.

He'd done some pretty fucked up things since their divorce ten years ago—like screwing married Georgia Carlton—but he wouldn't do that to Evie. He wouldn't cheat on her.

Even if they weren't together, they had committed to each other for the two weeks. He'd never—

Desperate, he remembered the one thing that would make her listen, that would make her go with him to confront his nude visitors.

He had needed it for the Vegas project. Had planned on using it then. But he had no choice.

"You owe me one carte blanche favor. I'm calling it in now. Come with me. Talk to them."

Her whole body vibrated in sheer wrath. "You're fucking two women in the room right next to mine and you want me to go speak to your two lovers?"

"Please, Evie."

Determination flashed in her brown eyes. Her chin tilted up. "Fine. Let's go. Let's see what your ménage a trois buddies have to say."

The two women were in the process of hastily pulling on their clothes when he and Evie returned.

"Who the fuck are you two?" Jackson demanded, closing the door, entrapping them all in his room. He didn't need the neighbors to come sightsee at the commotion. This was a classy hotel. The situation they were in was a far cry from classy.

"You called for us," said one of the women.

"I didn't call for anyone."

The other woman shrugged. "Say what you will. We were told to come here and fuck you. You gave us your room number. You even left the door open."

Panic engulfed him. Evie believed them. He could see it in her eyes. She looked at him like he was the lowliest scum of the earth. "I didn't!" He turned to Evie. "I swear to you, I didn't."

Evie's gaze fastened on his. He saw the betrayal etched in her features. She studied him closely. Whatever she saw in his eyes must have moved her enough to stay.

She turned to the women. "Who'd you speak with?" she asked. "Him directly?"

The women exchanged a glance.

The tall one shook her head. "No, not to him."

"We were told to come here and surprise him. Were told he was waiting."

"Who told you that?"

The bustier one shrugged. "Not sure. Some guy."

"It wasn't me," Jackson insisted.

"You got a name?"

They both shook their head. "He paid us cash downstairs. Some average-looking brunette."

Evie's gaze narrowed as she studied them. After a tense pause, she dismissed them with a jerk of her head toward the door. "Go."

The two women scurried away.

"Evie, you have to believe me, I'd never—"

"Order two hookers for yourself on your first day in Nice?"

She glanced at the still-made bed. Walking past him, she opened the balcony doors wide, letting in sea salt-scented air. "They had on some strong perfume."

He watched her as she stepped onto the narrow balcony, her eyes focused on the sea. Anger and frustration and fear clawed at him. He had told himself he had two weeks with Evie. He wasn't ready to let her go yet. Not after he'd only had the barest of tastes. His body still craved her. He couldn't let it all end now.

Who would dare send him a couple of hookers? He had friends with senses of humor, clients who were eager to impress—but this seemed out of character for them all. He'd get to the bottom of this. He wouldn't rest until he did.

He followed Evie onto the balcony. "I would never—"

She stopped him with a wave of her hand. "I believe you. But who the heck would send you two prostitutes? Who knows you're here?"

"My brothers know I'm here, Noémie, my Cannes club manager, my assistant, maybe the people they'd told… but that's about it."

"Do people send you hookers regularly?"

"This is the first time. I'll make sure it's also the last."

"You're going to have to change rooms. I can't unsee it."

"Done."

She finally faced him. "Did you have a hand in having your room so close to mine?"

He didn't see a reason to lie. "Yes. I called the hotel."

"Why?"

"Until our two weeks are up, I want you an arm's reach away."

He snagged her hand. For a second, it looked like she wouldn't allow his touch. Her whole body tensed at the contact. She searched his eyes, finally relaxing into his hold. He took a step closer. She allowed that too.

He wanted to kiss her.

Looking down at her—with the warm Nice air so reminiscent of their first meeting—he wanted to pull her into his arms and cover her mouth with his. He wanted to taste her, to hear her hum of pleasure as he slid his tongue inside the warm cavern of her mouth.

He watched her pulse quicken, her eyes darken.

He wondered if her thoughts had taken her there too—did she regret her "no kissing" rule now?

Slowly, he reached out his hand. His palm cupped her cheek, her skin velvet-soft and warm under his fingers.

Her lips parted.

He leaned down—

She turned her face, presenting him with her cheek.

Disappointment tore through him at the move. Reluctantly, he released her face. Took an unwilling step back, watched her walk away from him. The door snicked quietly behind her.

She had almost kissed him. Had almost drawn his head down and put her lips to his. How could he possibly have this pull on her? She had established the no kissing rule herself. How quickly she'd backtracked.

At least she had the presence of mind to move away.

Evie took a quick shower, trying to chase all thoughts of Jackson from her mind. The blind jealousy that had clawed at her when she saw the two naked women in his room—and the tidal wave of relief at learning that he had nothing to do with them—was concerning. She shouldn't care who Jackson saw or slept with. He could buy out a whole brothel of hookers if he so wished.

As she exited the glass stall, she heard Jackson's distinctive knock. Evie inwardly groaned. She needed time away from him to regroup. He wouldn't give her space.

She wrapped the waffle-weaved bath towel around herself, and went to see what he needed.

"I'm now on the other side of your other wall," he informed her, stepping inside her room and closing the door.

His gaze fastened on the towel that she held around herself. The material barely skimmed the tops of her thighs.

His gaze raked over her, from the rise of her breasts over the top of the towel to the full expanse of her legs.

Her thoughts scattered. "Glad they could… um… move you."

He stood frozen, apparently captivated by the water bead that began to slowly trail from her shoulder to her breast.

Evie's whole body heated at the look.

This might be the perfect time to try out her Parisian resolution—stay uninvolved emotionally and work him out of her system. She could do this. Just have the sex. No need for the feelings.

Before she could change her mind, she dropped the towel.

Jackson was on her in an instant. His mouth found her neck, nibbled to her ear. His hands roamed over her, tugged on her sensitive nipples before he moved to soothe them with the wet heat of his mouth.

He released her just as suddenly. Confused, she lifted her heavy lids, watched as he strode further into her room. He headed to one of the two plush armchairs that flanked a circular table by her balcony. His muscles flexed as he lifted the heavy chair.

"What…" Evie's thoughts scattered as he placed the armchair in front of the full-length mirror set against the wall.

"You said no beds. Just trying to keep you entertained, Miss Campbell."

Evie blinked at the chair.

"Sit."

Evie hesitated. She didn't know how she felt about sitting her naked butt onto a hotel chair. Who knew how many other naked butts sat there before hers? She grabbed the towel she'd dropped earlier, and placed it over the chair seat—a layer between her skin and the armchair. There, that seemed a little more hygienic. She sat.

Jackson had set the chair straight in front of the mirror. She faced her seated reflection in the silvered surface. Her chest rose and fell in rapid bursts, even as she tried to steady her breathing. Her cheeks burned red.

She watched in the mirror as Jackson positioned himself behind her. His large fingers curved into the back of the armchair. Their gazes met in the mirror.

Palpable desire rolled off him in waves. "Spread your legs. Show yourself to me."

Instinctively, Evie's thighs pressed close. Jackson had seen and kissed every part of her, but this felt different—this seemed too intimate—

I can do this. Keep it physical. No emotions. Make him want me as much as he makes me want him.

Evie's whole body burned and he hadn't even touched her.

He never shifted his intense gaze, never gave her quarter. Not pressing her, but not letting her retreat either. The desperate need in his eyes spurred her to do it. Slowly, she slid her thighs open, the thin cotton towel rough under her butt. The heat of the room—and Jackson's lustful stare—drew sweat to bead across her skin. She gasped the air that suddenly seemed too thin.

"Wider."

His command was low, but she heard it. The chair arms prevented her from moving her legs further apart. She glanced up at him over her shoulder.

"Watch yourself in the mirror. Spread yourself more."

Aroused beyond reason, Evie hooked her knees over the chair arms, pressing her back into the velvet fabric.

"So beautiful, spread for me. Do you want me to taste you?"

Evie mustered a feverish nod.

He prowled around the chair. Sank to his haunches. Evie's gaze slid to his face.

"Eyes on the mirror, Evelyn."

Evie's eyes moved to the image of her obscenely

spread-eagled while he sat in front of her, still fully clothed. The muscles rippled under the cotton of his shirt as he slid his palms along her legs, over her knees, to her inner thighs, until they framed her center. His fingers dipped into her pooling moisture, spreading the heart of her open before he lowered his head and put his mouth on her.

So softly at first.

She barely even felt him.

"You want this," he said. "You want me."

"Yes," she breathed. No use lying to either one of them. "Please."

"Please what?"

"More."

"More what? Tell me the words, Evie. What do you want me to do to you?"

"I hate you," she whispered, struggling to vocalize the words he demanded.

She didn't need him. She was so hot, so excited, she could… She slid her own fingers down—he caught them, immobilizing them quickly against her body.

"Say it, Evie."

"Jackson… kiss me there. Please."

"Oh, such manners," he cooed against her skin. "I'll try to be extra accommodating."

When he licked her, she almost came off the chair. He held her hands steady even as she struggled against the steely hold of his fingers.

He let her wrists go, using his hands to pull her closer to him as his mouth settled solidly on her. Evie's fingers curled into the silk of his hair as he tortured and pleasured and teased her, taking her to the edge only to slow… until she writhed and pleaded, her body dewy with sweat.

"Eyes on the mirror, Evie," he commanded again.

Her wanton reflection made her even hotter. The mirror focused her attention—made it impossible for her mind to wander to any safe space at all. He had placed her squarely into the experience and refused to let her think about anything else but him pleasuring her right there in her hotel room.

She moaned as his fingers entered her, his mouth continuing the pleasurable onslaught.

Evie couldn't look away. The flush had worked itself across her entire skin. Her eyes looked glazed, feverish in the mirror. She writhed helplessly against the thick intrusion of his fingers and the onslaught of his tongue until she came, biting her own fist to hold in her scream.

When he glanced up at her, satisfaction and need were flagrant in his features.

Tugging her off the chair, he directed her to stand behind it.

He stripped quickly before joining her. His heat seared her back as his powerful presence settled behind her.

His large hands trailed up her sides to cup her breasts. She watched him in the reflection as he squeezed her mounds. Her head fell back against his shoulder at the sensation.

"You want to watch me fuck you, Evie?"

He met her eyes in the mirror. Before she could respond, he bent her over the chair, pressing her hands into the soft edge of the chairback.

"Tell me, Evie."

She let her head drop briefly. "Yes."

She heard him tear open a condom he produced seemingly out of thin air. "Watch us," he commanded as he entered her inch by slow inch.

She lifted her head and met his passion-darkened gaze in the reflection. She could barely recognize herself. A mad flush had worked itself along her sweat-beaded skin. The feel of him inside her, around her, felt like coming home.

Jackson kept his movements maddeningly unhurried as he took her from behind, as though wishing to catalogue every sensation, every breath. She couldn't look away from the heat in his eyes, captivated by the desire in his face. It was like having a magical mirror to inside his soul.

She bit her lip from crying out as his movements stroked her need higher. He looked completely lost to the feel of her. An animalistic urge had taken over his features as he tunneled into her. Never. Breaking. Eye contact.

His hand snaked around her to find her throbbing clit. The added pressure was too much.

"I'm going to—" she gasped.

She tried to fight against the pleasure that unfurled in her, but she couldn't. Her world splintered apart, sending him over the edge as well. He groaned against her skin as his sweat-slicked body shuddered against hers.

The mirror had heightened their connection—inadvertently revealed a part of him he'd kept locked away. Panicking, she realized it had exposed her too. She had told herself that she could be physical with him while keeping her heart safely shut away, but she had been wrong. Feeling fractured apart emotionally, she steeled herself against the sudden feelings that bubbled inside her. Hoped her voice sounded steady even as she felt discombobulated. "I need to meet the parents downstairs soon. I'll see you later."

As Evie closed the door behind him, Jackson found himself hastily dressed and alone in the hallway.

She had dismissed him. Wham, bam, thank you ma'am dismissed him. The Evie he used to know would never—

But he didn't know her well anymore, did he?

His body still demanded her, even all these years later. The sheer force of her pulled him toward her, and he was powerless to stop the momentum.

He came hard just minutes earlier, yet he wanted her again. He wanted to bend her over the bed and take her. Hell, he wanted to throw her on the bed and pound into her until they both forgot their own names. She had a "no bed" rule, but the floor, the chair, the shower—the opportunities seemed endless.

He wished to test out every surface of the hotel room—no, every surface of the entire hotel. He hadn't been lacking for company the last ten years, but not a single person had ever stirred him like Evie did. He craved her more than his next breath. It took every ounce of his self-control not to storm back into her room and make love to her again and again until they were both spent and satisfied.

Chapter 16

Evie tried to put all thoughts of Jackson out of her mind as she met her parents and the Icefalls in the hotel lobby an hour later.

"How's your room?" asked her mom. "Ours has the most gorgeous view of the sea."

"So does ours," added Lisa. "It's so beautiful."

Evie, her parents, and the Icefalls set out to explore Nice. They strolled along the Promenade des Anglais, taking photos along the shore, to Cours Saleya market in Vieux Nice, the historic old town. Evie wanted to make sure they got to the farmers market before the vendors closed up for the day.

The fragrance of fresh flowers welcomed them to the market. Stands brimmed with blooms of every color and variety. Alongside the flower vendors, farmers sold just-picked fruits and berries, laid out in a spectrum of colors.

Evie purchased something at every stand—ripe strawberries, crisp peas, bright clementines—and topped it all off with a selection of nougat for dessert.

Her mom and Lisa bought several bouquets of sunshine-yellow mimosa flowers and an assortment of spices to bring back home to California.

They found a place to sit, and Evie spread out her treats. Once everyone ate through the fresh produce and sampled the nougat, they strolled to Place Massena, where Lisa and her mom took videos of one another.

Lisa and Rose twirled in front of the Fontaine du Soleil, posing at different angles. Her mom had always been shy, but Lisa seemed to bring out a playful side to her. The two acted like long-lost sisters. Leonard and her dad stood to the side, deep in a lively discussion. Apparently, Leonard had a keen interest in theology, and he and her dad had bonded over the topic. Evie learned that Leonard himself had contemplated studying religion, but life took him down the private equity path instead. She hadn't expected her parents to get on with the Icefalls so well, but somehow they clicked. Evie was also surprised to learn that Lisa and Leonard attended her parents' church every so often.

Evie glanced around the main square. She never allowed herself to think of her brief life with Jackson, not even during dark, sleepless nights. She had locked their time together away in the recesses of her brain and she never peeked through the peephole. Yet everything in Nice reminded her of him—the ocean air, the streets they had once crossed holding hands, the landmarks they had explored. The familiarity of it, layered with memories of the things she and Jackson had done to one another that morning, made it impossible to escape him.

She hadn't heard her parents and the Icefalls approach her, ready to continue their walking tour, until Lisa took a step closer.

"When was the last time you visited Nice, Evie?"

Evie's blood gelled in her veins. She never talked about it. "A long time ago."

"She got into a nasty car wreck when she was here," said her dad. "Took her months to recover."

"That's awful!" Lisa gasped. "What happened?"

Evie offered an apologetic smile. "I'm sorry, but I'd rather not relive it."

Leonard frowned. "Wasn't Jackson in a car accident in France a while back?"

"That's right," said Lisa. "He was. I don't exactly know what happened. I think he walked away unharmed."

His parents really didn't know his life at all, Evie realized.

They had a light lunch and continued exploring, Lisa and her mom taking long pauses to record Instagram reels. Evie didn't know her mom was such an avid social media user. Guess she learned something new about her parent on this trip.

Jackson tracked them down on the Promenade des Anglais on their way back to the hotel. He had gotten a haircut while they were busy sightseeing. Without the shaggy locks, the angles of his face became more pronounced, making him look like the old Jackson she knew. She tried not to stare.

"Ready for dinner?" he asked. "I made reservations at a seafood place just across the street from our hotel."

He led them toward the restaurant, chatting amicably with her parents. She could tell that they liked Jackson. He was charming, outgoing, well-read. He surprised Evie when he quoted a portion of her dad's church blog back to him. He didn't seem like the type to peruse church websites. Had he sought out her dad's online newsletter to impress him? What would that possibly get him? Her parents and she would return to California in nine days, and their paths would never overlap again.

Jackson's parents—so jovial without him—became

much more reserved when he'd joined. They made one another uncomfortable, that was infinitely clear. Evie wondered if they had questioned why Jackson had not said his goodbyes in Paris, why he flew with them to Côte d'Azur, yet they seemed to be taking his presence in unwilling stride.

When they reached the restaurant, a reserved maître d' showed them to a table on the outdoor deck that overlooked the Mediterranean. The whitewashed plank flooring, white tablecloths, and white chairs provided a stark contrast to the blue sea beyond. The sun had begun to set, spilling out watercolors over the Bay of Angels.

Jackson pulled out her chair. He had always had impeccable manners. It was one of the first things that had attracted her to him. His hand brushed her shoulder as he stepped away, charging her skin with an electric current she couldn't shake even as he sat down at the far end of the table.

The waiter brought their wine and took their orders. Evie tried to focus on the conversation flowing across the table, and not the memories of Jackson as he took her from behind in front of the mirror just hours earlier. His passion-glazed expression had imprinted in her memory, making it impossible for Evie to concentrate on much else.

When his fingers closed over the stem of his wine glass, images of the same fingers plunging into her as she watched herself come exploded behind her eyeballs.

Evie glanced away.

Not even the cooling evening breeze helped resettle her addled brain. She had to step away from Jackson's vibrant presence, to shake herself of the pull his presence had on her. Maybe she'd find the bathroom. Some cool water to her face might do the trick, stop her horny thoughts.

Setting aside her cotton napkin, she stood.

Jackson's inquisitive gaze found hers from across the table.

"I'll be right back," she told him.

He frowned, but didn't press further.

How long could this dinner last? How could she want him this much? Would it be completely inappropriate if she texted him to meet her right now? There had to be a supply closet somewhere in this place.

She headed inside the restaurant from the outdoor deck. "Do you know where the ladies' room is?" she asked a passing waiter.

He pointed to an archway at the back of the restaurant. "Through there, then down the stairs."

Easy enough. The archway opened to a compact square space, with a side door on the right and a steep stairwell leading down toward the cellar. A discreet sign indicated that the restrooms were located at the bottom of the steps. Maybe there was a supply closet down there that would be private. She'd go explore.

The shove surprised her.

A strong push sent her tumbling forward, down the hard stone steps.

Evie had been gone too long. Listless, Jackson reached for his phone. No text messages. How long could one spend in the bathroom? The need to check up on her seized hold of him until he gave in to the pull and stood.

The parentals, deep in conversation, didn't notice him stepping away from the table. He didn't provide an excuse, just traced Evie's footsteps into the restaurant.

He scanned for Evie as he strode through the near-empty indoor space. Not finding her, he stopped at the arched doorway, assuming the restrooms were through there. A small commotion from the lower level propelled him to move. His eyes zeroed in on the thick stream of blood that was clearly visible on the steps.

Please don't let it be Evie's. Let her be okay.

Panic gripped him as he ran down the stairs.

When he reached the bottom, he veered around the corner and saw three waiters surrounding her. Evie sat on a small bench set against the wall, holding a cloth napkin to her forehead—a forehead that bled profusely. Blood soaked through the cloth and trailed down her cheek.

He pushed his way through the group, and crouched down to be eye level with her. "What happened?" he demanded.

"She took a tumble," one of the waiters explained in French. "She says she's fine."

"Evie? You okay? You need me to take you to the hospital?"

"No hospital. I'm fine, I think. I've heard that head wounds bleed a lot. Turns out, it's true." Her lips tried to quirk up at her attempt at the joke, but the movement was fleeting.

He ignored her stab at humor. "You fell?" he prodded.

Evie didn't answer. She changed the hand holding the cloth to her head wound.

"I want to go back to the hotel," she told him.

"Come on. I'll take you home."

The small group of waiters, relieved to relinquish the victim to someone else, scurried away.

Jackson reached for her hastily made bandage. "Let

me see." He peeled the cloth away from the bleeding gash. "Ouch."

"Does it look very bad?"

"I think we should have a doctor take a look. You don't mess with head wounds."

"I just want to go home."

He wanted to argue. She needed medical attention, yet he knew how she felt about hospitals. Because insisting would be futile, he chose to agree instead. "Okay, I'll take you back."

"Don't tell my mom or dad, okay? They're going to flip out and they've been having such a great time with your parents."

"If that's what you wish. What happened? How did you fall?"

"I think—I think someone pushed me."

Her words chilled him to the marrow. Evie wasn't one for dramatics. Needing to touch her, to prove to his racing heart that she was whole and there with him, he laid a hand across her knee. "Tell me exactly what happened."

"I don't know—I was heading downstairs and I felt someone push me. Next thing I knew, I was falling."

"You didn't see who it was?"

"No. And none of the waiters seemed to have noticed either. The stairwell is so out of the way, no one saw a thing."

First the note in Paris, now this? He should have never let Tilly out of his sight. He hadn't even had a chance to question her about the penned warning before she slipped away. Would Tilly have traveled to Nice to shove Evie quietly from behind? She seemed more of an in-your-face individual. Either way, he would find whoever it was, and he'd make sure they'd never get close enough to Evie again. He cupped her bloodstained cheek. "You sure you don't want a doctor?"

"Positive."

"Can you walk or want me to carry you?"

"I think I've made enough of a scene here today."

He wanted to argue against her wishes, to scoop her up and carry her back to the hotel, but she was never one for drawing crowds. Fighting her on this, just like on the hospital, would be pointless. She'd never allow it. "Let me help you up."

When she placed her cold hand in his, her whole body trembled. She was probably still in shock from the tumble. He pulled off his sweater, needing to warm her. Although the material was thin, it would provide her with an additional layer. "Here. Arms up. I'll be careful."

Gently, meticulous to avoid the wound, he worked his sweater over her head until she was draped in the fabric.

"How do I look?" she asked.

He knew the question stemmed from not wanting her battered appearance to draw attention. The gash on her forehead was raw and bleeding. The blood caked down her cheek and neck, disappearing under the crewneck of his cotton sweater. She looked beaten up and frightened, but was still the most breathtaking woman that Jackson had ever seen.

"Beautiful."

She crinkled her nose in response. Pressing the dressing back to the head wound, she pointed upstairs. "There's another door to the outside at the top of the stairs. I don't want to walk through the restaurant."

The comment clamped Jackson's teeth together. Whoever had shoved Evie could have entered and left through that door without being seen by anyone in the restaurant. That meant that they knew this place—had been here before.

"You feel nauseated? Dizzy?"

"No, just still a little in shock. And very grateful that I didn't break something."

Intent on catching her should she fall, he walked behind her as they mounted the steps. Reaching the top of the landing, they slipped out of the restaurant through the side door. As they stepped outside, Jackson glanced around. No security cameras. Dammit. Anyone could have gone in this way and pushed Evie down the steps, with no one in the restaurant noticing.

Needing the contact, he reached for her hand. Her fingers felt like ice in his grasp. Their hotel was just a short jaunt away, and they managed to make it to Evie's room with a few curious looks but no direct questions.

Once inside, Evie headed straight for the bathroom. He followed, half-expecting her to protest his hovering. When she didn't, he couldn't decide whether to take it as a sign of her regained trust or her exhaustion.

She paused when she saw her reflection in the mirror. "Whoa. I look like I just got out of a fight, and the other guy won."

Jackson didn't find her comment amusing. "Need help with your clothes?"

"No, but there's a lot of blood on your sweater. We should get it out before it sets."

"Fuck the sweater. Let's get you washed up. I'll be right back. Going to go scour for some bandages and antiseptic."

"No need to go far. I have a travel-sized first aid kit in the inside pocket of my suitcase."

Of course she did. She continued to impress him. "Always prepared."

The corners of her lips curved up. "Like a Girl Scout."

He wanted to taste her smile. He shoved the thought away. "Let's get you on the bed."

"You wish."

"I promise to postpone any lascivious acts until after we patch you up."

Evie laughed, heading for her bed. "All right. I'll be holding you to that."

Jackson ran a washcloth under warm water. Sinking down next to her, he washed off the crusted blood with the damp cloth. He had to make several trips to the sink until he was satisfied. Finding her first aid kit, he unzipped the small case and pulled out butterfly bandages and antiseptic ointment.

He returned to sit beside her and glanced at her wound. "At least the bleeding has stopped. How you feeling? Any nausea? Dizziness? Confusion?"

"Nope. I got a thick skull."

He didn't smile. "Not thick enough apparently." Silently, he applied the ointment and the bandages. Once he patched up the gash, he studied her forehead. "You're going to have a nasty bump tomorrow."

"I'll survive."

Unable to help himself, he cupped her cheek. The cheek that had been blood-crusted just minutes earlier. Remembering how small and frightened she had looked on that bench in the restaurant made him angry. Someone had pushed her. Cowardly attacked her and ran. What if she had broken her neck? The thought made clammy sweat bead on his forehead.

"I'm calling the police."

"To tell them what? Not a single waiter saw what happened, and most of the diners were out on the deck. Do you think it was Tilly?"

"I'll hunt down whoever it was. And I'll make them pay." Evie nuzzled into his palm. The move twisted his gut. It was a far cry from her usual prickliness around him. "You okay?"

"I feel a headache coming on now."

Shit. It could be a concussion. "Let me take you to the doctor."

She blanched at the suggestion, moving away from him. "I can't go back to the hospitals here. I couldn't handle it—I just… it would be too much…"

"Shh," he soothed her. "It's okay. I understand."

"I could never ever again be in a French hospital. Even if I were dying."

He understood that. He felt the aversion too.

"No hospitals. What if I have a doctor do a house call?"

"Maybe if I feel worse. But I feel fine right now. Just a little achy. And hungry. We ordered, but didn't get a chance to eat."

She kept her hand between them on the bed. Powerless to restrain himself, Jackson covered it with his. "I'll go run across to the restaurant and have our food packed up to go. I'm surprised your parents haven't called you yet."

Evie stiffened under his touch. Pulling away, she reached for her phone and pretended to check for messages. The move stung. She still couldn't bear his closeness. The accident ten years ago had messed with both of their heads.

"They didn't message. They've been so wrapped up in their conversation, they may not even know we're gone."

"You going to be okay if I leave you for ten minutes?"

"Yes. Bring back some wine too though?"

"Deal. Bolt the door."

Jackson stopped by their parents' table to explain why he and Evie decided to take their food to go. He kept the account brief. "She's fine. Just a little scratch. But I'll take our dinner over to her room."

Rose stood instantly. "We'll go back with you."

"No, no. Stay. Enjoy your meal. The server is packing up our orders and a bottle of wine, so she'll be just fine."

Evie's mom didn't look convinced. Her husband tugged her back down. "Let the kids have an evening away from the parents," he said. "No need to hover."

The argument worked. Rose glanced up at Jackson and smiled. "Okay. You two have fun. But call me if she doesn't feel well."

"I promise."

Jackson grabbed their meals, wrapped to go, and a bottle of wine from the waiter. As a last-minute stroke of genius, he preordered soufflés for the parents to keep them at the dinner longer. He intended to make the most of his sanctioned time with Evie.

He returned to her hotel room a handful of minutes later. Evie had changed into her pajamas, and looked comfortable and relaxed as she let him inside. The bandages across her forehead seemed at odds with her calm demeanor and were a painful reminder of why they were eating in her room tonight.

"How's the headache?"

"Nothing some food can't fix. It smells delicious!"

"Want to eat in bed?"

Her entire body stiffened at the suggestion. "No, the table is more comfortable."

He set down their covered meals and utensils. The waiter had the foresight to include a wine opener, which Jackson used to uncork the chilled bottle of white.

Evie rubbed at her temples.

He noticed. "You should eat in bed."

She dropped her hands. "No, thanks. Brings back too many bad memories."

He knew the memories. He had them too. "Table it is."

When he pulled out one of the armchairs for her, her cheeks flushed. She must have recalled exactly what they had been doing in that chair just a few hours ago.

Instead of sitting, she walked over to the narrow table in the corner and grabbed two glasses from the hospitality tray, bringing them back to the table.

"What an eventful evening."

He poured the wine. "One I'd rather not repeat."

Evie folded herself primly into the armchair and pulled the covers off the food. Her sole, cooked in lemon and butter, and the accompanying vegetables, looked fresh and flavorful. As did his sea bass and mashed potatoes. He hadn't realized how hungry he was until Evie extended a fork his way. He took the utensil and sank into his chair.

"Mmm, this is delicious," Evie murmured, digging into the fish.

Instead of following suit, Jackson picked up his phone and pulled up a list of concussion symptoms. He rattled them all off. "Have any of those?"

"Just the headache… but that's to be expected. I did bounce off the step."

"Not funny."

"Who do you think it might be? The angriest person I've seen lately is Tilly. But I doubt she'd have made it to Nice so fast."

"What about Barnsley? Maybe he didn't take the breakup as well as you thought he did."

"It couldn't be David!"

"Why? Are you saying that only women can be crazy? Men are the nut jobs."

"How gender equitable of you. But that's not what I'm saying. David is too… kind. He's a gentle soul. He'd never push me down any stairs."

"You two dated for six months. That's not enough time to know someone."

"You and I got married four weeks after we met."

"My point exactly."

Evie sighed. "It's not David."

"I'll track down Tilly. Something is off. First the fire in Paris, then the note, now this. I don't like it, Evie."

"Maybe it's a coincidence. They caught the guy who set your club on fire. The note I got may be completely unrelated. And the shove… well… I don't know. Maybe some crazy waiter or something."

"You get a threatening note first and then you get pushed a day later. You don't think that's related?"

"No. Maybe. I don't know. I'm not sure." Evie set down her fork.

His eyes sharpened on her face. "Feeling queasy? That's a concussion sign."

"Or a natural reaction to the idea that someone wants to hurt me on purpose."

I would never let anything happen to you, he wanted to say. But his mouth wouldn't form the words. He *had* let something happen to her. Something that still haunted them both.

"I'm not taking any chances with your life," he offered instead.

Evie stood from the table, skirting it to stand in front of him. Surprise jolted through him as she planted herself in his lap. His arms tightened around her. This is where she belonged.

"Want to do lascivious things to me to distract me?" she asked.

Yes, he did. But he couldn't chance hurting her. "Not before we're sure you're not concussed."

She pressed the briefest of kisses to his cheek. "I feel fine… just headachy."

The warm, tropical scent of her perfume made him want to strip away her clothes and follow the trail with his lips. He pulled her closer against him. "Why don't you get in bed?"

"We said no beds."

"I won't join you—for you to rest."

"I don't want to rest." She closed her teeth over his earlobe. She didn't play fair. His dick, already hard, throbbed against the confines of his jeans, demanding release.

He fought to focus on their conversation. "Humor me?"

Pausing her teasing nibbling, she regarded him with resolute eyes. "I hate, *hate* lying in bed sick. After what happened… I just can't."

He soothed her suddenly rigid back, pleased as she relaxed under his touch. "I know you do. But you can't pretend like you didn't just fall down a flight of stairs."

She wiggled against his hardness. He tightened his hold, intending to still her, but his hips lifted instinctively, seeking to release the building pressure.

"We could play a game of cards?" she suggested too innocently.

"You got a deck?" His voice came out strangled.

"Maybe the front desk will have some. I need to do something. I feel so unsettled." Deliberately, she ground herself slowly against him. "Take my mind off it?"

"Evie—"

"You're watching me like I'm a sick baby bird. I feel fine. Here, I'll show you."

She reached for the buttons of his shirt.

He clasped her hands in his, staying her. "Evie, we can't. Not tonight. We can't risk it. What if you have a concussion and we make it worse?"

"What if I promise to be very, very careful?"

"No." Despite his vehement words, his grip loosened. The pad of his thumb traced slow circles across the smooth, warm surface of her wrist. "God, you're beautiful."

Her hand flew to his lips, stopping him from speaking further. "No love words."

"What about sex words?" he asked against her fingers.

She considered it. "Those are approved." She reached for the buttons of his shirt again. "You're wearing too many clothes, Monsieur Auclair."

He tucked a strand of hair behind her ear. "You sure you're up for this?"

Her mouth hovered near his. It would be so easy to move the inch and press his lips to hers, to dive inside and purge the last few hours from his memory. But rules were rules, and she'd never allow it.

Evie rubbed herself against him, the sensation sending the last, lingering ounce of blood to his dick. "I can feel that you are."

With a desperate groan, he slid his hand under her pajama top, seeking her warm, smooth skin—

Tap, tap, tap.

Go away! Not now! We are busy, he wanted to shout to whoever was at the door.

Evie leapt off his lap so quickly, she stumbled. He reached out to right her, but she scrambled away.

"Who is it?" Evie called.

"It's us, Evie. How are you feeling?" came Rose's voice.

Saved by the parents. She needed rest tonight anyway. He stood to clear their plates.

Evie hurried to the door and let her parents inside. As they stepped into the room, he stepped out. "I'll see you all tomorrow morning. Alain will take us to Saint Paul de Vence after breakfast."

Chapter 17

They arrived at the walled, medieval village of St. Paul De Vence, perched high on top of a mountain, late the next morning.

Evie had been there once before, with Jackson. It had been deep summer then, and the tourists had flooded the narrow, cobblestone streets, pressed close enough together to steam in each other's sweat. The crushing crowds had made it feel like Disneyland during summer vacation.

The town stood relatively quiet today. It was still early enough in May to lessen the visitors, giving the group space to tour the village. They sauntered up the stone-paved paths, exploring the shops, cafes, and galleries along the route. Lisa and Rose made several recordings as the group navigated along rue Grande.

"I want to buy some art work before we head home!" declared Lisa, stopping by a studio displaying beautiful French landscapes. The sign above the door, made to look like a painting palette, had *Cybèle: atelier d'artiste* written in bright blue. "Come with us?"

Evie's parents followed the Icefalls into the artist's studio and gallery.

Jackson's hand caught Evie's. She gave him a curious glance as he tugged her away from the parents down a vein of an alleyway.

"What are you doing?" she asked.

"Have you seen the views?"

"I've been looking at the views the entire time."

"I don't think you've seen this view quite yet."

He pulled her along narrow, stony paths down to an overlook. Evie had only a moment to glance out at the French countryside below them. She yelped as Jackson pulled her into a hidden alcove behind the cobblestone stairwell. The air was slightly cooler here in the shadows, fragranced with herbs that grew nearby. Birds chirped in the faraway distance.

"Oh no," Evie said, realizing what he had in mind. "Not here. Anyone can walk down here."

"No one will… it's perfectly private."

"What if our parents decide to come look for us?"

"They'll be in that art shop for hours."

"What if someone comes here to take photos?"

"They won't."

"Here?" she asked again.

He leaned down and nuzzled her neck. "Here. How's your head feeling?"

Jackson had been asking about her head every ten minutes the entire day. Despite her better judgment, she found his persistent concern touching. "Same as the last time you asked," she smiled. "Just fine. Not even a headache."

"Good," he murmured, kissing the curve of her shoulder.

The feel of his warm breath against her skin sent shivers to dance along each rib. Her body reacted instantly, a desperate need building from her core. Evie tried to fight it.

Sure, they were in a nook behind the stairs, hidden

from view of the village by the stone structure. Yet it felt wrong. It felt naughty.

Even more so when Jackson's hand cupped her breast over the thin material of her linen dress. His teeth found her earlobe as he pressed his body close to her back. Not fair. Evie fought a moan as he found her most sensitive spot below her ear.

"Tell me where you want my hand," he whispered against her neck. The heat of him burned into her.

"We should head back," she breathed out—then gasped as his fingers closed around her nipple. How had his hand slipped inside her dress and bra without her noticing?

"I think we should enjoy the view from here a while longer," he reasoned, his lips skimming down to her shoulder.

"All I see is a stone wall—" Words left her as he tugged down her underwear.

He turned her around to face him. "Feel how wet you are for me. Show me how much you want me, Evie."

She couldn't refuse the need in his gaze. Her own hand trembling, she reached for his, guiding it to her throbbing center. Her cheeks flamed as his fingers slipped through her pulsing heat.

"Do you want me inside you?" he whispered against her ear.

She knew she should say no, but her body quaked for him.

"Jackson—"

"Do you, Evie?"

"Damn you. Yesss."

"Well, since you asked so nicely."

He pulled down the front of her dress and fastened

his mouth on her breast through the lace of her bra. The sensation sent stars and fireworks exploding under her skin. She'd missed him, and these wild reactions he could stir in her. Her body reacted to Jackson like they'd known each other for lifetimes. Like a mere decade apart could do nothing to break their bond.

Frenzied, he kicked away his jeans and boxers, and rolled on a condom. She glanced at his face. His eyes were almost black with need. He studied her with a ferocious intensity. His uneven breath sounded too loud in the small cave of their shelter. He stepped toward her, pressing her against the rough wall. The cool stone was a marked contrast to Jackson's heat.

His fingers dug into her ass as he lifted her. "Tell me to fuck you," he murmured.

"Fuck me."

He didn't give quarter, entering her in one move. They both groaned as he filled her, taking her against the centuries-old stonework. As he moved inside her with deliberately slow thrusts, Evie felt suspended in time. She fought to return to the present, to stop the spell that had bound them to each other, to remember that they'd part ways soon.

"Please… Jackson…" she begged. *Faster. Harder.*

He whispered crude sex words against her neck, driving Evie mad with need. Desperate pleas fell from her lips.

She sobbed when he hastened his movements, hitting just the right spot every time, coiling the tension higher and higher. She buried her face against his shoulder to keep herself from crying out as she exploded. With a prolonged shudder of release, he came deep inside her.

When he slipped out of her, setting her back on the

ground, she felt the loss in every cell of her body. Her knees almost buckled. She'd have fallen if he hadn't held on to her, steadying her.

This was not good. She couldn't get attached to him again. The first time had almost destroyed her. They had wounded each other to the core ten years ago. How could this passion between them persist after that?

Evie took an unsteady step toward her discarded underwear, tugging them back on under her dress. She couldn't look at him.

"Evie?"

He stepped closer. His fingers tilted up her chin. She had to force her eyes to meet his.

His blue gaze looked concerned. "What's wrong?" She shook her head, but he persisted. "Evie? Talk to me."

"Why? We were never good at the talking part before."

She wanted to lash out at him, to run and ensure he never followed. She itched to fight him. To scream and yell as they did hundreds of times before. The writhing anger that began to swirl felt so good and familiar and heartbreaking. Yet when he cupped her cheek, his touch was a cool stream soothing the embers of anguish that unfurled inside of her.

She shook off his hand. "Don't."

"Don't what?"

"I don't want to get attached to you again. We are no good for one another. All we do is hurt one another. I can't… I can't do that again, Jackson. Every time we do this, my heart breaks open a little. I don't have that kind of strength."

"What are you saying?"

"I—I don't know."

"You do know. Tell me." A hot tear rolled down her cheek at his words. She swiped at it, angry with herself for letting the emotions break through the barrier she had constructed. "I keep making you cry. It's never my intent."

"You're not why I'm crying—well, you are, but it's not what you think."

"Tell me."

"Don't you see? *I don't want to fall in love with you again.*"

Evie gasped. She hadn't meant to say the words. Unable to face his shocked face, she did the only thing she could. She ran.

She dashed out of the alcove and back to higher ground of the medieval village. He couldn't chase her pant-less. She heard him curse as she hurried away.

What have I done?

Jackson's jaw twitched as he found his mother, stepfather, and Evie's parents in the exact same gallery.

His gaze darted around the space. "Where's Evie?"

"Oh, maybe she's shopping? We haven't seen her," responded his mother.

Jackson spun on his heel, and set out in search of his ex-wife.

He strode through the narrow streets, dodging the occasional tourist. He found her sitting at a small table in front of an ice cream shop, an ice cream cone in hand.

The panic that had gripped him since she'd run released its hold on him. Relief flooded every muscle.

"Can I join?" he asked, pulling up a chair.

Evie nodded. She didn't meet his gaze. "I don't think this is a place to talk about… us."

"What about a walk?"

She took a small bite of the ice cream. "Can we talk later? I feel too… emotional right now. Maybe tonight?"

He tensed to argue, but when her pained eyes met his, he couldn't. He wanted her to be ready for their talk. Now wasn't that time.

"All right. Tonight it is."

Chapter 18

The group returned to Nice for dinner. Evie had expected Jackson to skip dining with his parents, but he stayed. He seemed quieter than usual, but he sat through the entirety of the meal.

His parents tossed snide remarks his way as though they couldn't help but do so. Their comments made Evie angry. Lisa and Leonard Icefall failed to realize what an amazing son they had.

"Not my favorite food from the trip," scoffed Leonard, glancing at Jackson. "Where'd you find this place?"

"Jackson didn't pick this restaurant," Evie hurried to intercept. "I did. If you hate the food, blame me."

"Why?" Jackson's amused gaze landed on her. "You didn't cook it."

Leonard reached for his wine. "Jackson should have made suggestions—he's the Francophile of the group."

His stepfather really is a jackass. At least Jackson grew up with Valentin. Valentin was a good dad. He had even taken Evie under his wing, when he could have left her high and dry, young and divorced in a foreign country. Evie suspected that, had Leonard been in Valentin's role, he wouldn't have cared about her wellbeing.

Evie glanced at Leonard. "Once my mind is set on

something, no one can talk me out of it. Besides, I thought my meal was delicious."

After dinner, they strolled back to the hotel together as a group, Evie and Jackson rounding out the back. Jackson walked close at her side, his arm sometimes brushing hers. It would be so easy to take his hand, to feel his solid fingers grip hers. She kept her hands exactly where they were. Far away from Jackson.

Apprehension intruded as they reached the hotel. As much as Evie wanted to postpone the inevitable, she'd promised him they'd talk.

I owe him an explanation. Better to let it all out in the open tonight.

Jackson and Evie exited the elevator first, saying goodnight to their sets of parents.

"See you guys at breakfast," called Evie as the elevator doors pinged shut.

As she and Jackson approached their rooms, her gaze zeroed in on her door. Confused, she paused. *Did I forget to lock up?*

The door, the one she was sure she had locked, stood wide open. So wide open that anyone could walk right on in. *Crap! My laptop!*

Jackson beat her inside by a millisecond. They both froze at the door.

"What the hell?" said Jackson.

Her entire room had been… tossed.

The clothes, ripped off the hangers, lay in dejected piles across the floor.

Her bedding had been dragged off the bed.

The two chairs in the room were flipped over.

She raced to the safe. She had locked up her laptop and valuables, but what if the intruder figured out the combination?! Thankfully, the safe remained locked. Evie keyed in her code. Her laptop and passport remained untouched inside.

"Jackson, I always lock my door. You know that I check it a thousand times. It's muscle memory."

She walked through her violated space, reaching the bathroom. Her makeup littered the counter—most of it smashed and broken. What. The. Heck. Someone had broken into her room. Destroyed her things. Who would do that?

She stepped into the living area and faced Jackson. "You better call Tilly right now."

He looked grim. "Yes, and hotel security."

The call to Tilly went straight to voicemail. He called the concierge next. The hotel manager and head of security appeared almost immediately. They accompanied her and Jackson down to the lobby, where security checked the entry log for Evie's room. There was no record of anyone entering her room after she had left that morning. Jackson insisted they accompany the manager and security lead into the control room to review camera footage. The cameras captured nothing out of the ordinary.

"What about the lobby? The elevator? Can you pull that footage up?"

The guard did, but with the bustle of activity, faces proved difficult to track. They didn't see anyone they recognized.

"How's this possible?" wondered Evie.

The manager hovered. "I am at a loss. I'll send housekeeping up immediately. The hotel is completely booked for the night, but I can move you to our sister property a few blocks down."

Jackson's jaw tightened as he glanced at Evie. "You're staying in my room tonight."

"I am not. What would my parents think?"

"That you're a grown woman and can stay wherever the hell you want."

"I'll get a new room in the other hotel."

"Not a question up for discussion, Evie."

The manager hovered anxiously between them.

Evie considered her options. She really didn't want to pack her things and move hotels. She felt bone-weary from walking under the sun all day and, if she were honest with herself, freaked out.

"I'll stay put for now," she told the hotel manager. "No need for housekeeping tonight. I want to see what was damaged first."

"Give me a minute to replace your keys as a precaution," he said. "I'll bring you a fresh set of keycards."

When they returned to her freshly rekeyed room, Evie headed straight to the bathroom to survey the damage. "Darn, my favorite makeup too. You can't get this shade of Lisa Eldridge lipstick anymore." Someone had crushed it against the mirror. "It has to be Tilly."

Jackson dialed her again, but the call still didn't go through. "Straight to voicemail. I'll track her down. She can't hide forever."

Between the two of them, they made quick work of the cleanup. It pained Evie to toss her favorite lipstick, but she had no choice.

"Want housekeeping to do a quick vacuum?" Jackson asked.

"No. I can barely stand up straight. I just want to go to bed."

He extended his hand. "Let's go."

"Go where?"

"You're not staying in a room someone broke into and trashed. You either come stay with me. Or I stay here with you."

He could be so overbearing. She crossed her arms in front of her. "If you want to sleep on the floor, either option works for me."

He glowered. "I won't sleep on the floor in my own room."

"Then—"

"Nor will I sleep on the floor here."

Evie sighed. "Fine, I will."

"You're sleeping in a bed if I have to tie you down to it."

Heat flared. She remembered they had done that once before. She shook off the memory. "I'll put a pillow as a barricade."

"If that's how little trust you have in your abilities to resist me, how could I argue? Need to bring anything?"

Evie glanced around. "I'll grab a few things."

She tossed her pajamas and toothbrush into a tote, then pulled the toothbrush out. "I probably should get a fresh one. I shudder to think what could have been done to mine."

"Smart thinking. We'll have the hotel bring you a new one."

Evie added her phone charger to the bag. She extricated her laptop and passport from the safe. "Okay I'm ready."

He took the tote from her. "After you."

Exiting ahead of Jackson, she made sure that the door closed tightly behind them, testing the handle.

"I feel so violated," she admitted as they traversed the short distance to his room.

He stopped to face her. His expression looked resolute. "I'll get to the bottom of it."

A promise. She believed him. Jackson didn't make promises lightly.

When he held the door to his room open, Evie stepped inside. It felt strangely homey being in his hotel room like this, knowing that they would be crawling into the same bed, sleeping next to one another.

Panic gripped her at the thought. Their earlier interlude had left her emotions too fragile. Sleeping in the safety of his arms would undo her. She could never let that happen.

"How tired are you?" she asked, desperately seeking to prolong the inevitable.

"Why do you ask?"

"We could go to bed if you're exhausted. Or…" Her voice trailed off.

"Or?" he prodded.

"Or… shower sex."

Heat flashed in his blue eyes. "You do look in need of a thorough scrubbing, Miss Campbell."

Laughter bubbled from her as he swooped. His strong arms scooped her to his chest, and he carried her into the glass stall.

As they made their way into Jackson's bed quite some time later, Evie hesitated. She had promised herself to not let him crack open the barrier she had built around her heart. Yet sleeping in the same bed… it felt vulnerable, much more vulnerable than shower sex.

"Stay on your side," she mumbled, picking up a pillow and plopping it square in the middle of his bed. There. A solid barricade.

He watched her with a raised eyebrow. "I was just inside you," he pointed out.

"Well, if you ever want to be there again, you'll stick to your side of the bed."

Jackson eyed the pillow with disdain.

Ugh. I can't be a coward forever.

Evie knew it was time. Now or never. The guilt was eating her alive.

"Jackson, I do want to talk tonight… I… I've had so much to say… I didn't know how."

A guarded expression descended over his features. It made her want to change the subject, to move on to anything else. But she couldn't. She owed this to him, and to herself. Evie stood. She couldn't say what she needed to say from the bed.

Now or never. "I'm so, so sorry! I… I've been… this whole time, I've been so sorry—the things I told you when—in that hospital—I didn't mean them."

He sat up even straighter. "Evie—stop."

"No, listen to me. After the accident… after the baby died… I was angry at everyone and everything, but mostly at myself, and I lashed out at you. I didn't mean anything I said, Jackson. Not a word. It wasn't your fault. The crash wasn't your fault. If I hadn't started that fight, you wouldn't have been distracted, you wouldn't have swerved. You wanted to tell our families about our marriage—about our baby—from the beginning, but I didn't. I was terrified of disappointing my parents."

Her parents would have wanted her to be married in a church, with her father officiating. She, who had always told her parents everything, couldn't bring herself to share that she was married to a man they'd never met before, and pregnant to boot. She didn't want to disappoint them.

Tears burned her eyes, clogged her throat, as she continued. "I loved you so much. I loved our baby so much. But I was so scared."

The fight driving back from Monaco had been thunderous. She yelled. Jackson yelled. He glanced at her for a brief second, accidentally swerving into the opposite lane as he did so. Before a collision could happen, he corrected them back to their own lane, but he had overcorrected. The car hit the stone wall full-speed. Evie's side experienced most of the impact. She had broken and fractured several bones. She had also lost the baby.

He sat frozen. Expressionless.

She continued. "I was never angry with you. I was only angry with myself." She swallowed against the tears. "I loved our baby—as tiny as the little bean was. I know you loved our baby too. I wanted to hurt you as I much as I hurt inside, so I said awful things."

She had lashed out in that hospital room. Accused him of murdering their child. She hadn't meant it. Even as she had been saying the words, she herself didn't believe them. But she'd said them anyway.

He had yelled back with his own accusations. Accusing her of using him, of never loving him, of being relieved that their baby was dead. Because now she'd never have to tell her parents the truth.

Evie closed her eyes against the tears, remembering.

Valentin—who had met Evie earlier that week—had descended on the hospital like a benevolent whirlwind. He had hired a team of lawyers for them both, had seen to their speedy divorce and ensured that both sides had been fairly represented in the proceedings. Neither she nor Jackson at the time could afford attorneys. They couldn't even afford the hospital bills. Valentin had paid for it all.

He told them they had been too young to make such

a strong commitment that quickly. He had gifted them their independence back. That was his wedding gift to them—their subsequent divorce.

Jackson's accusations had burned her. Deep down, she was terrified they were true, even as her heart and brain screamed otherwise. She had loved their baby—had loved Jackson.

But it all fell apart so close to Monaco.

The memories returned now, fresh and raw and painful. As much as she had locked them away into the far recesses of her brain, they now burst forward, stinging her, and tearing at her all over again.

"Jackson, that accident wasn't your fault. You didn't murder our baby. Every time I see you, I want to tell you that—that I had been angry and hurt and I didn't mean any of it. It wasn't your fault. I never once thought it was your fault. We both know it was mine. I had started that fight, I had distracted us. I caused that accident. I caused our baby to die."

She could barely get the words out through the sobs that tore from her heart. She didn't see him move from the bed. When his arms closed around her, she turned and buried her nose against his familiar chest. His tight embrace made the tears fall harder.

"I'm so very sorry, Jackson. I'm the one that murdered our baby."

"You didn't murder anyone, Evie," he said, kissing the top of her head as his arms traced soothing circles against her back. "You were right. It was my fault. I was distracted. I was carrying precious cargo, and I was reckless."

"You weren't—"

"I was."

"No," she looked up at him with tearful eyes. "You

weren't, Jackson. It wasn't your fault. I'm so, so sorry that I accused you. I've been sorry since I said the words a decade ago. Sorry every day."

"Evie, you're not at fault here."

"You're not at fault."

"Maybe neither one of us is. Maybe both of us are. We were young and stupid and so in love. I had been furious with you for a decade—furious with myself. Maybe we can let some of that anger go? Maybe it's time to let go of the guilt too."

"I've lived with it too long. It's a part of me now."

"I think we can learn to let go of it together. Our child died in a tragic accident—we were young and stupid. We were just kids ourselves, Evie. We were both terrified. In over our heads. We fought constantly. It was a recipe for disaster."

"We were in love."

"Yes, we were. But I don't think we were mature enough to handle that powerful of an emotion. It had burned us alive then."

"I don't think I can handle it even now."

"Evie, we're much older now—"

"No. I can't. I refuse to put myself in that situation again."

"You weren't in love with David?"

She shook her head. "I don't think I could ever… ever be that vulnerable with anyone again." Evie looked at him, her tears starting to dry. "You and I really messed each other up big time, didn't we?"

His fingers ran over her cheek. "I think we frightened each other. Feelings that powerful can be destructive. I don't want to chance it ever again. Sex is easy. Sex is simple."

Evie froze. Stepped away. Or at least tried to.

"Not with you." He tightened his hold, bringing her back to his body. "Nothing is ever easy and simple with you."

"Thanks," she said, droll.

"Evie, I'm very sorry for all the things I said to you back then. Just as you hadn't meant a word of your accusations, I hadn't meant a word of mine either."

"I forgive you if you forgive me?"

"I forgive you."

His arms pressed her closer to his body. She laid her head against his chest, listening to the rapid beating of his heart.

"Now, can we remove the barricade?"

She laughed, the sound breaking through the emotional thunderstorm swirling around them. "If you promise to stay on your side."

He kissed the top of her head. "I promise."

Jackson couldn't sleep. He had never allowed himself to imagine that Evie Campbell would be in his bed ever again. Yet here she was, on the opposite side of his mattress, pretending to be asleep.

Their conversation released the hatred and resentment that he had felt toward himself for the last ten years. He had blamed himself for the crash that had destroyed their lives. He was shocked to learn that Evie blamed herself too. They were similar in that way, always taking full responsibility for everything. Now that they had talked about it, had apologized and forgiven, a decade's worth of emotions and self-blame lifted.

Having Evie lie so close to him felt like a precious gift, or a tragic curse. Jackson knew one thing—he wouldn't let anything happen to her. Whoever was targeting her had to be stopped.

He hadn't known Tilly long, but would she follow them all the way to Nice to trash Evie's room? To push her down the stairs? If so, what else was she capable of? He needed to get to the bottom of it fast.

Jackson reached for his phone on the nightstand. The screen burned brightly in the darkness of their room.

Hayes's connections had proven useful in the past. He texted his brother.

I need you to track down Tilly Harvey.

The response back pinged instantly.

Give me an hour.

Chapter 19

Evie opened her eyes to silvery morning light spilling in through the windows. She shifted her legs under the covers, her blood thrumming with energy. The morning felt like Christmas, full of possibility and joy. Her apology, and Jackson's acceptance of it, had chased away the heavy cloud of guilt that had churned inside of her for ten years. Today was a fresh start.

She glanced at Jackson. Sound asleep, he snored lightly on his side of the bed. He had respected her boundary. She wanted to roll over and press a kiss to his stubbly cheek, but she held off.

Rules were rules.

The kiss would lead to other things, and the bed remained off limits.

She tried to move quietly as she slid her feet to the floor.

Someone trashed my room last night.

Someone pushed me down the stairs.

She'd never had anything of the sort happen to her before. The incidents started when she had reunited with Jackson. Tilly was the obvious answer. But where did that girl go? Maybe if they talked, Tilly would stop her tantrum.

She found Jackson's sweater, hoping it would ward off the chill of unease. She pulled it on over her pajamas, pressing her nose into the soft fabric. God, he smelled good. She'd never been immune.

She knew that she should head back to her room and get ready for the day. They were heading to Villefranche-sur-Mer in a few hours and had plans to have breakfast in one of the Cours Saleya restaurants before their daytrip. Yet a stronger urge pulled her to climb back in bed and wake Jackson up in a way he'd never forget.

As she deliberated between staying or leaving, she heard Jackson stir.

"Come back to bed," he groaned. "It's the butt crack of dawn."

"Should I change rooms?" wondered Evie. "I can't stay here forever. I don't want to go to another hotel, but maybe they'll have a vacancy here today?"

"Stay. Sleep. Too early." He burrowed his face into his pillow.

A minute later, Evie heard him snore again. She smiled at his sleeping form. Jackson had never been a morning person. It warmed her to know that his habits hadn't changed even all these years later.

She fought the urge to crawl back into bed and snuggle close to him, but she had set the no bed rule for a reason. She opted for a shower instead.

Turning on the water, she hopped into the glass stall when she heard familiar steps approach.

Jackson looked sleep-rumpled and sexy as he slid open the shower door and stepped inside.

Evie couldn't help but reach for him. Her hands stroked his wide biceps. "I thought you were sleeping."

His lips trailed down her skin. "And miss this opportunity?"

Their conversation last night had ripped a fissure through the wall she had erected around her heart. She couldn't let this time with Jackson crumble her defenses. Loving someone as passionately and blindly as she had loved Jackson once had almost destroyed her. She had barely recovered. The pain from the accident had never even come close to the agony of the heartbreak. She could never repeat her mistake.

Jackson reached for the soap, lathering it in his hands. He shut off the stream before skimming the floral-scented bubbles down her body, grazing her most sensitive places. Evie gasped as his hand slid along the soft curve of her stomach and settled between her legs. He didn't linger in one spot too long, running his hands over her until her knees and ankles threatened to buckle.

She pressed herself close to him, rubbing her aching nipples against his hard chest. When he cupped her breasts, they both sighed. Evie wiggled out of his soapy hold, and reached for the shower gel herself. She worked the lather over his wide shoulders to his biceps and across his chest. Who knew that she had such a weakness for muscular men?

It's a weakness for Jackson, her brain tried to tell her.

She shook off the suggestion. Impossible. She would never fall for him again.

Her hand glided down to his massive erection, fingers closing over his length. His hips bucked into her, and she tightened her hold, stroked. His head fell back, revealing the stubble that trailed from his cheek to his neck. She pressed a kiss to the prickly area under his chin, then slid down to the shower floor.

He grabbed her shoulders, pulling her back up. "Nope. Floor's too uncomfortable for you in here."

Evie pouted. "Just for a minute."

"Bed's much softer," he murmured, but she wiggled out of his grip.

Holding his erection in her hand, she slipped down his body and pressed a kiss to the blunt tip. "No beds, remember?" she said, and closed her mouth over him.

"You're going to be the death of me." His fingers fisted at his sides. He let her play and explore, and she teased and tormented him until he grasped her under her shoulders and pulled her back up, reaching for the valve.

Water rained from the showerhead, surprising her. She yelped. He rinsed the soap from them both before yanking her out of the stall. He plunked her butt on the cold sink and sank down, his mouth finding her center and devouring. She wanted more. She wanted all of him. He stepped away briefly, returning with protection. She had expected him to carry her into the room, maybe lay her on the couch, but he took her right there on the bathroom counter as she dug the short moons of her nails into his back to hold him closer.

When her heartbeat steadied sometime later, he pressed a kiss to her cheek and plucked her off the sink. She needed an extra moment to steady herself.

"You okay?" he asked, keeping his hand wrapped securely around her waist.

"Yes," she assured him. "Just a little turned around."

He leaned close, his breath teasing her neck. "I like waking up with you."

Before she could process the quiet confession, he moved away, leaving her alone in his bathroom.

"It's your sister!" he called from the vicinity of the bed, returning with her buzzing phone. Distracted by the things he'd done to her on the counter, she hadn't even heard it ring.

"I'll call her back later."

The soft expression fled his face. "Afraid she'll know you spent the night?"

"Of course not. I just don't want to answer naked."

His jaw flexed. He strode over to the closet and yanked out one of the robes issued by the hotel. He thrust it into her hands. "Here. You want to call her back now?"

"Why are you mad?"

"All these years later, and you're still worried about appearances, about what other people will think."

"That's not true."

He gave her a look.

"All right," she admitted, shrugging into the oversized cotton bathrobe. "Maybe it's a little true. But you don't know what it's like to grow up a pastor's daughter! You were raised by a French actor. You could do whatever you wanted. My behavior as a child always reflected on my parents."

"You're not a child anymore."

"Joy is my little sister. I have to set a good example."

"Joy is an adult. She's in medical school. I'm sure she won't be scandalized to know that you spent the night with me." He turned on his heel as headed into the room. He sounded exhausted as he added, "I'm tired of being everybody's dark secret."

Evie wished she could argue otherwise, but she'd be a hypocrite. She had kept him—and their marriage— hidden. To this day, her parents knew nothing. As a sheltered twenty-two-year-old, she had been stupid. Deep inside, she had been scared that Jackson wasn't the man she could take home to her parents. She worried that he would disappoint them and, in turn, she would disappoint them. But she wasn't a child any longer. She was a grown woman, and she still sheltered the truth from them.

She hated the hurt that radiated from his body as he reached for the pants that had been tossed across his chair.

She glanced down at her phone, seeing the now-missed call from Joy. The decision came easily. She video called her sister.

Joy looked like she was on her couch and had accepted the call through her laptop. The blue light-blocking glasses she wore meant that she was studying. "Did I catch you in the shower?"

Evie crossed the distance to Jackson. "Sort of. But I wasn't there alone."

Joy's eyes rounded in delight. She clasped her hands together in front of her. "Please, please, *please* say you were showering with Jackson!"

Evie pressed herself against Jackson's side and pulled back the phone so that the video captured him too. "Your dreams came true today, Joy."

Jackson looked bewildered as he glanced down at Evie. He apparently hadn't expected her to ever tell her sister that she'd spent the night. Evie could tell that it took him a moment to process that she had. When he did, his whole body relaxed against hers and he planted a kiss to the top of her head before directing a smile at Joy. "Well, hello, stranger."

"I can't believe you are right there with Evie!" Joy practically jumped on her couch. "It's been too long. Are you guys finally back together? I miss having a brother. Please, *please* say you're back together."

"We're not together," interjected Evie.

Joy fell back against the couch cushions. "Ugh! Why are you doing this to me?"

"We're not—"

"Whoa, what happened to your head?"

Evie had almost forgotten about the butterfly-bandaged wound. "I fell."

"Fell where?"

"Down some steps. I'm fine. Jackson's been very helpful."

If Jackson even dared to tell her sister that she was pushed—

But he kept that part to himself.

"I'm glad to hear it. Evie needs a lot of TLC, Jackson. That bump looks bad."

"I'll do my best," he said, lips twitching.

"I can't believe I'm missing France! You know that I haven't been since I visited you guys when I was just a kid. I want to go back. As soon as I graduate, it's on my bucket list."

"Graduate first," said Evie.

"As soon as I do, the three of us can go wild in Europe."

"No one is going wild anywhere." Evie laughed. "Joy, we have to go. We are meeting the parents for breakfast."

"Do they know?" Joy asked.

"They know nothing."

Joy mimed locking her mouth and tossing the key. "It shall remain so. Bye, guys! Have a good time!" Her eyebrows jumped like suggestive caterpillars.

Evie hung up the call and set her phone on the bed. "I don't think I was ever that young at that age."

"That girl is pure sunshine," said Jackson. "It was good to catch up with her."

"I'm sorry that I treated you like a dark secret."

He pulled her into his bare chest. "I overreacted. It was your little sister calling. Of course you wouldn't want to answer naked. I think it just brought back—"

"I know." The hurt from their failed marriage continued to reverberate even all these years later. "Jackson, I can't ever tell my parents what happened—"

His hold tightened. "I understand. I don't expect you to. It was just a silly overreaction. I'm sorry."

She glanced up at him. "Look at us. Apologizing like adults and everything."

His lips curved. "Maybe we are growing up after all."

The salt-fresh air, warmed by the sun, danced across her skin as Evie explored Villefranche-sur-Mer with Jackson, her parents, and the Icefalls. Rows of houses, painted every color of sunrise, stretched along the shoreline. Evie loved their blue and green shutters. Potted plants, blooming with pink and white flowers, lined the paved streets. Evie had fallen in love with this town on her last trip there with Jackson. It hadn't changed much in the time she'd been away.

Lisa and her mom had apparently done their research ahead of this daytrip. They had mapped out the exact places they wished to photograph, and had each packed several outfits with them. They dragged the group from place to place like treasure hunters with a marked map, stalling for long minutes to take pictures and videos.

"Instagram will love this!" Lisa crooned as Rose posed in front of a colorful row of houses. Her mom's cheeks glowed as she laughed for the camera. Evie had no idea that Lisa was such an avid user of the platform. Maybe it was rubbing off on her mom.

Evie had expected Leonard to get listless from the long pauses, but he didn't seem to notice. He had brought his iPad with him. At every stop, he'd pull her dad aside and flip through something on the screen. Evie didn't know what they were reviewing, but the two remained so engrossed in their conversation, they never once complained about all the extra time the photo ops were taking.

She and Jackson stood on the sidelines, patiently waiting for their mothers to wrap up the photo shoot. He looked on with a mixture of amusement and confusion, but let them carry on.

"I didn't think our parents would get along so well," admitted Evie.

"Me neither. They seemed so different from one another when we discussed them." He glanced down at his phone. "Hold that thought. I have to take this. It's Richard. He manages Zohra Cannes." He answered the phone in French, listening for a few seconds before returning his attention to her. "I need to hop into a conference call. Don't go off by yourself. I'll be back in a few minutes."

She watched him walk toward the water, probably seeking a quite spot for his call.

Lisa and Rose grabbed their oversized totes that carried their additional clothes, waved over their husbands, and stopped in front of Evie.

"Should we go have lunch?" asked Lisa. "I have a spot in mind."

Leonard and her dad were eager to eat, and they didn't have a preference for where.

Lisa pulled up her phone to help navigate and led them toward the waterfront. As they approached the familiar row of restaurants, Evie felt panic rise.

Oh no. Don't let it be the same spot.

Of course it was. Out of the innumerable eateries in town, she had to pick this one. Lisa had taken them straight to Evie and Jackson's favorite restaurant, one they had loved—one where they'd made love—during their brief visit years ago.

I can't go in there. I don't need more memories of the past. Evie hesitated at the door, unsure of how to extricate herself from lunch.

The rescue came from an unlikely source.

"Evie?"

She turned at the sound of her name, twisting her head to see if she had heard correctly. It sounded like David, but what would he be doing in Villefranche-sur-Mer? Apparently, exploring just like them. He came up behind her, dressed casually in an outfit made for a hike or the beach. His cheeks looked ruddy, as though he'd been sunburned, making his familiar eyes glisten brighter.

David's arms closed around her for a moment. "What are the chances?"

Evie's parents and the Icefalls had already gone inside the restaurant. Evie took a step away from the door just in case. She wanted to be as far away from the place—and the memories she and Jackson had shared there—as possible.

"What are you doing here?" Evie exclaimed. She'd have expected to feel awkward around her ex-fiancé, but David had always made her feel comfortable. It was nice to see him look so happy and relaxed.

"I decided to take a solo trip to all our preplanned destinations. I was already in France, figured why not. I did swap out the Nice hotel. Didn't want to make it awkward by running into you in the lobby. How long are you guys here for?"

"Just for a day." Evie pointed to the restaurant. "Mom and Dad and the Icefalls are inside."

"I heard this place is pretty good." David glanced at it briefly before refocusing on Evie. "Do you have to join them or may I steal you away for a half hour? We can catch up."

Evie didn't hesitate. Anything to avoid going back into her past. "Sure! Tell me all about your adventures."

Jackson ended his call. He hadn't expected the license issue, which had never been a problem before. Zohra Cannes was three days away from Zohra's biggest party of the year, and getting shut down now was unacceptable. Legal would refile the paperwork today. He'd head down to Cannes tomorrow if the problem persisted.

Hanging up on the attorneys and Richard, he dialed Hayes. He knew it was the middle of the night in Vegas, but Hayes never slept and Jackson couldn't wait any longer. Last night, his brother had told him he'd have information for him within the hour, but the timeline dragged on.

Hayes didn't answer. Odd. He always picked up his calls. Frustration built at the lack of information. The slice through Evie's forehead had barely begun to heal. Her room was destroyed. It couldn't continue.

Where was Evie anyway? He hadn't meant to let her out of his sight for this long, but she was surrounded by both sets of their parents. They'd keep an eye on her. He sent her a text, then headed back to the spot where he'd left them. Knowing his mom and Rose and their love of cataloguing every aspect of the trip in a fresh outfit, they may still be there.

The town really was picturesque. He and Evie had spent a couple of fun summer days there, making out on the beach, along the walkways, in restaurants. A far cry from their relationship now. He glanced up a familiar street—

What the hell? Is that… Evie?

She sat at a wrought iron table outside a small café

at the top of the stepped street. Her laughter drifted toward him on the breeze as she conversed with someone across the table from her. He didn't recognize the back of the guy's head. He strode up the hill toward her.

As if sensing his approach, Evie's gaze shifted from her companion to him. The laughter stopped.

The back of the head turned.

What the fuck? Where did Barnsley come from?

"What are you doing here?" Jackson demanded, coming around the table to grip the back of Evie's chair. What he really wanted to do was grip the nape of David's neck and toss him down the paved steps.

"I was sightseeing and I ran into Evie. We decided to catch up."

"Consider yourself caught up."

Evie's warm palm covered his hand, still on the back of her chair. The gesture surprised him. The jealousy that had taken hold released. "Want to pull up a chair?" she asked.

He suddenly felt like an ass. Evie was loyal to a fault. She'd never do anything with David now that the two of them were together—

Yet they weren't together.

They had a week to her trip left.

A week until they'd part forever.

Maybe she wanted to keep her options open.

Didn't matter what she wanted. He wouldn't let anyone else have her. Emotions roiling, Jackson stepped back, shaking off her hold.

"You okay?" she asked, brow furrowing.

No. He wasn't okay. He didn't know what the hell he wanted.

"We need to go."

Evie hesitated. David glanced between her and Jackson. As the silence stretched, he stood. "I have got to head out. Evie, it was great to catch up. Jackson, good to see you." He merged with a group of tourists and disappeared down the street.

"That was rude of you," accused Evie. "David is a nice guy. I screwed him over, and he's still kind."

"Trust me, you did him a favor. You'd have screwed him over if you'd married him."

That came out wrong. She looked like he had slapped her. He hurried to explain. "That's not what I meant—"

She crossed her arms. She did that a lot around him. Protective gesture. He hated it. "What did you mean?"

Jackson sank onto his haunches in front of her. "You never loved him. Letting him go was the best thing you did for him."

She considered his statement. Slowly, her hand reached out and cupped his face. He wanted to turn and press his lips to her palm, but he fought the urge.

"I know. It wasn't fair of me to drag it out that long."

"But you had the guts to end it. That's what counts. You hungry? Where are the parents?"

Evie slid her fingers through his recently cut hair before she pulled back her hand. "Starving, but I can't go back to that restaurant—our restaurant. The one where…" Her voice trailed off, and her teeth sank into her lower lip.

He knew the exact place she meant. He understood why that restaurant would dredge up too much. They had been happy there. "We'll find another place to eat and meet them afterwards."

"There's a cute café around the corner, and I think they'll bring the food out fast."

He followed her into the café she'd mentioned. The compact eatery was just what they both needed—a place with food, and absolutely no memories. They ordered sandwiches at the counter, then settled at a table in front of the windows. A few diners sat at the outdoor tables, but inside remained empty except for the staff.

"What happened with Zohra?" she asked, uncapping a bottle of sparkling water and taking a sip.

"Unexpected licensing issues. A headache at the worst possible time, but it should be resolved by the start of the party."

"When will you go to Cannes?"

"I planned to go in three days, just before the event, but I'll drive over tomorrow if I don't hear back from my legal team by end of day today."

The waiter brought out their sandwiches and his coffee. Jackson could hear Evie's stomach growl as she reached for the food. "You'd starve before you'd return to that restaurant."

She nodded. "I remember our last time there too vividly."

He did too. The memories of their quickie in the opulent restroom had burned into his brain. He watched as Evie's cheeks pinkened. She must be remembering the same thing.

A couple entering the cafe caught his eye. Fuck. He recognized Sebastian and Georgia Carlton. Georgia, his worst mistake. And Sebastian, her husband. His affair with Georgia had ended as quickly as it had begun, but the couple bought a lifetime membership to Zohra and now their paths were irrevocably intertwined.

Were they simply glancing inside, he'd consider ducking under the table. That was how much he wished to avoid Georgia. But no escape routes were possible. The couple beelined for their table, Georgia's face beaming with recognition. "Jackson! We saw you through the window!"

He stood out of politeness. Her toned arms enveloped him in a perfumed hug, and she pressed a kiss to his cheek.

A brief burn of guilt flashed through Jackson as he shook Sebastian's hand.

The couple turned toward Evie, expecting Jackson to make introductions. When he didn't, Georgia cut in. "I'm Georgia Carlton and this is my husband, Sebastian. We're good friends of Jackson's. We go way back."

Evie gave Jackson a puzzled look. "I'm Evie. It's nice to meet you."

Georgia's gaze darted to the bandaged cut on Evie's forehead. "Oof. That looks painful."

Clearly reluctant to discuss the incident, Evie waved it off. "Took a little tumble. Do you guys want to join us for lunch? The sandwiches are pretty good here."

"We already ate," said Georgia. "But I'm so thirsty. Sebastian, would you grab me a water?"

"Certainly." He pulled over two chairs from the adjacent table, sat his wife, and headed to the register to order Georgia's drink.

Georgia scooted her chair closer to Evie. Jackson didn't like having her this near his ex-wife. He wanted to grab Evie and the sandwich she was clutching and leave.

"You arrive to the Riviera early for business or pleasure?" asked Georgia, turning to him.

"Playing tourist before the big event. Noémie said you're attending?"

"Wouldn't miss it. We're all about pleasure on this

trip," hummed Georgia, face glowing. "You can be the first to know." She cupped her barely there stomach, vibrating with excitement. "Babymoon."

Relief flooded him. He'd never fucked a married woman until Georgia. The one-night stand had happened years ago, but Georgia continued to drop hints that she wanted to resume their affair. The baby would put a swift end to that. He hoped.

"Congratulations," he offered.

"Boy or girl?" asked Evie.

Georgia flashed a wide smile. "We're going to wait to find out. It'll be a surprise."

Sebastian returned, setting a bottle of water in front of his wife before taking the remaining chair.

"I hear you have a potential investment opportunity," he said to Jackson. "Would love to discuss it."

The avaricious part of Jackson clamored to agree. Carlton's connections ran deep. It would be a smart partnership. Yet he could never work with the man whose wife he'd had. Even he drew a line somewhere. Besides, discussing Arlo in front of Evie was a no go. She knew nothing about it, and he'd ensure it stayed that way for as long as possible.

"Wouldn't be a good fit," Jackson kept his tone curt to end the line of conversation as quickly as possible.

"Oh, no business talk," Georgia swatted her husband's arm. "We're on vacation." She took a sip of her water before directing her attention to Evie. "How do you know Jackson?"

That was a hard question to answer. Evie wasn't sure where to begin. As she continued to hesitate, Georgia studied her with clear brown eyes. She was model-beautiful, with glowing skin free of makeup and perfectly arched brows. The flowy yellow dress she wore complimented her dark hair and golden complexion. Her husband looked like he could be on Polo Ralph Lauren ads. They were a gorgeous couple.

She didn't think that Jackson considered them as close as Georgia insisted, though. He looked like he wanted to be anywhere else but there. She tried for evasion. "We met a while back."

Georgia frowned when Evie didn't expand further. The Carltons waited for a beat longer. When Evie took a bite of her sandwich and didn't elaborate, Georgia offered a polite smile. "Well, that's nice."

Evie caught Sebastian's eyes skim over her chest as he leaned back in his chair. She found the move wildly inappropriate, given his pregnant wife at his elbow.

"Is Jackson taking you to the Cannes party?" A predatorial gleam accompanied his question, making Evie want to move as far away from his gaze as possible.

"No, Evie can't make it," cut in Jackson before she could respond. The sound of his voice had changed completely. She'd never heard such ice in his tone before.

"That's too bad. The Cannes gala is my favorite part of Zohra. And I'm a big Zohra fan. We both are."

"We were one of the first to get the lifetime membership," explained Georgia. "Keeps the romance alive."

I guess it's nice they have a shared hobby?

"Why aren't you coming to the Cannes party?" pressed Sebastian.

"Leave it, Carlton," Jackson warned.

"What'd I say? Just curious why one would want to miss it."

"Babe, she has her reasons. Zohra isn't for everyone. Stop prying."

"Not my thing," offered Evie. She hoped her curt response would spur a different topic.

When Sebastian's eyes drifted to her chest again, Jackson leapt to his feet. The chair scraped against the stone floor as he reached for Sebastian. Evie jumped to her feet too. "Jackson," she said before he could grab the well-dressed lecher. "I think we should go find our parents."

Georgia turned toward Sebastian. "See? Now you've scared Jackson's girlfriend."

"I'm not scared," clipped out Evie. "I don't enjoy being ogled by a stranger before I had a chance to finish my lunch."

Jackson came around the table, pulling Evie to his side. "Evie isn't my girlfriend. She's my wife."

Evie wasn't sure if he'd shocked her or the Carltons more.

"You're married!?" exclaimed Georgia, clearly stunned.

Unable to help herself, Evie leaned into Jackson. She plastered on a bright smile. "Ten years now, can you believe it?"

"My wife and I are leaving." He directed the next comment to Sebastian. "You ever look at her again, I'll yank your membership. And break your nose."

Sebastian sputtered. Guess Jackson knew where to hit so it hurts.

Evie pulled her purse from the back of the chair to her shoulder. She kept her smile artificially cheerful as Jackson drew her away. "Have a nice babymoon!"

They walked in silence for two blocks before Evie regained enough control over her raging emotions to face him. "You slept with Georgia."

"One of the stupidest things I've ever done."

"When?"

"After you and I got divorced. I was in a bad place, Evie. A dark place. I screwed anything that moved for a while. I met her at a party. I was drunk. Miserable. A one-night stand I barely remember. I knew she was married. I've regretted it and every interaction with her since. They joined Zohra a few years later. Became inescapable."

She glanced back, even though the Carltons were far out of sight. "I don't like them."

Jackson paused his stride. Evie instantly halted when he did. "You're not upset."

She really wasn't. She didn't like the idea of Jackson being with anyone else, but they had been apart for ten years now. She never thought the owner of a dozen sex clubs lived as a monk.

She also knew him and his abhorrence for cheating because of his childhood. It was wildly out of character for him to pursue a married woman because his mom had cheated on his dad with Leonard, and it broke apart their little family. Once his mom and Leonard had divorced and Lisa had married Leonard and had his kids, Jackson had been sent to boarding school until he came to live with Valentin. His mother and Leonard's affair had turned his world upside down. He must have been in a truly dark place to chase a married woman.

"It was a long time ago. Everyone is allowed a mistake. Besides, I know you're not lusting after her."

"I've only ever lusted after one woman," he said, his face serious.

Evie wanted to loop her arms around his neck and press her lips to his, but she fought the instinct. When he looked at her the way he did, she could almost believe they might have a future together. Then memories intervened. She couldn't ever reopen herself to that kind of pain.

She tugged him along down the paved street instead, changing the subject. "I didn't like Sebastian. He grossed me out."

"I didn't like him leering at you."

She laughed. "You made that crystal clear."

"This was the closest I've ever come to punching out a Zohra member."

"That makes two of us. For the record, I didn't like her either."

"You'll never have to interact with either one of them again."

They almost reached the restaurant where their parents were having lunch. She needed to ask the question now, or she'd agonize over it for hours. Her heart hammered as she did. "Why did you tell them I'm your wife?"

Jackson slowed his pace. "I don't know. I guess because girlfriend doesn't really describe your relationship to me."

"We have no relationship," she pointed out.

He stopped walking. The tourists behind them scurried around them with annoyed grumbles. Jackson's fingers grasped her upper arms, the hold tight enough to feel uncomfortable. "You're mine. No asshole gets to eye fuck you as though you're fair game. You. Belong. To. Me."

Evie's brain struggled to process the words. "We're done in a week, Jackson."

"We'll never be done."

Chapter 20

Jackson's vehement promise—or threat?—buzzed in Evie's ears for the rest of the day. They spent a stilted afternoon with their parents before returning to Nice. Everyone seemed exhausted from the daytrip. When Leonard suggested they dine at the hotel restaurant, everyone heartily agreed. She and Jackson asked for their meals to go, citing work.

Their parents, seated at a table tucked into the walnut-paneled corner of the hotel restaurant, exchanged a knowing glance. One Evie didn't want to see from them because they knew nothing. She could only imagine the romantic drivel her parents were spinning in their minds, yet setting them straight would require an explanation that was beyond Evie to provide.

Where would she even start to explain her relationship with Jackson? Their first meeting in Nice ten years ago? Their marriage and subsequent divorce? The baby they lost in a car accident? The sex tape? Jackson's blackmail? Their two-week contract? Her religious parents would be shocked all the way back to California. They'd look at her differently.

She would have to let them think what they wanted. She and Jackson had seven days left, and then she'd move on with her life.

They didn't have to wait long before the waiter brought out their meals, packed to go to their respective hotel rooms. Jackson took the covered dishes and motioned for Evie to precede him out of the restaurant. They wished their parents a good night and headed toward the elevators.

"Eat in my room?" he asked as they rode up to their floor.

She knew that she should refuse, but her mouth wouldn't form the words. She acknowledged his question with a nod. Although the hotel had assigned her a brand-new room after the break-in, Evie didn't want to be alone. She could pretend that the reason was safety. After all, someone could just as easily break into her new room too. But that would be a lie. Despite all logic and reason, she longed to spend just a little more time with Jackson. The man must have some powerful pheromones. She couldn't stay away despite herself.

Evie didn't say much as they reached his room. When he held the door open, she stepped inside. She watched him set the plates of food on the table and move his laptop out of the way.

She wasn't hungry. She couldn't stop thinking about Jackson's earlier words. Maybe he was right. Maybe they never would be done. Maybe they'd live on in each other's DNA like a virus. She'd be okay with that. But she couldn't allow herself to fall in love with him ever again. She owed herself that much.

He pulled her against his chest, his lips nuzzling her neck. "Spend the night." The dark rum offer warmed her blood. *Refuse. Run to your room. Staying here will lead to heartbreak and tears.* She let herself sink deeper into his arms. "I mean it, Evie. Stay here, or I'll go with you to your room. I don't want you alone."

She needed to decline, to go to her room, lock the door, and put Jackson out of her mind. Yet that's not what she wanted. "All right," she said. "I'll stay."

As he turned her to face him, triumph lit his blue eyes. *Maybe this was a bad idea. Maybe I should leave.*

"You going to put up the barricade again?"

She shook her head. "Not this time."

Terrible decision, Evie.

Emotions flitted across his face like a geomagnetic storm. Exultation. Desire. Others that she couldn't name.

She wanted him to kiss her.

The thought should have sent her running, but it made her press closer instead. Blood thudded in her ears, drowning out all logic and reason. Her gaze fell on his mouth. She missed kissing him, longed to feel his lips on hers and to give into the sharp pleasure only he could ever draw from her.

He stilled too. She moved even closer—near enough to feel his heartbeat against her skin. He lowered his head slowly, as if giving her every possible chance to reject the advance. His lips paused a hair's breadth away from hers, hovered. She forgot to breathe, her entire body coiled with anticipation.

He watched her for a moment longer, and then he closed the small distance and kissed her. The gentle brush of his lips against hers activated every nerve ending in her body. The memories flooded back in a pleasure-pain of sensation.

He kept the kiss brief, a mere touch of his lips to hers, before he lifted his head. When she raised her heavy lids, she saw him studying her with vibrating intensity. His eyes searched hers. She couldn't tell what he wanted from her, but she couldn't bear the crush of his unvoiced questions. She looked away. It was the wrong reaction. He dropped his hands, stepped away.

She didn't let him go far. She couldn't. Wrapping her arms around his neck, she stood on her tiptoes and kissed him. His groan echoed through her entire body as his iron-hard arms clasped around her. The hot glide of his tongue against hers caused a moan of her own. The kiss turned ravenous, an atmospheric river of need. His hold tightened until she thought her ribs would crack against him, but she didn't care. She wished the kiss would go on long past the one-week's time they had left together.

Jackson was the one that pulled away.

Evie blinked several times before her vision cleared enough to focus on his face. "What's wrong?"

"I want you in our bed."

She glanced past him at the large mattress. They'd slept in that bed last night. Kissed in front of it now. It seemed silly to refuse.

We only have a week left. One week of memories to take back with me to California.

"All right."

With a triumphant snarl, he returned his mouth to hers.

Food forgotten, they tore at their clothes until they were fully naked. He lifted her, her legs twining around him as he walked them to the bed. The plush mattress gave as he laid her across it, caging her with his arms.

Evie wriggled out of his hold. He reached for her again, but she pressed a palm against his chest, halting him from moving closer. She pushed at him until he lay on his back, and she hovered near him.

"It's my turn to give directions."

The want in his gaze made her unexpectedly

nervous. His chest rose and fell in an erratic rhythm, his fingers fisted the sheets, but he stayed still. And waited.

"I want to be on top," she whispered, moving over him. His hands reached out to steady her. She wagged her finger at him. "Nah-uh, you don't move."

"There's one part of me that's moving."

Evie glanced down at his considerable member that looked so ready for her before returning her eyes to Jackson's. Wiggling lower down his body, she closed her hand around his erection, lowered her head, and took him into her mouth. His entire body jerked as his groan echoed in the room.

How much she'd missed this—the heat they generated in one another, the magnetic force that seemed to surround just the two of them. Evie used her hands and mouth to pleasure him, taking him deeper on each downstroke as she knew he liked. He twisted the sheets under him but kept his hands where she had bid.

His heavy-lidded eyes never left her face. He watched her with barely leashed hunger.

"You want me in your throat or in your pussy?"

Evie's thighs clenched at the question. She maneuvered herself up his body, leaning down to take the lobe of his ear between her teeth.

"Kiss me," he whispered.

She obliged, letting her mouth skim his. His teeth sank into her lip, soothed the bite with his tongue. Skin feverish, Evie deepened the kiss. His hands framed her face, tangled in her hair as he adjusted her head to the angle at which he wanted it.

Evie pulled back, shaking her head. "You're not supposed to move," she chided.

"Put your breasts in my mouth," he countered.

Evie pressed his hands back to his sides. "I give the orders tonight."

"Killing me."

"You like it."

"I like you."

Evie's heart, already beating a wild staccato, threatened to overwhelm her hearing. She expected him to make a snide comment, to brush off the sudden tension, but all he did was watch her with hot blue eyes.

She didn't want this confession. She didn't want him to like her. She could never travel down the same path with him again. They had a two-week deal. They had seven days left on it. Seven days to work each other out of their systems.

She would never open her heart to anyone—*could* never. Even to him. Especially to him.

Seeking to get them back to safer territory, Evie wrapped her fingers around his member—

"Crap, condom."

His head jerked toward the nightstand. "Drawer."

Evie missed the heat of his body as she scooted away. Her hands trembled as she sheathed him. Moisture slicked her thighs as she slid down his length.

"Let me touch you," he pleaded.

"Yes, touch me."

His hands settled on her breasts, cupping and kneading the soft mounds before sliding down to her waist, to her ass, and sinking into the flesh of her buttocks. Evie set a rhythm, loving the hot pressure of his fingers as she moved on him.

He let her set the pace, let her take charge. She knew that he liked being in control in the bedroom. This relinquishing of power was not easy for him, yet he gave it to her because he understood that she needed it. They had broken every single rule that she had set in place. Their relationship had no boundaries now. Nothing to constrain or bind it. The limitlessness of it scared her. She couldn't allow it. She wouldn't let it tilt into the unknown. They had defined a two-week time frame. They had one week left. Then she'd walk away. She'd walk away because she had to.

Unable to stop herself, Evie leaned down and kissed him. The world spun. She found herself facing the ceiling—and Jackson's passion-crazed face as he began to move.

Evie fought the very air that separated them.

Tightening her legs around him, she clawed to bring him closer. She wanted nothing between them. She needed to feel his sweat-drenched skin moving against hers. She palmed his ass, needing all of him, all at once.

"Please. Jackson. Please."

"Easy. Easy," he soothed her. But she was beyond reason.

His mouth found hers. She bit at his lip as she desperately undulated under him, consumed in the sensations he drew from her. He changed the angle of his movements, sending new zings of sensation through her. Her inner muscles quivered in response. She was so close. Her body tightened, the sensation spinning and focusing, then bursting apart. One orgasm crested into another, and she came apart again and again as he moved inside and around her. She thrashed on the bed, wanting to pull him deeper, to never let go. Jackson buried his groan against her neck as he came, his weight pressing her deep into the mattress.

He shifted to move away. She tightened her hold.

Wait. Not yet. Catching herself, she relaxed her arms, letting him leave her body.

As he resettled her against him, his fingers twined through hers. The sensation of their clasped hands rammed against the barricades she had enacted around her heart. Her whole body went cold at the intimacy of the gesture.

She tugged away her hand, but that wasn't enough to slow the panic that began to gurgle in her blood. She moved to the other side of the bed, pulling a sheet around herself as an extra layer of protection against the tenderness that threatened to overwhelm her.

Jackson frowned. "What's wrong?"

"I can't do this."

"Do what?" Reaching out, he smoothed the tension between her brows.

She wanted to press her face into his palm like a cat. Instead, she swatted his hand away. "We said two weeks."

"Two weeks aren't over yet."

"Jackson—"

"I know you, Evie. I know you overthink. Don't overthink this."

"I can't just not think."

He pounced, encasing her with strong arms on either side of her body. "I guess I'm not doing my job well enough," he murmured and kissed her.

Thoughts scattered like butterflies. She framed his face, the shadow on his jaw rough under her fingertips. He slid lower, his teeth nipping at her skin.

"Jackson!" she yelped.

He soothed the bite with his tongue.

Nibbling along her shoulder, her arm, her inner elbow, he found her breast, drawing the tight bud of her nipple into his mouth. Evie arched into him, her fingers tangling in his hair. His lips traced down her stomach as he settled between her spread thighs.

"What are you—"

His fingers spread her open for his mouth. The raspy slide of his tongue against her sensitized bud was too much. She tried to shift away, but he held her steady, his touch turning feather soft as he pressed a gentle kiss to her center. He continued to tease her, his ministrations a gossamer glide against her sensitive core. Soon, she needed more. She tugged at his hair, moving restlessly against his mouth. With a satisfied groan at her increasingly frenzied movements, he closed his lips over her clit. Evie came instantly.

She was boneless by the time he shifted up the bed and pulled her once again into the safety of his arms. She couldn't lift her heavy lids as he settled her against him and tugged a blanket around them both.

Evie knew that she needed to move away.

To put the barrier back between them.

To sleep on her own side of the bed.

But as his fingers once again threaded through hers, she didn't want to be anywhere else.

She ignored the stinging tear that escaped her lid as she slowly slid into sleep.

An hour later, Evie blinked open her eyes in the night-darkened room. Jackson's heavy arm held her securely to his body as he curled around her like a big spoon. For a brief moment, she surrendered to the sensation, to the feeling of safety only he could provide. She allowed herself to enjoy their evanescing time together. Soon, she'd return home to Manhattan Beach alone.

She wiggled closer to him, seeking his heat. His arm tautened, pulling her even firmer against him in one smooth move.

"I think I can do something about that frown," he murmured against her skin.

She glanced back at him. "How do you know I'm frowning? Your eyes are closed."

"I can feel it." His hand skimmed lower, tracing the seam at the juncture of her thighs.

"That's not where I'm frowning." She smiled, spreading her legs to make room for his hand.

His lips curled against her skin as his finger dipped lower. Moisture pooled at his touch. She shifted in his arms, seeking his mouth, welcoming him as his weight moved over her.

I'm in big, big trouble here.

When Jackson's mouth settled on her breast, Evie's thoughts gave way to sensation.

The sun hadn't broken the horizon yet, but Jackson couldn't sleep. Holding Evie felt too fragile. Too temporary. He loved the weight of her fully relaxed against him. Savoring the feeling, he watched Evie dream soundly in his arms. There was nothing he wouldn't do for her.

As stupid and fucked as it made him, he was still in love with his wife.

His ex-wife.

His ex-wife, who someone was targeting—most likely because of him. He'd ensure she was safe. Even if she wanted nothing to do with him after their two-week contract ended, he'd do everything in his power to make sure that she was protected.

He couldn't do it from a random hotel, with no backup. He needed to get her somewhere secure, surrounded by people he trusted, and he knew just the place. He reached for his phone.

Having sent the last of a series of texts, he replaced his phone on the nightstand and let his lips graze Evie's cheek. He couldn't resist the pull she had on him, even asleep. His heart leapt as she blinked open her eyes. Her fingers threaded through his hair as she drew him closer.

He kissed her with every emotion he was too afraid to name, knowing that the week they had left together would never be enough time to work her out of his system. Centuries wouldn't be enough.

Chapter 21

"Change of plans," Jackson announced to the group at breakfast the next morning.

Evie glanced up from her eggs. They had chosen to eat at one of the hotel restaurants for efficiency, ahead of the scheduled tour of Grasse, Gourdon, and Tourrettes-sur-Loup. Alain would be picking up both sets of parents at nine for the tour, arranged by Jackson. Evie suspected that he had plotted to have the parents away on purpose, and would drag her back to his hotel room as soon as they were alone.

"I know you had a few excursions planned while in Nice," Jackson continued, "but I have a suggestion. My aunt has a house less than half an hour northeast of here. It's fully restored, has several gardens, a pool. She's not using it this month. She's letting us all borrow it while we're here."

Jackson's aunt didn't have a house on the French Riviera. His father did. Though saying so would probably set his parents instantly against it.

"We already have the hotel reserved," said Rose.

"The house is much nicer than a hotel. Èze is nearby, and we can explore it tonight, once the tourists leave for the evening. We can move to the house once you're back from the tour today—would that work?"

"How's the internet connection?" asked Leonard.

"A thousand times faster than at the hotel. There's a private office and a library. You can work from either place."

"It sounds very Instagrammable," said Lisa.

There was that word again. Had Lisa and her mom just discovered social media? What was with their recent need for reels, boomerangs, and thousands of pictures of the exact same pose?

"I defer to Rose," said Evie's dad.

Rose glanced at Lisa. "I say we go."

"Seconded!" Lisa exclaimed.

"Great. We can head out as soon as you're back."

The conversation picked up quickly at the short timeline. Taking advantage of the parents' focused conversation, Evie leaned over to Jackson. "What are you doing?"

He replied in an equally low tone. "Until I can figure out who's behind this mess, I want you in a private, secure space. The house is under twenty-four-hour surveillance."

"We know it's Tilly. We just need to find her."

"You stay at the house until we do."

"I'm here on vacation. I don't want to live like a prisoner."

"I hardly think a saltwater pool qualifies as prison."

"You two okay?" asked Leonard from across the table.

"Yes, all good," Evie assured him, reaching for her coffee. She couldn't let Jackson have the last word though. "We're not done with this conversation," she murmured.

"Far be it for me to assume you'd ever agree to anything easily." Jackson projected his next announcement across the table. "I have also invited Hayes, Nate, and

Oliver to join us. Nate and Oliver said they'll be here tomorrow. Haven't heard from Hayes though."

"You invited the boys?" exclaimed Lisa. "That's just marvelous! We haven't seen Nate in months!" She beamed at Rose and Michael. "You'll love them. They're go-getters, wildly successful, and still such gentlemen. I'm excited for you to meet them."

Evie didn't point out that Jackson was all those things too. It didn't matter to his mom or Leonard. They only had eyes for their three younger sons.

Alain scooped up the Icefalls and her parents at nine o'clock sharp. Evie's instincts had been correct. As soon as the car pulled away from the hotel, Jackson's hand closed about her wrist and he pulled her toward the elevator. They ran to his room, stripping before they fell into bed. Neither one anticipated the knock.

Evie glanced at the door. "Think they forgot something?"

"Who is it?" Jackson called from the bed.

"It's me. Open up. I'm tired and hungry."

Evie recognized the voice instantly.

"Hayes? Hold on!" she called, untangling herself from Jackson and hopping off the bed.

Jackson pulled on his pants. He waited for Evie to get her clothes in place before he opened the door.

Hayes Icefall looked drained and grumpy. He strolled inside, dropping his leather duffel bag to the floor. His eyes scanned across her and Jackson before his head fell forward with an exhausted exhale. "Don't tell me you're back together."

"We're not back together!" Evie assured him. She wanted to rush over and give him a hug, but Hayes wasn't a hugger.

Evie got along with Jackson's brothers. Although all three were as tall as Jackson and had inherited their mother's bright blue eyes, each one had a wildly different personality. Hayes, the eldest of the three, was the prickliest. Whip-smart, he had launched—and sold—several successful businesses. He preferred to limit his interactions with people because, in his words, "people are annoying." It continued to surprise her that he had made a distinct effort to stay in touch. She suspected that he had input "text Evie" into his calendar for every twelfth Friday because that was when the brief messages always arrived.

"Good," he said. "Because there's not enough Xanax in the world."

"Why haven't you replied to my messages?" demanded Jackson.

"I had nothing to report. Tilly doesn't want to be found. Her phone is off, she hasn't used her credit cards."

"How do you know all this?" asked Evie.

"I looked into it," he explained in a way that clarified nothing. "I do know that she never returned to the States. It's safe to assume she's still in Europe. I came to see if I can track her here better."

"That's above and beyond, Hayes," said Evie.

"You're my ex-sister-in-law. I don't want to see you hurt."

"I don't know if you saw our text thread, but Oliver and Nate are landing tomorrow," said Jackson. "We're moving to Valentin's house as soon as the parents are back from their daytrip."

"Good. I could use some pool time. I'm going to shower here, then I need food."

Once Hayes showered and changed, she and Jackson took him to a small café on the quieter side of town. The bistro had set out a handful of tables along a private alley outside. Jasmine-covered trellises separated the tables from the rest of the alleyway and scented the air with white blooms. Evie walked over to the chair closest to the trellis that separated the walkway from the awninged seating area. As Jackson pulled out her chair, he planted a brief kiss to her bare shoulder.

Hayes noticed. "Stop that," he said, waving at them as though they were two dogs in heat. "Don't make me get a hose." Hayes had been a witness to their tumultuous relationship, and he clearly remained traumatized.

Evie set her purse at her feet. "We'll try to behave ourselves."

Hayes ordered a sandwich, which he ate quietly and without looking up.

"How's work going?" asked Evie, wishing to break the silence—and to distract herself from Jackson's proximity.

He had scooted his chair close to hers, leaving his knee glued to hers. She wished the mere feel of his jeans against her skin didn't activate every one of her pulse points, but it somehow did. She felt hot and restless all over, and all she wanted to do was to drag Jackson back to his hotel room.

Hayes glanced briefly at Jackson before responding. "Work's going fine."

"Whatcha working on?" prodded Evie, trying to draw out a conversation.

"I'm launching a hospitality business."

"Whoa! That's new. How'd that come about?"

"Wanted a challenge."

Chatty, Hayes was not.

Evie glanced at Jackson, hoping he'd help fill in the

blanks, but Jackson sat preternaturally still. A muscle ticked in his jaw. "You okay?" asked Evie.

His gaze darted away. "I'm fine."

Oookay. Both brothers were acting stranger than normal. She decided to change the subject. "Do you think your parents will figure out we're going to be staying at Valentin's home?"

"Dad's asking his staff to remove anything that may give it away, and he's giving them a paid break so we can have full run of the place. We should be okay."

She reached for her espresso. "Where's Valentin anyway?"

"He's been in Rio with his new girlfriend. I think he was supposed to return this week, but he's letting us take the house while we're here. He said they'll either extend their trip or add on another leg to it."

"That's very nice of him."

"His new girlfriend is old enough to be his younger child, so I think he's trying to keep her as entertained as possible."

"Valentin has always loved love," said Evie.

"Let's just hope he doesn't marry this one. I can't have another stepmother younger than me."

Evie didn't notice the teen at first. He walked at a leisurely pace, just another passerby cutting through the secluded alley to get to his destination. She was too distracted by the sprucy scent of Jackson's cologne, and the way he casually rested his palm on her knee.

The teen's hand darted out quick. He grabbed the purse she had left at her feet and ran.

Jackson jumped up before Evie could react.

"Stay with her," he called and took off after the purse thief. Evie, acting on sheer instinct, took off after them.

She heard Hayes's groan as he set off after her. The teen ran fast, zipping around the corner. Jackson turned after him. Hayes caught up to Evie. "Will you stop?"

"He has my wallet!" Evie gasped out, mid-sprint.

The teen leapt into the back of a beat-up sedan, yelling something at the driver, and the car sped off. Seeing them disappear with her things made Evie's heart sink. She stopped along the road, trying to draw air into her burning lungs. Hayes flanked her, panting. Jackson didn't give up. He raced after the car, as though determined to catch it. When it disappeared at the turn, he stopped, doubling over to catch his breath.

Several pedestrians asked Evie what happened. One offered to call the police, but it would be of no use. The teen had been too fast. She declined their offer.

Jackson stormed back to her and Hayes, eyes pinning Evie. "I can't believe you ran after him! He could have had a gun."

"*You* ran after him. I ran after you both. I can't believe he took my bag. It had my wallet—my credit cards, my license. They're going to be a pain to replace. Ugh, my memory stick was in my purse." Panic flashed through her. "Crap. I back up my writing on it, and now they have parts of my next book."

"Where's your cell?"

"Crap! I left it on the table!" Evie took off back toward the restaurant. Jackson and Hayes followed.

"Will you stop darting away," grumbled Jackson. "I'm not twenty-six anymore."

"I don't think I've run this much since high school," said Hayes. "And that was only because I was being chased."

The waiter hovered at their table.

"I saw what happened," he said in rapid French. "I stayed to make sure no one took your things."

"Thank you!" Relieved at seeing her phone safe and sound, she almost hugged the waiter.

"I'll get you some water," he said, and hurried into the café.

The waiter brought out three ice-cold glass bottles. Evie twisted off the aluminum cap and took a long sip. "We should head back to the hotel. I need to call the credit card company and my bank. Maybe even my agent, in case they realize what's on my USB drive and leak it online."

Jackson reached for his wallet and pulled out several bills, which he handed to the waiter. He twined his fingers through Evie's, and the three walked back to the hotel.

They took the elevator to Evie's floor in silence. Evie tapped her keycard to unlock the door. She blinked twice before her brain processed what her eyes saw.

"What the fuck?" Jackson spat out.

"Shit," said Hayes.

She'd barely moved into her room yesterday, hadn't even unpacked yet. When she woke up early that morning, she didn't wish to disturb Jackson's sleep, choosing to shower and change in her new room instead. Taking advantage of some free time after the shower, she'd pulled out her laptop from the safe to squeeze in a writing session. When Jackson had come to grab her for breakfast and started to kiss her instead… time got away from them and she forgot to return the computer to the safe. How foolishly careless of her!

Now, her smashed laptop lay in the middle of the otherwise-immaculate room.

Evie fell to her knees in front of the notebook. It looked like someone had stomped across the screen. The glass had shattered in a web pattern. Her most recent work—the parts of the story she had written on this trip, which was almost half of the next installment in her series—lay destroyed on her floor. She had backed up everything except what she had written that morning on her USB drive, but that had been stolen with her purse. Tears burned her eyes.

"Where are you going? Jackson?" she heard Hayes call, but she didn't turn to see. She tried to click on the keys, hoping it might turn on. But the fragmented screen remained black.

Hayes placed a comforting hand on her shoulder. "The chassis looks intact. Maybe we can fix it."

She wanted to believe his words, but looking at the sad state of her laptop drained her of all hope.

"Can I take a look?" asked Hayes.

She reached for the laptop, carefully picking it up off the floor. She placed it in Hayes's hands. "Here… but I don't think it's fixable."

"Are any of your other things damaged?" asked Hayes, moving the laptop to a nearby table.

"I'm always so careful about keeping my laptop safe. I can't believe I left it out."

She surveyed the room. Nothing seemed out of place. She stopped at the safe, testing its door. Still locked. She keyed in her code, and found her passport safe and sound inside. If only she had remembered to replace her laptop into the safe's metal confines.

Jackson's agitated voice from somewhere in the hall grew louder. He was speaking in rapid, angry French as he strode back into the room, the hotel manager behind him.

"How did this happen?" he demanded, jerking his finger to the broken laptop. "What kind of hotel can't guarantee security? Someone's now gotten into her room twice."

"I'm sorry," stammered the manager. "This has never happened before. I can't imagine how it could have happened twice in two days. Please, be assured that your entire stay is on us. We must go speak with security immediately."

"They were useless before."

"I will personally review all camera footage," the manager promised. "I will check the log again myself."

"Go." Jackson waved him off. "I'll be down in five."

The manager threw an askance glance at Evie and hurried out of the room.

"He thinks I'm the one doing all of this," said Evie. "I can see it in his face. No one goes into my room but me, but it's destroyed every time."

"Hayes, stay here. Evie and I are going to make him show us every single recorded angle of this hotel."

Jackson took her hand and pulled her along with him to the elevator. "What if you had been inside? What kind of fucked up place is this?"

"They destroyed everything I wrote on this trip," said Evie. "I back up everything on my USB, but that's gone now too."

"Soon as we're done here, we're getting your files out of that laptop. You're not losing your work." The promise hung in the air as the elevator doors pinged open.

She wished she could believe him, but she doubted anyone could salvage her files from the demolished device.

Evie followed Jackson out of the elevator.

Is that… no. That guy looks like David. No, wait. That is David.

She watched her ex-fiancé stride through the lobby to the exit. He certainly wasn't dressed casually today. He wore dress slacks and a white-collared shirt, and had gotten a fresh haircut between yesterday and today.

Evie hurried after him.

Jackson beat her to it. Reaching David, he spun him around.

"What—" The bewilderment on David's face morphed into chagrin. "Oh. Hello."

"What the fuck did you do to Evie's room?" demanded Jackson, towering over her ex-fiancé.

David held up his hands. "I didn't do anything to Evie's room. I don't even know which room is Evie's. What's going on?" he directed the last question to her.

A few interested guests glanced their way.

Evie lowered her voice. "What are you doing here, David?"

He dropped his gaze. "I… I… er… don't want to say."

Jackson looked enraged at David's response. Not wishing to have Jackson make a scene, Evie stepped between her ex-husband and her ex-fiancé. "You're going to have to," she told him.

"This is embarrassing. You sure you want to hear it?"

"Positive."

His words rushed out quickly on a breath of alcohol-scented air. "I was here to meet Tilly, but she stood me up."

Evie thought she'd misheard.

"Why the fuck are you meeting Tilly?" demanded Jackson. "Where is she? I haven't been able to reach her for days."

"Listen," said David, glancing between her and Jackson. "This is really awkward to say… but… Tilly's hot. I'm single now. So is she. She asked me to meet her at the hotel bar for a drink. I came, and now she's not responding."

"How did she get your number?" asked Evie.

"She and I ran into each other very briefly in Paris after… well, you know… after she and I checked out of the hotel."

"So you asked her out on a date?" Evie clarified.

"I only asked for her number. She said she had plans to stick around France. Since we were both single, I suggested we meet up for dinner sometime if our paths crossed. We both happened to be in Nice."

"Tilly is in Nice." Evie turned to Jackson. "See? I told you it's her."

"It's her… what?" asked David.

"Someone keeps breaking into my rooms, destroying my things."

David looked appalled. "But this is a nice hotel. Did you tell security?"

"No," drawled Jackson. "That didn't occur to us."

"Do me a favor?" said Evie. "Can you text her? Tell her that I want to talk to her. If she's upset, maybe we can… just talk. She doesn't have to keep stalking my rooms."

"Of course. I'll do it right now." David reached for his phone, and tapped out the text. "I'll let you know what she says, though she didn't respond to my last three questions about her ETA."

"You were in the lobby the whole time?" asked Jackson.

"I've been sitting at the bar for two hours. You can ask the bartender. Guy started to feel sorry for me."

The manager approached, looking grim. Evie already knew what he was about to say. They couldn't find a record of anyone entering her room.

Chapter 22

Evie would have preferred to wait for the parents to arrive before moving to Valentin's house, but Jackson had refused to loiter around the hotel. Too despondent over her laptop and stolen USB to argue, she acquiesced.

She had never before visited Valentin's restored eighteenth century home. The four-story mansion perched atop a hill in Eze Bord de Mer. Jackson had shared that it boasted a state-of-the-art security system, 24/7 camera surveillance, and a pretty insurmountable, electrified fence. Good. She couldn't handle any more damage to her property.

They drove through a heavy wrought-iron gate and up a winding path until they reached the main house. Palms, cypresses, olive trees, and blooming bougainvillea surrounded the bright yellow, four-story home. An expansive green lawn ran from the front of the house to the edge of the property, where it dropped sharply. The view of the Mediterranean spanned out beyond.

"Wow," Evie breathed, stepping out of the car.

"Hayes, take the fourth floor. The entire floor is dad's suite, so you can keep the parents out of there and you get a hell of a view. The two rooms on the ground level next to the pool are mine and Evie's."

"Got it," said Hayes. "I have work to catch up on, so I'll see you later." With that, he took off into the house.

"What if Lisa and Leonard figure out this house is your dad's?" Evie asked as they followed Hayes inside.

"Doubt they will. The staff put away all proof before they left." He gave Evie a sideways look. "He also had them lock up his Aston in the garage. Didn't want Leonard driving it."

"Smart man."

They walked through the living room, with its pale wood flooring and cream-colored furniture, until they reached the suite of bedrooms on the ground floor.

Jackson stopped at the first door. "This is my room. Stay here with me."

As much as Evie wished she could agree, she couldn't. "I'm not going to scandalize my parents."

He grinned. "Figured you'd say that." He reached around her to open the door of the room next to his. "I had this one prepared for you."

The bright space was tastefully decorated in cream and pale rose. Glass made up the entire opposite wall, leading out to a patio and the pool beyond. An ornate bed took up one corner, but the antique desk facing the window caught her eye. A bouquet of peonies sat atop its polished surface.

"Thought you'd like this desk for your writing while you're here," said Jackson. "Had it brought down from upstairs."

Touched, Evie laid her hand on his arm. "I love it. Thank you."

"I'm putting the parents on the third floor to give you and me as much privacy as possible. I plan to do things to you they won't want to hear." He set her luggage at the armoire and walked to the sliding glass wall. "This slides open all the way. That way, you can write and enjoy the breeze at the same time."

He motioned for her to precede him through the sliding glass door and followed her outside. White chaise lounges flanked the shimmering blue pool. A thicket of cypresses against the opposite edge provided privacy from neighboring houses.

Jackson waved toward the back of the property. "There are a couple of small gardens that way. I can take everyone on a tour once the parents arrive. I think you'd like the citrus grove on the other side of the house."

Lavender grew in earthenware pots next to the sliding doors. The scent of the lavender and citrus blossoms mixed with the salty tang of the sea wafting toward her on the sun-warmed breeze.

Evie inhaled a fragrant lungful. "I can't wait to swim here."

"I have an idea of what else we can do here."

She laughed. "Not with Hayes upstairs. Maybe the next time we're back."

Evie hadn't realized what she had said until the teasing spark fled his features. "Will there be a next time?"

"That's not what I meant…"

He swallowed. "We're sticking to the two-week agreement?"

It hurt her to say it, but she powered through. "Yes."

She must have imagined the hurt that flashed across his face. The icy gleam that settled there was easier to read. "Then we have to make the most of it."

She couldn't help herself. She kissed him. How would she ever say goodbye to him less than a week from now? His hands settled on her hips, pulling her into his body as his tongue teased hers.

"Hey, cut it out!" came Hayes's distant voice from the window four stories above. "I need the Wi-Fi password."

Evie pulled away. Jackson's fingers on her hips tightened, keeping her near for a moment longer. Then, with a reluctant sigh, he let her go.

Alain dropped off the parents and their luggage a few hours later. Evie and Jackson greeted them at the door.

"This is *beautiful*," breathed Lisa. "I had no idea your father's sister owned something this breathtaking. Rose, imagine the photos we can take here!"

Evie's mom and dad loved historical homes. They peppered Jackson with nonstop questions about the original owners of the mansion and its history. Surprisingly, Jackson knew quite a few facts. Her parents were enchanted.

"Let me take you all on a tour—" The insistent ring of his phone interrupted the offer. He glanced at the screen. "I should take this. I'll be back." He disappeared toward his room, just missing Hayes who came downstairs to greet his parents and to meet Evie's.

"Hayes! We didn't know you were here!" Lisa gasped and rushed to embrace her son. Hayes, not one for shows of affection, stood stock-still and bore it. His father hugged him too. Lisa and Leonard practically glued themselves to Hayes, introducing him to Evie's parents, describing his recent successes in colorful detail. A far cry from their treatment of Jackson.

Evie wished the Icefalls had treated their oldest son with the same admiration, but it seemed beyond them. Hayes escaped upstairs soon after that, preferring his spreadsheets to small talk.

"What's the plan for the rest of the day?" asked Leonard.

"We're going to have dinner in Èze Village in a few hours," Evie replied. "But we can relax until then."

The parents appreciated the break. Her mom and Lisa

pulled out the outfits they had purchased in Paris, got dressed up, and went to pose against the Mediterranean backdrop in the front yard. Her dad and Leonard discovered Valentin's putting green and took full advantage.

Evie made quick work of unpacking. Her heart lurched as she pulled out her broken laptop and set it gingerly on her desk. She didn't think her work could ever be salvaged from such a crushed computer, but she'd try. First thing tomorrow, she'd find a local repair shop.

Was Jackson done with his call? No one would be within earshot of her and Jackson's rooms for at least an hour. Maybe they could put that hour to good use.

Jackson really had thought of everything—being in adjoining bedrooms makes this so much easier. She slipped into his room through the sliding glass wall, expecting to see him at his desk. Although his laptop was there, he wasn't.

Good. Now she could surprise him. Where should she greet him upon his return?

The desk.

Did she dare text him to come find her in his room? Then wait for him naked, sprawled across the gleaming surface?

Feeling a zing of excitement at the prospect, she approached the desk. She just had to move his laptop and then find a sexy pose before texting him.

He had left the laptop open. As she picked up the device, the screen lit up. *Guess he forgot to lock it.*

What is this? Evie tilted her head.

ARLO LAS VEGAS: BY AUCLAIR-ICEFALL HOSPITALITY GROUP read the tagline on what looked like a presentation deck of some sort.

What the heck?

She knew that she shouldn't snoop, that she should respect his privacy, but the leaden feeling that settled low in her stomach made her scroll down to the next slide.

A business plan for a new club in Vegas?

No, this is an investor deck.

Evie scrolled lower, reading quickly through the pitch deck. *Is Jackson opening up a nightclub in Vegas?* Her confusion dissipated as she saw a quick bio on him and Hayes. *He's opening a nightclub with his brother.*

Blood pounded in her ears. He wasn't allowed to be in Vegas. Had he orchestrated her visit to France so that he could redraw their borders? So that he could open a club in the state previously forbidden to him?

How did he manage to get her parents to take a trip to Europe—to have them invite her to join? He really was a master manipulator.

Then, when he knew he had her, he blackmailed her into sleeping with him on top of that. She had fallen for it. Hook, line, and unsuspected sinker.

The Jackson she knew would have never manipulated her this way. She really didn't know this new Jackson at all. How could she ever trust him?

Betrayal tore through her. He had been using her the entire time. Even using her parents! Using her pastor dad.

Was the letter, the fire, the attacks—oh God, her destroyed laptop?!—all part of some sort of master plan to get them all into this house? Her entire world—made up of facts she'd known to be true—was falling and crashing around her, like crumbling brick and concrete. Everything had been a ruse. Fake.

Disappointment and anger crashed through her. She felt like she had walked into a beautiful snowstorm only to learn that the swirling snowflakes were nothing but mashed potato flakes, and the beautiful scenery nothing but a set.

Tears burned her eyes. She wouldn't cry over him ever again. He didn't deserve her tears. They had hurt each other immeasurably ten years ago. While she had been wracked with guilt over all the horrible things she had said to him then, he had no such qualms. Instead, he had been using her to get his business with his brother off the ground.

Betrayal lashed at her. Stunned by his deception, she could barely breathe.

She desperately wanted to run back to the States and to never see his face again. Yet how could she drag her parents back home with her without telling them everything? She had kept her marriage a secret for so long, she couldn't tell them now, but she refused to leave them in Jackson's lair.

Fool me once, fool me twice… shame on me for both instances.

She didn't know whether she should stay in his room and confront him, or find an attorney to yank away his access to Nevada, or return home and never think of him again.

She thirsted to hurt him as much as he had hurt her. This was her chance. She could contact his investors, or ask her publicist to share that a sex club owner is sinking his claws into the Vegas Strip. The city had invested a lot to become a family destination. She doubted they'd want a sex club owner taking over a chunk of the Strip. The bad press and the outcry from local groups would kill his deal.

This is it.
This is payback.

The time to act.

She didn't want to do any of it.

She looked up at the antique mirror that had been set into one of the walls. It reflected the pain in her eyes. Her entire trip here—her parents' trip—had been orchestrated for his business dealings.

They had never played games before. They had always been open and honest with one another, even when it led to horrific fights and screaming and tears. They had always trusted one another, but how could she ever trust him after this? She felt so stupid.

The footsteps at the door startled her. She had great reason to be in Jackson's room—she had meant to surprise and seduce him. Now that he was about to walk in, the situation looked bad.

She didn't care. She stayed where she was.

Jackson didn't expect to find Evie behind his desk, his open laptop in front of her. The hurt and betrayal on Evie's beautiful face froze him. Panic slammed through him. She knew.

He understood that she'd find out eventually—he'd planned to tell her eventually—but he wasn't ready for the stark pain he saw in her face. He had never meant to hurt her.

He needed to confirm what he already suspected. "You know."

"You were behind my trip to France. You made me feel terrible for breaking our contract—yet you were behind it all along. *All of this*, it's all stage-managed by you."

"I can explain."

"Explain *what*? That you're a jerk? I understand if

you wanted to hurt me, but getting my family involved in your scheme? That's low. Even for someone like you."

"I had no choice."

"You always have a choice."

"You'd never have let me open Arlo in Vegas. You know that you wouldn't have."

"So instead of taking no for no, you planned out this elaborate fake trip? *Jackson,* you blackmailed me into sleeping with you. The layers of manipulation… I don't know you at all."

"Please, hear me out. You're right. It started out as a means to an end, a way to get my club launched. But when I saw you again, everything changed. I wanted you more than my next breath. It stopped being about Arlo. I'd have done anything to have you back in my life."

"Except asking me?"

"I was afraid you'd say no. Evie—"

"No. Don't speak. I don't think I have room in my brain for any more of your lies. You can have Vegas. You know what? The entire boundary is lifted. Open a hotel in California. A restaurant in Venice Beach. I don't care anymore. Do whatever you want. *Just never come near me again.*"

He had intended to use the carte blanche favor to get her to listen to him when the shit hit the fan. He didn't have that favor now, had used it up in Nice.

Panic rose like a tide he couldn't stem. She spoke the words with such finality, he didn't know how to make her reconsider, how to make her understand.

He knew he was a jackass. He had manipulated her and her family, even his own parents, into being in Europe. Where would he even begin to ask for forgiveness? But he couldn't let it end like this.

She turned to go. He leapt forward, grabbing her elbow.

He had expected her to fight or pull away. Instead, she stopped. Her sad eyes lifted to his. She sounded resigned. "What more do you want from me?"

Terror rioted through him. He was losing her. They had always had trust between them, and he had broken that with his greed. He didn't want Arlo if it meant losing Evie. He only wanted her. "Please. Stay. Talk to me."

She shrugged. The defeat in her face broke him. "Were you ever going to tell me about Vegas?"

"Eventually. I didn't know how."

"You lied to me. This whole time, everything was a lie."

"Not everything."

"What was real? How could I possibly trust you now?"

"You know that our feelings are real. The passion between us. The need. You know that's real."

"It's chemistry. It's fleeting."

"Has it fled in the years we've been apart?"

"You betrayed my trust. I thought my future was over—my career, my livelihood… you made me feel that. How could I possibly ever get over that?"

"I'm sorry. I'm sorry that I did that. I didn't know what else to do. I wanted that club."

"You wanted it more than me."

"I've never wanted anything more than you."

"Well, that's hard for me to believe. Considering you overlooked my feelings to be able to operate in Nevada."

"I thought that's what I wanted. I thought it would make me happy. That was before."

"Before what?"

"Before I saw you. When I saw you at that café in Paris, everything changed."

"You went through with your plan anyway. Well, good news. You got what you desired. You get to open your club. Anywhere in the world."

"I don't want the club, Evie. All I want is you."

"You've made that impossible. You used me. You used my family."

"Evie, please, listen to me. You're right. I did manipulate you. From the beginning. When I'd learned that the house next to your parents in Coronado was being put up for sale, I made Hayes float the idea to Mom and Leonard. After they'd moved, I had Hayes suggest they visit your dad's church. I bought my parents' tickets to Europe if they invited your parents to go for the same dates and locations."

"And they agreed?"

He looked away. How could she possibly not hate him after this?

"What?"

"I had to twist Leonard's arm, but he agreed eventually."

"How?"

"Couple of tax things he didn't want people to know about."

"You blackmailed your stepfather into getting my parents to go to Europe with them." A statement, not a question, as though she finally understood how low he'd stooped.

He answered anyway. "Yes."

"And my parents, unknowingly, invited David and me. You puppeteered everyone because you wanted to sell Zohra and start a new business."

"I'll never sell Zohra. After our divorce, when my life fell apart, I was depressed. Deeply depressed. I fucked woman after woman in an attempt to forget you. I was spiraling. Zohra pulled me out of a dark place, Evie. It put an end to all the fucked up shit I was doing—like screwing Georgia. Zohra gave me purpose. I owe my life to Zohra."

"Then stick with it. Why open a night club?"

"My parents don't acknowledge me because I run a sex club. I want a business I can discuss in polite company without people blushing and turning away. I want the opportunity to work with my brother, to have something we can show off to family and friends. I want something legitimate." He released a sad puff of a laugh. "I guess in a way I'm still seeking my parents' approval, silly as that sounds. Hayes has been looking to start a business in Vegas for years now, and it finally came together. I couldn't partner with him because of our boundaries before. It was a once-in-a-lifetime opportunity."

"To lie and manipulate and blackmail me to become your fuck buddy in France? To make me break up with my fiancé?"

"You never loved him. You were using him."

"Like you're using me!"

"Don't pretend like you don't want me—like you don't want this."

Before she could say anything, he swooped down and took her mouth with his. He released his hold on her elbow, giving her freedom to move away, to escape, but she didn't. She stayed. His tongue traced the closed seam of her lips, beseeching entry. Her entire body zeroed in on the sensation. The urge to kiss him back, to get lost in the taste of him, overwhelmed her, but she had to stay strong, to not succumb to the mistakes of the past.

She wrenched her face away.

As though unwilling to let her go quite yet, his lips found her cheek, nuzzled against her flushed skin, even as he held his fisted hands at his sides. She appreciated his heedful attempt to not confine her. When he lifted his head, a myriad of emotions flashed across his eyes—disappointment, need, sadness, hope. She looked away.

Neither one seemed to be able to catch their breath.

She yearned to step into the safety of his arms, to feel them wrap tightly around her and hold her close, even as she wanted to yell and scream and lash out at him.

"What can I do to make it better? I'll pull out of Vegas. Hayes can pursue it on his own. Tell me what it'll take for you to forgive me, and consider it done."

She knew it was a foolish move.

Not sound in the least.

Yet being so near him made it impossible for her to fight it. Despite it all, she ached for him. He lied and manipulated and prevaricated, but her body didn't seem to care.

Surprise flashed in his eyes as she stood on her toes, curled her fingers into his shoulders, and kissed him. His arms wrapped around her like steel bands. His tongue dove inside, finding hers. They kissed ravenously, the past and the present and the future swirling around them.

"God, Evie…" he whispered, before returning his lips to hers.

The world moved as he lifted her, his strong arms setting her butt on his desk. He pulled off her shirt over her head, unclasped her bra. His mouth fastened on her nipple. Evie's fingers tightened in his hair, pulling him closer.

"Evelyn!" Her father's distant howl made Evie jump. He wasn't a yeller. He sounded angry.

Evie scrambled to put her shirt back on. What in the world happened? He called her name again, this time even louder. Uncertain of what to expect, she ran out of the room.

Jackson followed her into the living room, where Leonard, Lisa, Rose, and Michael faced off across the travertine floor.

Evie glanced around the group. "What is going on?"

"You stay away from him!" Her father's finger made it clear the him in question was most definitely Jackson.

"Why? What did he do?" asked Evie, glancing back at Jackson.

"I… I don't know how to tell you this… but…" Michael's chest heaved as he spoke. "But… I can't say it."

Rose stepped forward, taking her husband's hand. "Evie, he's…" She lowered her voice. "He's a pervert."

Evie frowned. "What do you mean?"

Rose moistened her lips. Her voice remained low as she explained. "He owns a sex club."

"I can't believe you didn't tell us!" Michael redirected his finger at Leonard and Lisa.

"We didn't know how! We're so ashamed of his profession—we don't feel comfortable talking about it," said Lisa.

"Ashamed of my profession," repeated Jackson. "Yet you didn't mind the swanky hotels and restaurants my profession paid for on this trip."

"We didn't ask for any of that," Leonard pointed out calmly. "Besides, after what we spent on your education—"

"You mean the boarding school you shipped me off to as soon as your other sons were born?"

"You needed a stern hand. We couldn't provide the discipline you needed," said Leonard.

"We sent you to the best school, Jackson. You could have been anything. Yet you're… you're a brothel-keeper," Lisa added.

Evie rolled her eyes. "He doesn't own a brothel. He owns a chain of sex clubs—the most exclusive, coveted sex clubs in the entire world. That's nothing to be ashamed of. You should be proud of him."

"You knew?!" Her parents demanded in unison.

"I did."

"You didn't tell us either," her dad accused.

"I knew how you'd react."

"You willingly let us stay at the house of some… pimp?" asked her mom.

"He's not a pimp. There's no prostitution involved. Think of it as an exclusive country club—only instead of tennis, people go there to explore their fantasies."

"You stop speaking, young lady. What will happen if anyone sees us? Knows that we are vacationing with a sex club owner? My career would be ruined. Your mother and I would be made a laughing stock. We have a position to uphold—people look up to us to spiritually guide them."

"You're in the middle of the French Riviera, in a private house. Who'll find you here?"

"What about when we leave the premises?"

"Jackson's parents go to your church," Evie pointed out. "You're on vacation with friends, not with entertainers from Spearmint Rhino."

Her dad frowned. "What's Spearmint Rhino?"

"I'm not ashamed of my line of work—I didn't tell you what I did because I don't broadcast it. People react to it in different ways."

"Lying by omission is still lying," Michael pointed out.

"I know, sir. I'm sorry I didn't tell you."

"You've put us in a really difficult situation."

"Difficult how?" Evie asked her father.

"We'd never agree to any of this if we knew it was being paid for by a business we wholeheartedly stand against."

"He doesn't run a brothel. He runs a club. Every member is a willing participant. They pay hundreds of thousands of dollars to be a part of it," Evie explained.

She never thought she'd be in a position to willingly justify Jackson's job. She herself wasn't sure she approved of it, though she couldn't tell if that was how she truly felt or if the ideas drilled into her during her upbringing skewed her opinion.

Evie's mother directed a hurt gaze at the Icefalls. "It's hard not to feel like you were all lying to us."

"Rose, I never tell anyone about what he does," said Lisa, expression pained. "I just can't bring myself to say it…"

"I'm their darkest kept secret." Jackson's face remained impassive, but Evie knew he ached inside.

Evie spoke up. "That's a true shame, Lisa. You and Leonard have been such *buttholes* to Jackson, and all he's done was show you a great time across Paris and the South of France."

"Evie!" her mother cautioned.

"Your son runs a multinational company that he built from the ground up. He's kind and generous, and he still somehow brings himself to be around you despite how you treat him." Leonard began to sputter something, but Evie interrupted him with a raised brow. "Save it,

Leonard. I don't want to hear any more of your grumbling. You two will never understand what an incredible person Jackson is, and that's a true shame." The silence lay heavy in the hall. It appeared she'd muted everyone. "Now. Let's all take a breather. Alain is about to pick us up to take us to Èze. We'll cool off, have dinner, walk around, explore, talk like adults."

"With a sex club owner?" her dad scoffed.

"With Jackson, whom you've gotten to know over the last week. Is there anything about him in particular that you don't like?"

Michael's head dropped. The pause dragged on. He finally lifted his gaze. "She's always been wise. Jackson, I apologize. That was uncalled for. You've been nothing but kind to us this entire time." He extended his hand. Jackson shook it.

"Apology accepted, sir. I'm sorry that I didn't tell you sooner."

Evie, unsure what drew her to do it, slipped her hand into the crook of Jackson's arm. After a brief pause, he covered her hand with his, his warm palm engulfing her.

"How did you find out?" asked Evie.

Michael pulled out his phone. He shoved it into Evie's free hand. "This article was texted to me by an unknown number."

Evie glanced at the screen. "What number?"

"I don't know. American though. Charleston area code."

Jackson's lips thinned. "That's Tilly's number."

Evie had to bite her lip to keep the "I told you so" from erupting. Her blood curdled in anger as she remembered her destroyed laptop. She used her dad's phone to dial Tilly.

"Straight to freakin' voicemail," Evie groaned. She gave Jackson a frustrated look. "Dad's number is listed on his church website. She's been on the site to find it, Jackson. That's so creepy."

"What's going on?" asked Rose.

"Nothing. Tilly is throwing a tantrum." Evie sent a text. It bounced back. "Darn." She handed the phone back to her dad. "If she texts anything else, call her instantly. I need to speak with her."

"Thank you for what you said back there," said Jackson, closing the door to Evie's room.

"I meant it. You should be proud of what you've accomplished."

Slowly, giving her all the time to pull back, Jackson cupped her cheek. She lifted her head, eagerly meeting his mouth. Being part of a family that hides you from the world couldn't be easy. Jackson was the child his parents only discussed behind closed doors, while they spoke so openly about Hayes's, Nate's, and Oliver's accomplishments. No wonder Jackson wanted to go the legitimate route—of course he still yearned for his parents' approval.

Jackson loved his brothers—she knew how much they meant to him. The opportunity to work with one of them would have been impossible for Jackson to refuse. Had he come to her, explained his goals, she'd never have allowed it, as ashamed as she was to admit it. She'd feel too fearful that letting him west of Colorado would someday make them run into one another—and she had always been terrified of that. Their drawn map ensured that they could avoid one another forever.

She hated that he'd used her as a pawn in his game—even worse, had used her parents—but seeing her parents' reaction and hearing his parents' comments made her realize why Jackson had needed this so much. He strived for legitimacy, for his parents to see him on the same level as his half brothers. She understood why he did what he did.

He wrapped his arms around her, drawing her closer to his body. "Evie, I really am sorry. I never meant to lie or manipulate, but I did. And I hurt you, the last person in the world I would ever want to hurt. I need to tell you something else."

She pulled back to look at him. "Oh boy. What now?"

"I never had the sex tape. Never. I destroyed it a decade ago, when I told you I did. I lied because I saw you and I wanted you and I knew you'd never agree to—"

"I know."

"You know what?" His brows drew together.

"When you first said you didn't destroy it, I believed you. I was so mad. But the more I thought about it, the more I realized you wouldn't have done that to me. That's not you. I knew you didn't have it even before I broke it off with David."

Pain and realization flashed across his features. "You trusted me, and I betrayed you with Arlo."

"If you had told me about your plans for Vegas, I'd have never allowed it. The bitterness from earlier… it was so strong inside me. I'd have never let you gain access to Vegas. I understand why you did what you did. I don't like it. You used me. But in a way, I'm sort of relieved. We got to talk through what happened back then. It released all that pent-up anger and resentment. I don't like that you manipulated me into coming to France, but I'm so glad that you and I finally talked. Even all these years later."

"I'm glad we talked too." Jackson's smile broke through the tension that had descended on the room. "Also, that was impressive, what you did back there," he said. "No one stands up to my mom and Leonard like that."

"I've spent a week with them now. I'm surprised I didn't explode sooner. They're so… rude to you all the time."

He shrugged. "I'm used to it."

Despite his lackadaisical response, Evie could tell that their treatment of him had continued to smart. "Well, I'm not. I'm still mad on your behalf. And after all you've done to impress them on this trip. The night at Le Grande Contrôle must have been astronomical, not to mention the private car services and the fancy restaurants."

"I didn't do any of that to impress them."

Her face scrunched. "You didn't?"

"I did that to impress you. And, more recently, to get them distracted enough so you and I can have alone time together."

"Well, I did appreciate the alone time. But I don't need you to buy me things to impress me. You do that just by being you. I'm glad I'm on this trip with you. I think it'll help both of us move on."

His hands fell away as though she had tossed a glass of crumbly dry ice at him. She watched his throat move as he swallowed. "And that's what you want us to do? To move on after this?" he asked, his voice even.

She nodded.

He didn't say anything more.

Jackson had been to Èze Village plenty of times. It perched on a mountainside like an eagle's nest, a preserved piece of history turned tourist destination. He was glad they had waited for the sightseers to drain out before arriving for dinner. It would have been a crush otherwise.

Hayes had opted out of joining them. He wasn't much for small talk and chose to have a quiet evening alone instead. Evie walked ahead of the group with her dad, pointing out the medieval architecture along the route. His mom, Rose, and Leonard followed close behind. He held to the back, ignoring the views of the Mediterranean unfolding far below.

The whole trip was one unfortunate event bleeding into another, and his gut told him it was far from over. He didn't believe that the hotel hadn't captured a trace of Evie's trespasser. Between the cameras and key access logs, it would have been easy to identify the culprit, yet the hotel failed to produce a shred of evidence. If Tilly were behind it, she knew someone who worked at that hotel. He suspected Evie's purse being stolen wasn't a coincidence either. She was now in another country with no access to her debit or credit cards, even if her bank had assured her that they'd put a security freeze in place. If she had carried her passport on her, it would have been an even bigger mess.

Rose slowed her pace to join Jackson. She waited for the group to walk on ahead before turning to him. "We really don't fault you for your line of work. I apologize we had been so rude earlier. We were just a little shocked."

"It's a common reaction. That's why I don't much share about it."

"As long as you love what you do, and your job doesn't hurt anyone, then you should be proud."

"Thanks, Mrs. Campbell."

"Call me Rose. I think we're past the formalities. After all, you are sleeping with my daughter. Oh, don't look so shocked. I wasn't born yesterday."

Jackson, who'd never been at a loss for words before, didn't know what to say. He wanted to assure Evie's mom that his intentions were pure, but were they really? He had blackmailed her into sleeping with him. Had lied to her to do so. They had six days left before they'd part ways.

Could I let her go?

Neither Zohra, nor Arlo brought peace to the restlessness inside him. Only Evie did that. With her, he felt whole.

He offered the only thing he could. "I care for your daughter."

Rose smiled. "That, my dear, is vividly obvious. And, if it helps, I've never seen her look at David the way she looks at you. I think the two of you are good for one another."

Jackson's heart beat in his ears. If only her daughter agreed.

Chapter 23

The next morning, Jackson followed Evie to the kitchen. He had never been a morning person, but being woken up by Evie's eager hands and mouth was a hell of a great alarm.

"I want to make pancakes," she announced, looking bed-rumpled and kissable despite the pressed, prim dress he had helped her zip up just minutes earlier. The neckline dipped low enough to reveal the creamy tops of her breasts. Pancakes were the last thing on his mind.

"I'll help," he said, pulling her into his chest, enjoying the way she fit so perfectly against him. "It'll be like a treasure hunt, since I have no idea where dad's staff keeps anything."

He felt her smile against his T-shirt as she wound her arms around his waist. "We won't get to breakfast at this rate."

"Let's spend the day in bed," he suggested, his hands sliding down to cup her ass.

Evie laughed. "And tell the parents what? Besides, aren't Nate and Oliver arriving today?"

"Yes. They can keep one another entertained while we're otherwise occupied."

"I may be able to be convinced."

He mock-gasped. "You normally never agree with my suggestions."

Evie gave him a sardonic look from beneath her lashes. "I think I agreed plenty with your suggestions last night."

His dick jumped. "Screw pancakes. Come back to bed with me."

"Pancakes first. And coffee. Maybe some eggs and bacon too… I'm starving."

"Well then, let's get you fed." He let her go, watching the sway of her hips as she approached the fridge.

"Fully stocked." Evie's eyes ran over the neatly organized food. "Do you know if he has flour?"

Jackson opened the pantry. "Let's find out." He scanned the shelves. Locating what he sought, he pulled it from the shelf. "Got it. Sugar too."

"Great. What about vanilla?"

Jackson added the vanilla to the growing pile in his arms. He set the ingredients on the counter.

Evie glanced around the kitchen. "Where would bowls be?"

He found the bowls stacked in the cabinet. "Here you go."

As Evie started on the pancake batter, Jackson figured out his dad's espresso maker. The appliance must be new, because he didn't remember it from his last visit. It had more nobs and nozzles than could possibly ever be used. After some trial and error, he succeeded in making a decent shot of espresso. He made one for Evie too.

"Here. You like small, bitter drinks in the morning," he said, handing her the cup.

She laughed. "Makes the day seem sweeter in comparison."

Jackson reached for the milk in the fridge. He poured a generous dose into a frothing pitcher, bringing the contents to the espresso machine and playing with the nozzles. The machine steamed the milk with a reluctant hiss. Once it was sufficiently warmed, he poured the contents into a cup, added his espresso and a generous helping of sugar.

He took a long draught, watching as she whisked. "Need help?"

"Want to make eggs while I finish up the pancakes?"

Draining his coffee, he set the empty cup to the side. "On it."

He and Evie had cooked breakfast together many times before. It seemed like centuries ago now. The moment reminded him of how happy they'd been, cooking and dancing to whatever was playing at the time. He pulled up a playlist on his phone and cast it through the kitchen's built-in speakers.

The cheerful beat made Evie laugh. "This brings back memories."

They worked to the rhythm of the music—her ladling the first batch of pancakes onto the cast-iron griddle while he chopped ingredients for a crustless quiche. As he set the onions to sizzle in the skillet, a sense of longing shot through his body. This was the future he wanted. Sunny mornings first making love, then making breakfast with Evie.

He watched her dance to the music projecting through the speakers as she flipped pancakes, sadness flooding his mouth like bitter syrup. Evie would go home in less than a week, and he'd return to his life. He'd manage Zohra, launch Arlo, work nights, sleep days. He was used to his nocturnal existence. The fact that he'd be reverting to it in just five days shouldn't faze him, yet it did.

"You okay?" she asked. "You're staring."

He cleared his throat against the gathering tightness. "It's hard to look away from you."

Wariness entered her features even as she smiled. She refocused her attention on the pancakes, flipping the three on the griddle with more focus than the task required.

"Your onions are burning," she pointed out.

Shit. He tossed the charred pieces into the trash and reached for a fresh onion. Evie left three pancakes to finish cooking on the griddle as she located strawberries in the fridge. She skirted around him to wash them in the sink.

"Our contract ends in five days."

Her hands froze under the water stream. Her teeth sank into her lower lip. It took two beats before she resumed washing the berries. "Yes, it does."

"What if we extend it?"

She turned off the water in the sink. Drying her hands on a nearby towel, she faced him. "No."

"You don't want to even discuss it?"

"By how long would we extend it? A week? Then what? Another week? Why postpone the inevitable?"

"Because I still want you."

"You have five days with me. Get it out of your system."

"And you'll get it out of yours?"

"Yes. Within the next five days."

"You're counting down the time because you're dreading saying goodbye."

The smell of scorched batter stung his nostrils. "Crap." Evie turned to her now-burned pancakes, waving away the smoke as she scooped them up with the spatula and tossed them straight into the trash. "Do we have to discuss it now?"

"Now seems as good a time as any."

"I agreed to two weeks. That was our deal."

"I want to update our terms."

She shook her head. "Impossible."

"Why are you fighting me on this? I know you don't want this to end in five days either."

"It doesn't matter what I want. I'm heading back to California. I'm not twenty-two anymore. I can't just stay in France."

"I'll go to California with you," he offered.

"We both signed the contract. You are not allowed in California."

"You're going to hold me to that?"

"A deal is a deal."

"The Evie I knew was never a coward."

"The Evie you knew doesn't exist anymore. You and I don't exist anymore."

"What about meeting me in Nevada? Neutral territory. Nevada doesn't count."

"Nevada would count. You can't change the rules now, Jackson. We both knew what we were getting ourselves into."

"We made up the rules! We don't have to stick to them."

Her voice was cool when she responded. "I prefer we do. A clear end-date."

Jackson refused to accept it as such. He and Evie had something special. He'd never been able to replicate the feelings with anyone else, nor did he wish to. He knew that Evie didn't want to replicate them either. She was scared, and understandably so. What they had before had overwhelmed them both. They were older now, mature enough to handle the power of the feelings they drew from one another. Evie would see that eventually. She had to.

"What the hell are you guys doing?" asked Hayes, waving his hand through the murky tinge of smoke in the air. "You decide to set the kitchen on fire?"

"We burned some onions and some pancakes," said Evie. "But we're on track for breakfast now."

Hayes eyed the small number of ready pancakes. "I better help."

"Here," said Evie, handing him the bowl of strawberries. "Slice these while I focus on the pancakes."

Conversation temporarily over, Jackson returned his attention to chopping the onions.

With Hayes's help, they made quick work of breakfast. As Jackson set the quiche in the oven, Evie plated their pancakes. "I'll save the rest of the batter for when the parents wake up."

"They've been clamoring to go to Monaco," said Jackson, helping her bring the plates to the table. "What do you think about sending them there tomorrow?"

Hayes glanced up from studying the espresso machine. "I'm not going."

"You weren't invited," Jackson pointed out.

"Think your mom and Leonard would still want to go once Nate and Oliver are here?" asked Evie, taking a seat.

Jackson sat too. "I can tempt them. I have to be in Cannes tomorrow, but my brothers will stay here with you."

"For my home confinement."

"You're not confined. You're out of Tilly's reach."

"Can't track her even here," said Hayes, waiting for his cup to fill with espresso. "I've called in every favor I had around here."

"I don't want to stay here for the rest of my trip. You'll be at your party… and I'll be stuck behind an electrified fence."

"You'll have my brothers for company," said Jackson.

Hayes set his coffee on the table and pulled out a chair. "We're fun. We can make a pool day of it tomorrow. The beach is a three-minute walk from here."

"You're not to leave the premises until I return," Jackson told Evie.

"You don't trust me to go out with just your brothers?"

"No. You're staying here until I'm back and can watch you."

"I'm not a child. I don't need to be watched."

"You were pushed down the stairs in Nice. I think that warrants someone watching you at all times."

"Okay, okay, stop arguing," Hayes cut in. "How about this? We all go to Cannes. I'm sure Nate and Oliver would want tickets to the party, and Evie and I can hang at a hotel or something."

Jackson's gaze never wavered from Evie's. "I got Valentin to loan us his house to keep Evie as far away from hotels as possible. I'm not going to drag her to Cannes because she doesn't want to be bored for a day."

"I have a say—" Evie began.

Jackson didn't let her finish. "No, you don't."

Her chin tilted up in defiance. Although her cheeks flushed with anger, she kept her voice exquisitely low. "I want to discuss this somewhere private."

"Oooh, you're in big trouble now," said Hayes, pulling his pancakes closer.

Jackson ignored his brother. He shoved back from his chair, grabbed Evie's hand, and dragged her outside.

Jackson didn't say a word until they reached the flower garden, a small section of Valentin's property jigsawed with neatly planted boxes of roses, peonies, foxgloves, delphiniums, and an explosion of yellow blooms Evie couldn't name. The scent of flowers and the buzz of bees hovered around them as Jackson pulled her toward a small wooden shed. Painted the same color as the house, it must have been used by gardeners to store their supplies. He didn't try to open its doors, but rounded its corner until they were in a shaded area behind it.

"I want you."

"We're not done talking yet," she protested.

He pressed her against the side of the shack, anchoring her to it with his pelvis. The painted timber felt rough against the exposed areas of her skin. She glanced beyond Jackson's shoulder to gauge how exposed this location left them. The steep slope of the mountain behind him and the trees that grew on all sides kept them safely hidden from prying eyes. She couldn't help herself; she wound her leg around his to bring him closer.

"We'll never be done," he growled before crushing his mouth to hers. The rough kiss gave no quarter, demanding surrender. She refused to back down even as she opened to him, letting him deepen the kiss. He tasted of the sweetened coffee and cream he'd had earlier. Evie cupped his neck with her hands, and let her tongue explore against his.

She wanted more.

You can make love with him without falling in love.
It's not hard.
People do it all the time.

His strong hands glided over her, from her hips to her ribcage to the sides of her breasts. They curled around their fullness, skimmed lower, finally settling around her waist as he tore his mouth away.

She closed her eyes against the feelings reflected in his blue depths. She didn't want to see them, refused to accept them.

Sweat beaded her skin even in the cool morning air. His hand dove under her skirt, cupping her over her underwear, moving the small triangle of fabric aside. His fingers found her, stroked through her wet heat.

Her head fell against the siding as she struggled for air. The sensations he drew from her caused every one of her nerve endings to hyperfocus on him. The bright morning light, the buzz of the insects, the scent of the flowers around them disappeared. She was surrounded only by Jackson. The uneven gusts of his breath against her skin, the wintry scent of his cologne, the delicious feel of his thick fingers as he entered her made her feverish.

"I need—I need…"

"I know what you need." He sank to the ground, tugged down her underwear, and settled his mouth on her. Her hips canted toward him, her hands reaching down to tangle through his hair. The strands felt cool against her hot skin.

When he pulled away, she wanted to drag his face back to her center, but he was already towering over her, murmuring low instructions in her ear. His hands wrapped around her elbows to steady her as she stepped out of her underwear. He shed his own pants before threading his fingers in her hair and kissing her. His kiss burned through her like an unleashed river of molten glass, one she didn't wish to escape. She gave in to the sensation.

"The quiche is ready!" Hayes's voice reached them from the house.

Jackson's forehead fell to her shoulder. "Fucking cockblocker."

Evie struggled to control her own breathing. "I think that's his code for the parents are awake."

"I'm sending them away today. No questions asked."

She laughed. "As long as I don't get home detention."

His face turned serious as he studied hers. "I don't want to see you hurt. This whole shit is my fault. I'll be busy in Cannes. I don't want you in a hotel. Can't you just stay here with my brothers? I trust them with my life. Otherwise I wouldn't insist."

Evie knew he was right. She didn't want to go to a hotel and be subjected to another room break-in. Tilly had clearly known the location of her Nice hotel room. It was safe to assume she'd figure out any possible Cannes lodging as well. "If it means that much to you, okay. I'll stay."

"You're not really going to leave her with us, are you?" Hayes asked Jackson as they cleaned up the dishes after breakfast. They had declined Evie's and the parents' offers to help.

Jackson stacked the dirty plates on the table and carried them to the sink. "She'll be safer here."

"I remember you two together too clearly," Hayes said, taking the top plate from the stack and setting it in the dishwasher. "You fought constantly because you always thought you knew better. Like a stubborn ass, you'd never give in."

Jackson began wiping down the table. "I do know better most of the time."

"No. You don't. She didn't feel comfortable telling her parents about you guys. Yet, you kept pressing. If you had fucking backed off, you probably would still be married, God help us all." Hayes set another plate on the dish washer rack.

"I flew Nate and Oliver out to watch her."

"And she insists she doesn't want to be watched." Hayes reached for a cup from the sink. "Listen, I get it. You want to protect her. But she's a grown ass adult. She doesn't want to be locked away in here."

"It's for a day."

"It doesn't matter. It's her decision."

Jackson straightened the chairs around the table. "We still don't know where Tilly is."

"Again. Doesn't matter. She wants to be with you. Meanwhile, you keep insisting she stay with your brothers. What message does that send?"

"That I trust you guys."

Hayes shook his head. "That you don't trust her to make her own decisions about her life."

"You didn't see her all bloody after the push down the stairs."

"I'm sure she recalls it well. She also recalls how you'd never let her make a single decision without arguing with her about it. You need to learn to trust other people to make their own choices in life. Oliver barely spoke to you for months because you kept trying to talk him out of his degree."

"Look how well that turned out. He now has a PhD in Art History. What's he going to do with that?"

Hayes moved a handful of dirty forks into the dishwasher. "It's his choice."

"No one ever offered me any sort of guidance growing up. I wish they had. I'm just trying to set safety bumpers for you all."

"I know you mean well, but it's not appreciated. That's why you two set each other off all the fucking time. Her dad's been controlling her behavior her whole childhood. Now in adulthood, you're trying to do the same."

Jackson studied his brother. "For a guy who claims to hate people, you're quite observant."

Hayes shut the dishwasher door and started a cycle. "I'm observant, and that's why I hate people."

After Hayes retreated to his floor to work, Jackson's phone pinged with a text message. Sending off a brief reply, he strode out of the house to the front yard, where Rose and his mom sat at an umbrellaed table, hunched over a laptop. He hurried past them to the gates, where he met Alain.

"That was fast," he told the driver.

He handed Jackson a large bag. "Your name carries weight in these parts."

As Alain got back in his car and reversed his way out of the driveway, Jackson retraced his steps into the house and headed to Evie's room.

She'd left her door open, but she wasn't inside. He strolled through her room toward the pool. Just as he'd anticipated, he found her on one of the loungers, a paperback in hand.

"I got you something," he said when she looked up at him.

She set her book aside and sat up in the lounge chair. Her gaze narrowed. "What is it?"

"Why so cautious?"

"I don't want it if it comes with strings attached."

"No strings." He plunked himself down next to her on the lounger, the bag between them. "Here."

Evie's movements seemed reluctant as she reached for the bag. Maybe Hayes was right after all. Maybe his overbearingness alarmed her.

"Did you get me a new laptop?" she asked, sounding perplexed as she withdrew the box.

"I did. The tech guy was able to recover and extract all your files from your broken one. They're all on your new laptop."

Realization dawned quickly. Her gaze softened as she processed the words. "I can't believe you did that," she breathed, falling against him to hug him with one arm while the other held the boxed laptop. She lifted her face to his and brushed a soft kiss against his lips, but pulled back before he could deepen it. "That's beyond anything I could have asked for. Thank you."

"I know how much your writing means to you. I'd have moved mountains to get those files back for you." His phone rang. He checked the screen. "Shit. It's Richard. I'll be back."

Chapter 24

Evie took the laptop to her room, still processing the gift that had meant so much to her. Jackson had recovered her files and had moved them to a brand-new computer. She had thought her work had been smashed beyond repair when Hayes's attempts to recover her files had failed, and hadn't had the time or opportunity to find a repair shop herself, yet Jackson had rescued her book. The thoughtful gesture filled her with overwhelming gratitude. As soon as Jackson finished his call, she'd drag him to her room and thank him any way he wished.

Eager to see her files, she took the computer to her beautiful desk. The peonies in their cut crystal vase smelled especially fragrant as she opened her new laptop.

She found each one of the Word docs, all looking as good as new, as though someone hadn't smashed them to smithereens just yesterday. She hoped Jackson's call would end soon, but while he was occupied with Zohra, she'd work on a chapter or two.

The knock on her door startled her. She glanced up as Jackson strolled in. "I brought you a late lunch."

"A late lunch? It's morning."

"It's already two."

She glanced at the clockface in the corner of her laptop. "Wow, I lost track of time."

"I didn't want to interrupt you while you worked, but I did make you a sandwich."

She accepted the plate from him. She realized how hungry she was as soon as she saw the *jambon beurre*.

"Everything okay with Zohra?"

He sat at the end of her bed. "It will be. I'll drive down there tomorrow morning. Make sure it's all set up before the big event tomorrow night." He hesitated. "Do you… would you want to come?"

She spoke around a mouthful of ham, bread, and butter. "You'd let me outside the secured perimeter?"

"I don't want to strong-arm you into anything. It's your call."

She didn't have to think about it. "I want to come with you."

"All right. Done."

"What about your brothers? Won't they be upset you flew them all the way down here for nothing?"

"Are you kidding? They get to laze around the pool and the beach while we're gone. It's a dream vacation for them. I'll have Alain bring you back here when the Zohra party starts. Would that work?"

She thought about it. It did.

"Jackson," she said, standing up and brushing the crumbs off her hands. "Where's everyone?"

"Hayes is probably upstairs. I think our parents went to the beach or are about to go. Why?"

She walked over to the door and locked it. "Thank you for recovering my files."

His eyes darkened to a stormy blue as she approached him. She tried to walk as sexy as possible. The spike in his breathing indicated that she had succeeded. He widened his legs to make room for her, but she directed her steps to the glass wall instead, pulling the panes shut and drawing the curtains closed.

She shed her clothes as she closed the distance between them, standing fully naked in front of him in the dimmed room. His eyes never left her face, the intensity sending a prickle of unease to pluck at her marrow. "What?" she asked as she straddled him. "Why are you looking at me like that?"

"You're so beautiful. I still can't believe you're here." He cupped her breast with a tender reverence, sending her head to fall back at the sensation. His lips skimmed her neck, kissed her jaw, the corner of her mouth. "Evie, I—"

Not wishing to hear any tender sentiments, she slipped her hands under his shirt, reveled as his muscles flexed under her fingertips. "You're wearing too many clothes."

"I want us to revisit our earlier discussion," said Jackson as he and Evie returned to the kitchen some time later. The parents were still away from the house, providing them with the perfect opportunity to grab the orange juice that Evie was craving.

Evie's fingers stilled on the fridge door. "What discussion?"

"I'm not forcing you into anything, but is there any possibility—any way at all—you'd consider just one date with me when we're back in the States? It'll be your choice entirely—pick the time, the location, the day."

"You know that I can't do that."

"Two weeks was an arbitrary amount of time—I am not ready for this to be over yet. You don't want it to be over either."

"That's why it has to end," said Evie, turning to face him. "Don't you get it? I can't be around you for much longer."

"That's not what it seemed like ten minutes ago."

"The sex is great. It's spectacular! And every time, it breaks my heart. Jackson, I can't let this go on. I'm not strong enough to survive it. You can take sex casually—God knows you've had plenty of it since our breakup. I haven't. I don't have the ability to enjoy our time together without fall—without developing feelings. I don't have the experience to do that. That's why this can't continue. What happened between us traumatized me. It took me years to recover, and I don't think I've succeeded yet. I need space. I need space once we're done here. I need to put the pieces of my life back together again because our contract has knocked them all out of place." She didn't know she was crying until Jackson's familiar fingers wiped at her tears. "You keep offering this casual continuation of what we have, and I don't have it in me to keep it casual!"

"I don't want casual. I've only offered that because I thought that's what *you* wanted. Tell me what you want and it's yours. You're mine, Evie. Have always been mine, always will be. Tell me what it'll take."

He demanded too much from her. He didn't understand why they couldn't continue, why she couldn't let it go on. She'd tried to explain it so many times, but he refused to hear it. She shook off his hands. The tears streamed down her cheeks with a relentlessness she couldn't control.

"Evie—"

"Don't touch me. Please. I can't bear it right now."

"Jackson is making Evie cry again!" came Oliver's voice. Evie hadn't even heard them come in. She leapt back in surprise, bumping into the fridge.

"Did we accidentally go back in time?" asked Nate, coming up behind Oliver.

"Guys, you're here!" said Evie, swiping at hot tears as she headed to embrace Jackson's youngest brothers with the brightest smile she could muster.

She hugged Nate first. An attorney, he lived in Manhattan full time and she hadn't seen or talked to him in at least a year. Releasing Nate, she embraced Oliver. She and Oliver lived in Los Angeles and would meet up from time to time for a coffee or dinner, though she hadn't seen him in a few months.

"You two okay?" asked Oliver.

"All good." Evie smiled through the burn in her eyes. "I can't believe you two are here."

"How could we turn down staying at a mansion?" deadpanned Nate. "Catch us up. What'd we miss?"

Once Nate and Oliver duked out who got which room, complaining about Hayes's palatial accommodations the entire time, Evie joined Jackson and his brothers outside for a glass of wine. The parents were still at the beach, giving them time to catch up in private.

The soft breeze rustled the leaves around them, birds chirping high above their chairs. If Evie closed her eyes and forgot about the reason for their stay at Valentin's home, she could almost believe they were on a poolside vacation. She accepted a glass of wine from Oliver. "Tell me—how has it been officially being Dr. Oliver Icefall?"

Oliver chuckled. "So far, it's been great. I accepted a post doc position at UCLA, and I've secured a research grant to Greece next semester. But my news isn't as big as Nate's."

Evie took a sip of wine as she turned toward him. "What's your news, Nate?"

Nate reached into a box of cookies he had snatched from the kitchen earlier and now balanced on one knee. "I quit my job."

"What?"

"You quit?"

"When?"

"Why?"

Jackson and Hayes exploded with questions. Evie wasn't even sure who asked what.

"I'm tired of it. The billable hours. Barely sleeping. Not having the time to go outside. I'm exhausted. I'm done."

"What are you going to do?" Evie asked.

"I'm not sure. I'm going to take some time and figure it out."

"Wow," she said. "I always thought you wanted to be a lawyer."

"I did too. Funny how that works out. When you reach your goal, sometimes you realize it's not what you wanted after all."

"Whoa, whoa. Were you offering me legal advice as an unemployed lawyer last week?" asked Hayes.

Nate threw a cookie at him.

When the Icefalls and Evie's parents returned to the house, introductions, then excited catch-ups erupted. Evie stood next to Jackson as he watched his mom and stepdad laugh with his brothers. Unlike their nonchalant treatment of Jackson, they practically climbed all over their younger sons. They'd been happy to see Hayes, but the radiating delight from having all three of their sons around them was overwhelming. Evie's heart hurt for Jackson, who looked on from the periphery.

For someone who'd always grabbed for what he wanted, this family dynamic seemed forever out of his reach. Lisa and Leonard had ensured that.

Oliver turned toward Jackson, an attempt to include him in the conversation. "Has Jackson been showing you a good time?"

"He made us move out of a hotel and into this remote house," said Leonard.

"You mean the mansion with a pool and a putting green?" asked Nate. "There's a wine cellar I've yet to raid."

"The hotel was central. Now we're outside Nice and have to rely on his driver for excursions," explained Lisa.

"I think the home is lovely," said Rose in a quiet voice. "He's been very generous to include us too."

"It's the least he can do," mumbled Leonard.

"Speaking of excursions," cut in Jackson, directing his next statement at Evie's mom. "Since you wanted to see Monaco, I have a tour booked for you all, with a night in Monte Carlo."

"Oh, you didn't have to do that!" said Rose. "We could have arranged our own trip."

"Alain will take you, not a big deal."

"Evie, have you been to Monaco before?" asked Lisa.

"Evie isn't going, but you guys will have a grand time."

"Why can't Evie go?" asked her mom.

"I don't want to," Evie hurried to clarify.

Her father looked dumbfounded. "Monaco is one of only six European micro-states. How could you not want to go see it? Don't you want to see Monte Carlo?"

As much as Evie wished she could explain her aversion to the area, she couldn't. She had buried the truth ten years ago. How could she ever share her story now? It would crush her parents. "I've seen it before, and I have a lot of writing to catch up on."

"Finish it today," suggested her dad.

"One day isn't enough. Don't worry, I don't feel left out. You all go and enjoy yourselves, and I'll see you when you're back."

"Fine, fine," grumbled her father. "You still have time to change your mind."

I won't.

"What about you, boys? Will you join?" Lisa asked.

"Nah," said Nate. "I'd rather stick around the pool tomorrow."

"Same," agreed Oliver.

"I got work," said Hayes, "so can't."

"Alain will pick you guys up tomorrow morning," Jackson said. "Bring nice clothes. I made dinner reservations for you too."

With a few hours left until dinner, everyone scattered around the house. Hayes returned upstairs, while Nate and Oliver popped open a bottle of champagne by the pool. Jackson assumed that Michael and Leonard were out on the putting green, but he didn't care enough to check. Rose and his mom hunched over a laptop at the kitchen table. As he walked through the house, he still couldn't find Evie.

She had slipped out of the living room quietly once he announced the Monaco trip. He thought she had returned to her room, but when he knocked on her door and peeked inside, she wasn't there. She didn't seem to be anywhere else in the house either.

On a hunch, he made his way to the flower garden that was the pride of his father's gardener. The blooms had been imported from flower shows all over Europe, and were tended daily by his gentle, age-gnarled hands.

Jackson assumed a lot of negotiations had gone into sending him away for a few days while he and Evie and their families were here.

His guess turned out to be correct. He found Evie typing on her laptop on one of the benches amid the blooms. Two tiny yellow butterflies fluttered above a peony bush next to her.

She glanced up at his approach. "You know, I can recognize your footsteps with my eyes closed."

"Good," he murmured, pressing a brief kiss to her lips as he joined her on the bench. "I hope my footsteps aren't the only things you recognize with your eyes closed."

She laid her head on his shoulder, hugging his waist and burrowing closer. He loved her snuggling into his side. He hated the exhausted-sounding question that followed. "Did you come to argue some more?"

"No," he said, tracing languorous circles down her back. "I came to make a request."

Wariness drew her brows together. He loathed seeing her look so guarded. "What kind of request?"

His brother's counsel still rang through his brain, and he intended to trust him. Evie was too important for him to ignore sound advice. "Come with me to the Zohra party tomorrow night."

She looked confused. She studied him closely, as if wondering if she'd misheard. "To your sex party?"

"It's not my sex party. It's a Zohra party. I have to attend, but I don't partake. Dad's house is secure. You'll have Hayes, Nate, and Oliver here if you choose to return tomorrow night. But I'd like for you to join me and stay in Cannes."

Evie considered the options: to return to Valentin's

home before the Zohra event or to be Jackson's guest at the sex party. The first option would leave her under the watchful eyes of his brothers and whatever security company Valentin employed to monitor the cameras. She'd relax by the pool and write at the desk Jackson had set up in her room. Meanwhile, Jackson would attend the Zohra party alone. The idea of naked, attractive women throwing themselves at Jackson made her feel as achy as the flu.

She craved to go and be mysterious and sexy, and have him want no one else but her. The sheer idea was ludicrous. They only had a handful of days left before they'd part forever and never see each other again. She couldn't fall in love with him again. She wouldn't be able to bear their breakup a second time around.

She chose option two regardless. She'd go to Zohra Cannes, to a sex party—*the sex party of the year*—with Jackson. The idea sent a dark thrill reverberating through her kneecaps. It wasn't something she'd ever done, but Jackson would keep her safe and respect her boundaries. Of that, she had no doubt.

"I want to go to the party. I don't want to do anything with anyone but you, but I want to see it. Everyone is masked, right? No one will know it's me?"

"I'll make sure that no one does."

"I'll need to buy a dress. What do people wear to it anyway?"

"Black tie. Sometimes women wear lingerie."

"What if I want to wear lingerie?"

"You can wear whatever you want when we're alone. At the party? You'll be as covered up as a nun at Christmas mass."

Evie didn't want to be ogled by horny men paying a

quarter million to have wild monkey sex with strangers. "That works for me."

His darkened gaze skimmed down her body. "How about we head back to your room and get you out of your clothes now?"

The low timbre of his voice sent tendrils of anticipation unfurling through her.

Five days to go.

She could work him out of her system by then.

She had to.

Chapter 25

The next morning, Jackson stayed in his room while the parents packed for Monte Carlo. He, like Evie, refused to ever set foot there again. The crash, loss of their child, and collapse of their marriage all happened too close to Monaco. He would never go back. He didn't even want to listen to the Campbells, or his mom and Leonard, discuss the upcoming trip.

When he heard Alain arrive and, soon after that, the parents leave, he went to seek out Evie. She had made herself comfortable at the desk he had installed in her room, a cup of espresso next to her open laptop. Her fingers flew over the keys.

"Ready for Cannes?"

Her entire body froze, the typing halting. "A little nervous."

"I need to put in an appearance, but we don't have to stay."

She shook her head. "No. I want to do this."

"You can always change your mind. I can take you to our hotel and have one of the Zohra security guys stay with you."

She closed her laptop and faced him. "You got us a hotel? I figured we'd spend the night at your club."

"You're not sleeping at Zohra."

"I wouldn't mind."

"I would. I got us a nice room at a beachfront resort. We'll come back here the following night. We may even beat our parents."

"They can never know."

"Definitely not. Your dad would skin me, then shoot me."

"What about your brothers?"

"I bribed Nate and Oliver out of wanting tickets. They'll be fine here. Hayes only needs his laptop to be happy."

Evie and Jackson hadn't spent any time in Cannes during their brief marriage. Because the city held no memories for Evie, stepping out of the car brought no anxiety.

"I love how warm it is here," she told Jackson as he handed the keys to the hotel valet. He chose to drive them to Cannes himself, breaking out his dad's Aston to do so.

They checked into the hotel before retrieving their car from the valet and continuing on to Zohra.

Zohra Cannes was located not far from Vieux-Port de Cannes, a harbor lined with sleek yachts of all sizes. Although smaller than its Parisian counterpart, Zohra Cannes looked just as exclusive and discreet. Jackson navigated past the three-story building, with wrought iron balconies and mint green shutters and no visible signage. He pulled around to the back alley and drove through tall wooden gates. "It's closed for the day, only staff are on the premises. No one will know you're here."

A tall, serious gentleman with thick-rimmed glasses met them outside. "You're here."

Jackson introduced her to Richard Guiliano, Noémie's Cannes counterpart.

"Did the paperwork get sorted?"

"It has all been settled," said Richard in formal, accented English. "Come see the acrobats practicing."

Richard led them through the back room toward the grand foyer. Evie glanced up, captivated by the skylights set in the roof three stories above. Sunrays fell through the circular panes of glass and bounced off the marble flooring to illuminate the space. Part of the light was blocked by rigging for the upcoming acrobatics show. Two aerialists, suspended on silk scarves high above the makeshift stage, spun and twisted against each other in the air, practicing the choreography for their upcoming performance. A small group that looked to be part of the set-up—most looked like technicians, one like a trainer or choreographer—watched from below.

Florists bustled around the space, setting elaborate arrangements along polished tables. Production staff moved furniture and tested lighting.

A short woman in a fitted suit and high heels clicked her way toward them across the marble. Jackson introduced her as the events director, Margaux Martin.

"Margaux's planned every single one of these now. They're always spectacular."

"They're always a pain in the ass," said Margaux in an American accent. She turned to Jackson. "I scrapped the salmon for the halibut. I know you prefer salmon, but at the price of the ticket? The guests will want halibut. One of your guests is allergic to honey, so that party favor is out. They'll have to drizzle each other in chocolate instead. Which will stain your furniture, so I made it white chocolate."

"This is what makes Margaux the best," Jackson told Evie. "She anticipates everything."

"The ticketing staff are arriving in an hour. One staff member will check in every twenty guests to avoid a jam. I usually go one staff member per fifty guests, but this is a special occasion—and we have a waiting list going. I've upped the security too. Discreetly, of course. Given the fire in Paris, didn't want to chance it. Whatever happened there anyway?"

"They're still investigating."

"We won't hear for months then." She tapped her nails against her clipboard. "I have to go. The musicians will be doing a sound check soon, and I need to make sure they're set up in the right place. Richard, grab someone from the production company. They may be needed to work the sound system."

Margaux and Richard weaved through the marble columns and disappeared out of sight.

Jackson took Evie's hand. "Everything is on track. Let's go get you your dress. Unless you changed your mind and want to bow out? I can call Hayes, Nate, and Oliver to meet you."

"And miss the acrobatics show? I don't think so."

"How about I take you to Cirque du Soleil any time you want instead?"

He'd asked her to accompany him, but now he was having second thoughts? "You think I can't handle myself?"

She noticed that the muscle in his jaw began to tick. "You really want people like Sebastian Carlton leering at you?"

"No one will leer. I'll be with you."

"Everyone will be leering at you. Have you seen you?"

She smiled at his petulant response. Was Jackson preemptively jealous? Resting her hands on his chest for balance, she pressed a kiss to the pulsing muscle in his jaw. "You're biased. I want to finish up my wild two weeks with you by being your date at Zohra Cannes."

"And I can't convince you otherwise?"

She shook her head, wrinkling her nose impishly at him. "Nope. My mind is set."

The sounds of an argument from the front of the Club interrupted Jackson mid-sentence. "Stay here."

Evie kept pace with him as they followed the racket. They both stopped short. Two security men tried to block and restrain a screeching woman from entering further. Evie would recognize that voice anywhere. Tilly.

"Let her through," said Jackson, striding forward. "I've been trying to reach you for a week. Where have you been?"

Shaking off the guards' hold, she leapt at him. "I'm filing charges!"

"Charges for what?" demanded Jackson.

"For what you did to me."

"What did I do?"

"You hired some goons to threaten me and take my phone."

"What the hell are you talking about?" asked Jackson.

Evie skirted around Jackson, coming face to face with a raging Tilly.

"Be careful, girl," warned Tilly. "This one is dangerous. He lured me to France and then threatened to strangle me."

"Jackson did no such thing. He wouldn't do that. Tell us what happened."

Evie hadn't noticed Richard join them until he cleared his throat. "You're disturbing the performers and production crew. Please take this to my office."

"Will you come talk to us in private, Tilly?" asked Evie, trying to sound as reasonable as possible.

Tilly glared at Jackson from beneath her lash extensions. A few of the lash clusters were missing since she last saw her, and the remaining extensions hung for dear life in patchy clumps. "Fine. But you do anything I deem threatening, I'll have the local police on your ass immediately. I'm done running and hiding from you."

Jackson motioned for everyone to follow him to Richard's office, which was tucked away behind the dual staircases. Once everyone entered the tastefully decorated space, he jerked his chin at Tilly. "Start from the beginning."

"Yes," Evie couldn't help but add. "Like how you shoved me down the stairs in Nice, and left that nasty note in my hotel, and trashed my room *twice*."

Tilly looked confused. "I didn't do any of that. I admit, I was upset… Jackson had invited me to France only to dump me the same night I met his parents. I was mad. I was *furious*. I went to confront him at his club, but his annoying manager kicked me out. Then I found you in the hotel." Tilly stabbed her finger in Jackson's direction. "I know you were responsible for that scooter hitting me. Trying to keep me away from your new flavor of the month."

"I didn't get anyone to run you over, Tilly."

"Well, someone did. They did it purposely too. They came straight for me. I didn't see their face. They had that stupid helmet on. Then you sent your henchmen to my hospital room. Scared me enough to run. Well, I'm no runner. I'm here to confront your ass. I'm not scared of you—or your threats."

"What henchmen? What threats?" asked Jackson.

"That night the scooter hit me and I was in the hospital room, you supposedly left to get your stuff. Then you sent two assholes to find me. They took my phone. Said they'd strangle me if I ever saw you again."

"I did no such thing. I came back from the hotel and you were gone."

Tilly scoffed. "Liar. Who else would send them?"

"That's why you left the hospital," said Evie.

Jackson turned to Evie. "I told you it's Barnsley."

"Why would David be threatening your ex-girlfriends?"

Tilly tilted her head, Evie's words finally resonating. "Wait, you were threatened too?"

"Yes. Even pushed down the stairs once." Evie pointed to the almost-healed cut on her forehead.

"I didn't do that!"

"What about the licensing issues I've been having with Zohra Cannes?" Jackson asked. "You behind that?"

"I don't even know which licenses you need." Tilly studied Jackson, reassessing him. "It really wasn't you who sent the goons?"

"No. I thought it was you behind all the shit happening to Evie."

"Then who sent those men?"

"David said you and he had plans to meet up in Nice," Evie said. "If you didn't have your phone on you, who made a date with him at the hotel?"

Jackson gave her a sardonic look. "If there even was a date."

"David asked me for my number in Paris, and I gave it to him, but I haven't had my phone on me since then."

What the heck kind of mess are we in?

"Tilly," said Jackson. "It'll be safer for you to go

back to the States. I can get you on a flight out today. Go back to Charleston. If you need to stay somewhere safe, I'll get you a hotel room."

"No, no need. I was going to visit a friend in Atlanta for a bit. Now that I know I'm not running from you, I feel better about going back stateside."

"I'll get to the bottom of this. I promise."

"Were the men who threatened you French?" asked Evie.

"No. American."

"Would you feel comfortable going to the police and filing a report?"

"No. All I want is to go home."

"Someone used your phone to text my parents a story about Jackson," said Evie.

"They did? Well, text them back and tell them I want my property back."

Chapter 26

Jackson and Evie took Tilly to the airport before returning to their hotel to drop off the car.

As the valet took the car away, Evie turned to Jackson. "I was so sure it was Tilly. Knowing that it's someone else is… oddly unsettling. Tilly was a known entity. Now I'm really creeped out! That means someone other than her had texted David to meet at the hotel? Why would someone do that?"

"To fuck with him? Or he made the whole thing up. Either way, you're not to leave my sight. You understand?"

"Yes, sir," said Evie, playfully pecking his cheek. "Which means you're going to have to go dress shopping with me."

"The Zohra event couldn't come at a worse time."

Evie shrugged. "We might as well make the most of it. Come on, we need to start getting ready soon."

She pulled him toward the shops on Boulevard de la Croisette. Aware that they only had a few hours before they had to be at Zohra, she hurried along the window displays until a narrow wedge of a local shop caught her eye.

"Stay out here. I want my dress to be a surprise."

She was in and out in under fifteen minutes. Jackson carried her shopping bag as they returned to the hotel.

Evie showered and curled her hair to fall down her back in loose waves. Leaning close to the bathroom mirror, she applied heavier eye makeup than usual and went ham on the highlighter. Satisfied with her work, she pulled the dress she had chosen off the hanger.

The shimmering dress had been cut from two-tone fabric, flickering between a lavender-blue and iridescent silver. The deep V-neck stopped at a banded waist. Thin spaghetti straps crisscrossed low on her bare back, showcasing a generous swathe of skin. The heavy skirt fell to the ground, swirling around her four-inch heels as she stepped out of the bathroom.

Jackson, who had been typing into his phone, looked up and froze.

"Fuck," he groaned. "You look gorgeous."

The short compliment sent blood racing to all her pulse points. Jackson looked debonair himself, in his tuxedo and bow tie. She wanted to strip him out of them immediately. "You look very handsome," she said. "We clean up well."

Her heart beat rapidly in her throat as he stalked toward her, his stride as slow and focused as that of a wild cat. His hand reached out, as if to trace the lock of hair curling over her breast, but he snagged it back. "We'll never leave this room if I touch you."

"You can touch me all you want at Zohra."

"You don't play fair, woman."

"Is this the time I tell you that I'm not wearing underwear?"

He lunged for her. "Screw the party."

She evaded his grasp, rushing for the door with a laugh. "Come on. We can't be late to your own event."

***

Jackson wanted the party to be over, and it hadn't even begun. Not that his dick didn't harden at the thought of fucking Evie at his sex club. He had rejected the idea before, but now that she was accompanying him to the Cannes event, anticipation filled him. He wanted her anywhere, anytime, but the thought of having her in his lair heated his body with savage intensity.

Nevertheless, the niggling feeling at the base of his skull grew stronger the closer they got to Zohra.

None of the incidents had been the result of Tilly's jealous tantrum. Tilly was just as much a victim as Evie, and he was the common denominator. But who'd want to cause this much havoc? As far as he knew, he had no enemies. His competitors in the sex club space wouldn't push his ex-wife down the stairs. As much as teasing Evie about Barnsley amused him, he knew the guy wouldn't hurt a fly. Yet someone had tracked him from Paris to Nice— knew enough about his life to text his ex-wife's father.

"You okay?" asked Evie as he pulled up to the back alley again, foregoing the main entrance to avoid attention on Evie.

"Something feels off. I can feel it. I just don't know what it is yet."

Evie touched the mask tied securely around her head for the tenth time before she exited the car. Jackson assured her that she was unrecognizable. She hoped he was right. She couldn't afford bad publicity. Attending a sex party was the worst kind of exposure for an author of young adult books.

Sensual music streamed in through hidden speakers

260

from the stage as they slipped through the back entrance. Low, glimmering lights gave the party a sensory feel. Discreet guards with ear pieces spread out along the perimeter. Waiters and waitresses dressed in black lingerie carried trays heavy with drinks.

Couples chatted in groups, sitting along the clusters of low couches or standing by the bar. Jackson had mentioned that Zohra had a two-alcoholic drink maximum for each guest to ensure consent and safety.

The party had just started, but some women had already stripped down and sat on their partners' laps. Their chosen companions, some also naked, stroked their bodies as they chatted with other guests.

At the main entrance, Evie saw innumerable staff checking in guests, taking their mobile devices and coats, and directing them into the party. The aerialists spun in tune to the music high overhead.

Evie stepped forward, drawn by the carnal movements above.

A familiar hand closed about her elbow. Jackson pulled her away from the show and the increasingly touchy-feely couples around them into a small alcove, fastening his mouth to hers. She kissed him back, her body reacting to his touch as eagerly as it always did. The feel and scent of him made her ravenous, and she whimpered to get closer.

"I need you," he murmured against her lips.

She arched into him. "More."

"Not here. Upstairs."

He dragged her up one of the two curving staircases to the row of private rooms on the third floor. He stopped at the furthest one. The room, decorated in earthy tones, centered around a tall, four-poster bed. Evie didn't get a chance to explore further. Jackson slammed the door shut with his foot, and pulled her into his arms. His mouth skimmed her neck as he dragged down the thin straps of her evening gown.

He tried to tug the dress lower, but it didn't budge.

"Zipper," Evie said, lifting her arm to show him the hidden fastening.

His fingers closed over the zipper tongue and tugged it down. Evie took a full inhale as the fabric fell away.

She stood in front of him wearing only her lotion and a spritz of perfume.

"Killing me," he groaned, and reached for her again.

His palm slid down her skin, sending pleasure to shimmer across her nerve endings. His thumb teased across one distended nipple as he studied her with an intensity she hadn't seen before. The emotions etched in his features frightened her. They were too raw. Too real. She wanted to see lust. Desire. Physical need. Not this devastating tenderness that threatened to break through the last of the grit she had erected around her heart.

She cupped him through his suit pants, stroked his erection over the expensive fabric. "Pants off, Monsieur Auclair."

He helped her divest him of his suit and undid his bow tie as she reached for the buttons of his shirt. The crisp fabric fell away, and they both stood naked in front of one another. He was beautiful. She still couldn't get used to the musculature of his body, the chiseled planes she wanted to trace with her fingertips and mouth and tongue. Her fingers explored his abs, the muscles jumping under her touch.

"I can't get enough of you." He scooped her up to carry her to the bed. The mattress barely gave as he set her onto its wide surface. The sheets felt cool and slick against her heated body. She rolled against them, the sensation pleasant on her sensitized skin.

Jackson watched her with a frozen expression, a muscle jumping in his jaw. She reached out her arms, desperately needing to feel his skin on hers, yet he ignored the supplication.

She knew he wanted her. His eyes looked almost black with need. Yet he didn't move, just watched her with that unsettling intensity. A flush of desire heated his skin and gathered high on his cheekbones. Evie drew her legs together and sat up—suddenly uncomfortable with his attention.

"Lie down," he commanded, his voice so guttural she barely recognized it.

She leaned back on her elbows, the position thrusting her breasts forward. His eyes followed. "Come here and make me."

Challenge glinted in his eyes as he joined her on the bed. Brand-hot hands spread her legs as he made room for himself, trailing unhurried, open-mouthed kisses along her inner thigh, stopping just short of where she needed him. "Jackson," she breathed, falling to her back in frustration.

She felt his grin against her skin just before his mouth dove down and settled on her. *Yes. Make me come. Make me forget. Don't look at me like that.*

She arched off the bed at the hot press of his tongue. Her legs tightened around his head as he teased her, maddeningly ignoring the bundle of nerves that pulsed for his touch. She tried to shift her hips, wordlessly begging him to stop his torturous evasion, but he eluded the move. When she lifted toward him, he pulled back, moving off the bed and pulling her with him until her butt hit the very edge. "What—?"

Thoughts scattered as he slid one thick finger inside her soaked channel, then two, and his mouth—*finally*—settled on her throbbing peak. He curved his fingers, unerringly finding her G-spot. The combined assault on her senses left her suspended in space, deafened and blind to anything but the feel of him inside and around her. Her inner muscles clamped hard on his fingers, her back bowing off the bed as she came.

He withdrew and moved away. Her legs splayed open as she watched him stroll over to one of the cabinets, lined with a collection of packaged sex toys. What did he intend to do? Evie had never tried any toy before, and his sure search along the line-up made her nervous.

The span of his shoulders blocked her from seeing what exactly he had chosen from the shelf.

"Jackson?" she asked, uncertain.

He strode back to her. His fingers pulled apart the small box, revealing a silicone-covered rose. "Trust me. You'll like this."

"What is it?"

He held up the bright pink toy. "You wanted the full Zohra experience."

She glanced at the innocuous-looking flower. Her teeth sank into her lip as she considered.

"We don't have to use it." Jackson, watching her closely, moved to set it aside.

"No!" Evie blurted out before he could put the toy away. "I want to try."

He swooped down, caging her with one arm as his lips descended to hers. He kissed her deeply, pulling back as he pressed a button that set the flower to buzz. He traced the purring bud along the curve of her cheek, down her neck, grazed her collarbone. The sensation was foreign, but not unpleasant. The low vibration caressed her skin as he rounded each nipple, lighting up nerve endings with the unfamiliar resonance. As he grazed a sensitive peak, Evie arched into the sensation.

She felt lightheaded, so absorbed with the foreign object's teasing path that she had forgotten to breathe. Forcing her lungs to relax, she gasped in air even as Jackson continued his teasing trail. He moved the toy in a maddeningly slow caress to her belly button. Her body coiled, hyper-focused on its path as he circled the sensitive dip, skimming lower.

Her mouth went dry. She licked her parched lips as the bud teased the delicate skin of her mons.

"Tell me you want this," he murmured.

She nodded feverishly against the silk sheets. He—and the vibrator—moved away. *Where is he going now?* Desperate to have him—and the toy—back, she craned her neck to watch him grab one of the pillows. Returning to her, he propped the pillow under her head, shifting her angle of view higher.

"I want to watch you pleasure yourself." His whisper was a low rumble against her ear. She turned her head, seeking his mouth, but he was already gone. He resumed his position between her splayed legs, his eyes almost black as he surveyed her.

The new angle changed her experience. She could no longer close her eyes and rely solely on sensation. She was now an active participant, required to watch as Jackson dragged the vibrating rose low across her belly.

She'd never used a vibrator, not even in the privacy of her own bedroom, under a nocturnal veil. Now, Jackson expected her to perform such an intimate act in front of him.

His gaze dared her to decline as he placed the toy in her sweat-sheened palm and curved his fingers around hers. He'd used the cool silicone toy to tease her earlier, and the heat of his skin finally touching hers made her want to twine her fingers through his and hold tight.

His hand lingered on hers, his thumb tracing a warm path as he relinquished control of the vibrator. He pressed a hidden button, shifting the low purr to a soft pulse.

Her fingers tested the soft surface of the sex toy. Her eyes anchored to his as she placed its cool petals against her stomach.

Jackson's entire body had gone rigid. His hands clenched and unclenched at his sides, his chest rose and fell in jagged breaths. He looked like a wild beast struggling to hold on to his quickly unraveling threads of control. She wanted those threads to snap, craved to feel the full burn of his lust as he took her on this silk-covered bed at his club.

Yet it wasn't his barely leashed desire that spurred her to move the toy. It was the other emotions she saw reflected in his eyes. He'd always made her feel safe, treasured. Cherished. Shedding her reserve was easy when he looked at her this way. She trusted him. She couldn't imagine being this vulnerable with anyone else.

She trailed the vibrator to between her legs. His gaze followed. The low pulsating sensation felt odd and scintillating as she moved it across her sensitive flesh. The rhythmic pressure spurred her to press it tighter against herself. Jackson stepped closer—

"Fuck." He inhaled sharply.

Startled by his low curse, she sat up. "What is it?"

He crouched down, rubbing at his shin. "Bumped the bedframe."

She couldn't contain her laugh. "I'm glad you can test drive your furniture tonight."

He swooped down and kissed her, pressing her back onto the pillow. "Me too. Imagine the injury lawsuits back in the States."

"Is your leg okay?"

"Already forgotten. Continue. Please," he ground out, moving her hand—and the toy—back to the juncture of her thighs, but keeping his hand firmly over hers. He found the hidden button again, increasing the speed and strength of the pulsating vibrations.

Evie gasped at the intensity of it.

"You want me?" he demanded.

Distracted by the new sensations below, Evie couldn't form the words to answer. She focused on the insistent throb against her body—sinking her teeth deep into her lip to contain her moans.

His hand pulled hers—and the toy—away. She gasped at his audacity, struggling to focus on his face. "Jackson…"

"Tell me you want me."

"I want you. I always want you."

He released his hold on her hand. She didn't bring the pulsating object back against her. The vibrator lay forgotten in her hand as her eyes glued to the sight of him sheathing himself.

She wanted him now. If he didn't join her soon, she'd leap off the bed and climb up his body. He spared her the gymnastics. He tugged the pillow out from beneath her head and tucked it beneath her hips. They both groaned when he sank hilt-deep. He gave her a moment to adjust and then he was moving, each thrust a promise of a future she was too afraid to want.

"Put the vibrator back," he rasped.

Evie's trembling hand moved the buzzing toy to her center. The dual sensations assaulted every one of her senses. Sweat beaded her skin as she tried to hold on to the vestiges of her lucidity. She couldn't hold back. Her body had always recognized only him. He fell forward, his mouth finding hers.

"I love you," he whispered against her lips. "I love you."

Evie let his words wash over her as she came apart in his arms. She clasped his body to hers as he came hard inside her, held on to him even as she knew she should let go. When he attempted to move away, she held on tighter. She wanted to feel every inch of him for as long as possible. *We have four days left on our agreement.* The thought intruded into her subconscious. She tried to shake it off, but couldn't.

Too soon, he pulled out. She wanted to protest, but she was too boneless to do so. Shifting her higher up the mattress, he joined her on the bed. As she settled herself into the crook of his shoulder, his fingers twined with hers.

He pressed a kiss to the top of her head. "That was… wow."

"You pipe something into the air here?"

He didn't acknowledge her joke. He pulled back to glance at her. "I meant what I said, Evie."

"I don't think you could have possibly meant that."

"Evie—"

She struggled up. "Stop. I can't… I can't… not ever again. The last time nearly broke me."

He sat up next to her, his body unyielding. "It won't be like that again."

"How do you know that? How could you possibly promise that?"

"We were silly kids then. We're grown ass adults now."

"I don't feel like an adult when it comes to you—I still feel like that overcharged girl running around the country with you."

"I'm in love with you, Evie."

The words burned her throat, but she had to protect herself. She wouldn't survive a second Jackson Auclair breakup. "I'm sorry, Jackson, but I can never love you back again."

The quick flash of pain in his eyes disappeared quickly. Had she imagined it? "So, this was all just sex to you?"

She couldn't lie to him. "It never, ever was just sex between us."

"What would it take for you to consider giving us another try?"

Her heart broke open at the hope creased into his eyes. "I don't know. I'm scared."

"Can you at least think about it?"

She wanted to refuse, to tell him that her mind was set, yet her tongue couldn't form the falsehood. She owed them both to at least consider the possibility. "Okay. I'll think about it."

His shoulders relaxed a fraction—

The familiar ringtone of his cellphone echoed in the room. His head whipped around at the sound.

"Hold that thought," he said, moving off the bed. He searched his pants for the phone. "This is Jackson." Evie's heart dropped when she saw his face pale. He listened to the voice on the other line. "I'll be right there," he said in French. His shocked gaze met hers. "It's my dad. He's in a hospital in Monaco. He had a heart attack."

Chapter 27

They tugged on their clothes in a hurry. Evie didn't bother to zip her dress. Stepping back into her shoes, she reached for the door.

Jackson beat her to it. "We'll take the back way. It'll be faster if no one sees us."

That made sense. The guests were there for Zohra's party of the year. Of course they'd want to stop and speak with Jackson. He was the only maskless guest at the party for that exact reason—he was the man of the hour.

Jackson peeked his head into the hallway. "Coast is clear." He took her hand. "Come on."

The back stairs were conveniently located at their end of the hall. They were accessible by a key card, which Jackson scanned before swinging open the door. Evie preceded him down the simple stairwell. It spat them out to the back alley where they had left their car. Valentin's Aston was the only vehicle parked in the small space. Jackson acknowledged the security guard keeping an eye on the lot.

He opened the passenger door for Evie, then jogged around to his side of the car and slid inside.

"Do you know which hospital?"

As Jackson gave her the name, she typed the directions into her phone and connected it to the car's navigation screen. The GPS indicated that the drive would take over an hour.

Jackson pulled out of the courtyard, weaving in and out of Cannes traffic. Evie drew up her knees in front of her on the cognac leather seat and hugged them tightly to her chest, an attempt to warm her chilled frame. She had sworn she'd never return to Monaco, but they had no choice. After everything that Valentin had done for them, being there for him was the least they could do. *He'll be okay. He has to be.*

When traffic cleared on A8, Jackson sped up, keeping his attention on the road. They drove in silence, Jackson navigating around the occasional slowed vehicle while she fought against the nausea roiling her stomach. The Aston brought them closer and closer to the scene of her worst nightmare, and she braced for the moment they'd actually reach it.

Her brain didn't catalogue the shadowed scenery that whizzed by them in the night. It was too dark to see much beyond the road anyway. She focused on keeping her breaths slow and even, while her heart turned into a thirty-pound weight thumping against her ribs. Her reluctance to return to Monaco blended with her concern for Valentin, a man who'd done everything he could to support her during the most difficult time of her life.

She had seen Valentin a decade ago. He had been young and so full of life. How could someone who jogged, swam, played tennis have a heart attack? Her brain couldn't process the information.

"Have you seen him recently?" she asked.

"A few months ago. His new girlfriend's been keeping him busy."

"Busy enough to give him a heart attack?"

"Maybe."

"He'll be okay. He'll pull through."

Jackson didn't respond. Evie saw the stress etched across his brow. He needed to be there for his dad.

"Have you… driven up there… since…"

His hands tightened on the wheel. "No."

Evie curled her legs under her and tried to think of anything else but Valentin's heart attack and the looming site of their accident.

They drove for a half hour before Jackson spoke. "I haven't told him about opening up Arlo with Hayes."

Evie turned her whole body toward him. "How come? Would he approve?"

"I know he would. I guess… I wanted it to be a done deal before I told him. Wanted us to celebrate together."

She reached across the center console and placed her hand on Jackson's thigh, squeezing the taut muscle. "You will. Knowing Valentin, he'll be there on opening night, popping champagne and charming the ladies."

Their drive whisked them closer to the curve of road where their lives had changed forever. A part of Evie wanted to shove open the door and roll out before they reached it. Only her love for Valentin kept her buckled in her seat.

Just focus on your breathing. In and out. Just like meditating. Focus on the breath—

It wasn't helping.

Sweat beaded her skin and soaked through her dress. She hated this. Hated their drive to Monaco. Hated that they'd have to drive right through the site of their accident to get to Valentin. Hated that vivacious, kind Valentin was sick. As they approached the turn that changed their lives forever, she reached for her phone. Maybe there were alternative routes somewhere? Before she could look for a bypass, she set her phone back down. Valentin needed family around him—they didn't have time for detours.

Jackson slowed. She wondered if he did so instinctively, as there were no cars ahead of them to mandate braking. This was it. They were getting closer. Evie's vision blurred. She couldn't breathe. Air seemed just out of reach. She gasped for it, but failed to catch enough into her lungs.

As if sensing her panic, Jackson settled his hand on hers. His palm, a warm, solid presence, jarred her out of her panicked hyperventilation. Their fingers intertwined. He squeezed. She squeezed back.

They reached their crash site—a sliver of a curve, almost imperceptible to others, yet an anvil to them. Evie felt grateful for the night, for the darkness that cloaked the scene from her view and helped cushion the despair that clawed through her. They had both avoided this road for ten years. Now they traversed it together. Evie let her other hand settle on top of Jackson's as they passed the turn and continued on to Monaco.

"You okay?" asked Jackson. His gaze never strayed from the curvature of the road.

"I don't know. It's still so fresh in my memory. I don't think I could bear seeing it in broad daylight, all perfect and fixed and clean and… scenic." She glanced at him. "Are you okay?"

"I hate this road. I don't ever want to drive it again. But maybe it's okay that it is fixed and clean and scenic. Maybe it's a reminder that we can't live in the past forever."

She glanced behind her. It was too dark to see the mountainside that almost took their lives and killed their baby and marriage. "Let's try to figure out another road to take back anyways. I don't want to see it in daytime."

***

Jackson parked the car illegally in front of the glass-fronted hospital. Evie reached for his hand as they hurried toward the building. As someone who spent most of his life alone, it felt rare and precious to have her near as his brain fought to process what happened. He tightened his clasp on her hand.

Maybe it was the quiet of the evening or the unfamiliar location, but time seemed to slow around them. The air gelatinized into a thick substance they had to fight through to reach the entrance. He was grateful to have Evie with him.

A nurse directed them to the correct floor. The woman seemed overly polite and friendly, at odds with the leaden dread that had settled low in his stomach. As he and Evie exited the elevator, Jackson realized they were in a corridor lined with private rooms. Why wasn't his father in intensive care? Were they so lackadaisical in Monaco?

The doctor had just stepped out of Valentin's room as they approached. She glanced at them curiously as they surrounded her.

"Are you Monsieur Auclair's family?" she asked.

"Yes," Evie spoke up before he could. "How is he?"

"He'll be just fine," said the doctor.

"Just fine?" Jackson questioned. "He had a heart attack."

"Originally, we thought that, yes, but it wasn't a heart attack. Monsieur Auclair experienced a panic attack."

"A panic attack?" Jackson thought he'd misheard. "What does he have to be panicking over?"

The doctor hesitated. "I'll let him tell you himself."

274

She hurried away, her steps fading as she moved further down the wide corridor.

Evie looked as confused as Jackson felt. He opened the door, and they walked into his father's hospital room.

Relief that flooded his body at seeing his father alive and well almost buckled his knees. Valentin sat in bed, typing something into his phone. Jackson detected no tubes or beeping machinery. His dad looked up as they entered. A smile broke across his tanned face. He tossed the phone to the side, opening up both arms in greeting.

"Jackson, I didn't expect you to be here so fast. Evie, you came too! I'm touched. And look how dressed up you two are."

"How could I not come see you, Valentin? How are you feeling? The doctor said you had a panic attack?"

Valentin waved off Evie's questions. "It's all silly. Come sit next to me and tell me about your trip. Has my son been giving you any trouble?"

"Let's start with you," cut in Jackson. "What happened?"

"Nothing happened. Just a small… panic attack."

Now that he knew his dad was fine, Jackson wanted to shake him. How could he be so blasé? "A small panic attack? You're in the hospital."

"I'll be fine."

"Tell us what made you panic in the first place, Valentin," pressed Evie. "Maybe we can help."

He shuffled his feet under the thin hospital blanket. "Erm, you two better sit down."

"You're scaring me," said Evie. "Please tell us what happened."

"It's all right. It's not bad. Just… unexpected."

Evie sat at the foot of Valentin's bed.

Jackson's feet refused to move. "I'll stand."

"Suit yourself. You see, I'm… You're… This is odd to say. I'm going to have another baby."

"What?!"

Jackson wasn't sure if he, or Evie, or the two of them simultaneously blurted out the word. It bounced off the walls in the spacious suite.

He couldn't process the information. "How can you possibly have a baby? You're—"

"If you say old, I'll disown you."

"Who're you having the baby with, Valentin?" asked Evie.

"My girlfriend, Daniele. You'll like her."

"You have a lot in common," said Jackson. "She's also thirty-two."

Evie rolled her eyes at him. She turned back to the patient. "Are you excited?"

"I barely remember what it's like to raise a baby. This feels like whole new territory for me."

Evie scooted closer to him, taking the older man's hand. "You'll be fabulous at it. You really stepped up for Jackson when he was a kid. You stepped up for me too."

"You're sweet."

"Valentin, I don't think you realize how much you did for me during… you really took care of both of us."

"You were my daughter-in-law. I had to watch out for you both."

"You're a born father. You'll be wonderful with the new baby too."

"Imagine it, having a kid at my age. Jackson, how are you feeling about all this?"

A good question. "I'm going to have another sibling. Never thought I'd say those words."

Chapter 28

Valentin made them promise that they wouldn't drive back in the middle of the night. As much as Evie wanted to sleep in her own bed, Valentin was adamant. She couldn't say no. Besides, she could barely keep her lids from closing over her gritty eyes. She expected Jackson was just as exhausted. The adrenaline of their mad dash to Monaco had slowly dissipated into fatigue. It wasn't safe to drive back this late, even if Eze Bord de Mer was only a twenty-minute hop away.

Jackson selected a hotel nearest the hospital. They could have stayed in the same hotel as their parents, but Evie didn't want to explain her sudden appearance in Monaco wearing only a formal evening gown. Jackson didn't seem eager to tell his mother that her ex-husband was in town, and having a baby with a woman four years younger than Jackson. Avoiding their hotel was the perfect solution.

They left Valentin to rest in his private chambers and made their way to their hotel for the evening.

"You're going to have a little sister or brother," said Evie as they entered their room. "How does it feel?"

Jackson dropped the small package of toiletries they had requested from the front desk on a nearby table. "Surreal."

She approached the windows, and shut the curtains tight against the night. "You meet Daniele?"

"Not yet. Want to meet her with me?"

Evie's hand stilled on the curtain pull. Panic prickled through her. She had to force her muscles to move, to turn her head and face Jackson.

His face remained carefully blank, as though he anticipated her no, and was prepared to not react.

"I shouldn't. I'm heading back to the States soon."

"In four days."

"In four days," she said, letting go of the curtain pull.

"I want to talk about our relationship."

Evie's shoulders drooped. "Now? All I want to do is to crawl into bed and go to sleep. I'm so tired."

"We only have four days left. You said you can't love me, but let's talk about it. I understand that you're scared. I'm terrified too. I need to know if there's a chance."

"A chance to do what exactly?"

He took a step toward her, but stopped, as though afraid that getting too close to her would derail the conversation. "To date. To see where this goes."

"I told you I'd think about it. Don't push me."

"Thinking about it is not good enough. I want us to talk about it."

"Any other time," she implored, not ready for any discussion of the future. "I'm *exhausted*."

"If I let this go tonight, all you're going to do is run away from it."

"If you insist on talking tonight, I'll tell you where my head is now. Jackson, I already know where our relationship will go. Nowhere good. You and I are not meant to be. We're a disaster together."

His eyes gleamed with a mixture of hope and uncertainty. "These last ten days haven't been a disaster. They're the first time I've felt alive in a decade."

Pain sliced through her. "I'll always remember this time. I just… I can't repeat the past. Please don't make this harder."

"You're closing the door forever."

Evie knew that he'd tossed the statement out as a challenge. He expected her to argue, to reason. He expected too much. They had been so in love and so happy once, and it had all come to a screeching halt. The drive across the meridian of her nightmares had reminded her of that. She couldn't let herself be that recklessly happy again. The plummet would shatter her, and she'd never pick up the pieces. She couldn't let their foolish infatuation with each other continue past their established fourteen-day contract. "I think it's best we end this. After I leave, we can't ever interact again."

The statement hung between them. She knew it was harsh, but it was necessary.

He looked angry. Emotions flashed behind his eyes like a lightning storm. "You're a coward. You're too scared to trust your own heart."

"Yes! Yes, I am! And I'm okay with that."

"You'd rather be all alone than to trust that there's a future here?"

"Don't make this difficult, Jackson," she pleaded.

"I won't. I will make it easy. I'll sleep on the couch." He grabbed the toiletries and stormed into the bathroom.

All Evie wanted was to crawl into bed, close her eyes, and sleep. Brushing her teeth and washing her face evaporated any remaining droplets of energy. If she could have curled up on the floor of the bathroom, she would have. Instead, she dragged herself to the king-sized mattress. There was strange comfort in the crisp cotton sheets that enveloped her, a barrier between her and reality. She tucked her legs to her chest and pulled the top sheet closer to her chin.

From her side of the bed, she could see Jackson's back. He lay facing away from her on the sofa. She had taken one of the pillows and the duvet and left it on the couch for him while he was washing up. He had flipped the pillow over twice before he had settled.

She'd never see Jackson again after her return to the States. The burning sensation that started deep in her stomach spread to her heart and throat. She swallowed against the welling tears. Four more days and they'd be parted forever. How could she possibly let him go?

She loved him. She'd loved him since the moment she met him ten years ago. Every cell in her body was his.

But it didn't matter.

Sometimes love wasn't enough.

She tunneled her face deep into her pillow, hoping the down feathers would stifle the sobs that poured out of her. She mourned their impossible marriage, their impossible love. Mourned the fact that she was a coward. That she was too scared to trust herself. They had turned on each other so quickly once. What if that happened again? What if she retreated into herself once more? Ran like she had done a decade ago?

Her whole body shook with the tears she tried to contain. In the stillness of the evening, a sob broke free, but it wasn't hers. The heart-wrenching sound came from Jackson. It echoed in the quiet room, and made her cry harder.

Jackson slid the curtains open early the next morning. Evie twisted away from the light that slapped her face. Her ribs ached from the sobs that had torn her apart during the night. She sat up in bed, rubbing at her swollen lids. Gathering her courage, she glanced at Jackson.

He looked as haggard as she felt. His cheeks looked sunken, his eyes red and swollen. Coldness blanketed him like mist from an Icelandic waterfall. When he caught her gaze, his lips thinned. "Time to go."

He headed to the bathroom before she could respond.

Evie sighed. She didn't have any clothing with her except for the dress she wore last night. The sparkly dress that she had picked out in anticipation of Jackson's reaction to her wearing it. The dress he had stripped her out of before making love to her, before telling her that he loved her.

Without any other choice, she put it back on. It felt rough and uncomfortable against her skin, and all she wanted to do was get home and get into her pjs. When he exited the bathroom, she went in to brush her teeth. Her reflection in the mirror startled her.

The crying had made her face swell to twice its size. Her skin looked pale and blotchy at the same time. The splashes of cold water didn't help.

Jackson waited at the hotel room door as she exited the bathroom, his face withdrawn. She followed him down the corridor to the elevator and endured the silent ride that took them to the lobby. The air-conditioned air was only slightly cooler than the remoteness radiating from Jackson.

She wanted to explain why she couldn't be with him.

Wanted to make him understand.

Yet as she looked at his set face, words escaped her.

They took the exact route back home. She didn't know why. Maybe he had searched for alternate options but couldn't find any. Maybe he wanted to get back as soon as possible and escape her presence in the car. Maybe he wished to see the road at daytime after all. She herself couldn't gather the energy to find a bypass, so she sat quietly next to him as he drove.

As they approached the site of the accident, she laid her hand on his shoulder. His whole body jerked at the contact. His head whipped around to look at her.

"Can you pull over here?" she asked.

He didn't say anything, but he did pull off the road and parked at the spot of their accident.

As she had suspected, the place had moved on, and this sliver of road looked just like any other. Wild blooms cascaded down the rocky hillside into which they had crashed so long ago. The early morning lull made it look almost… peaceful. Nothing marked the place where their baby and marriage had died.

Without looking at him, Evie reached for his hand and slipped hers into his much larger one. His fingers closed over hers instantly. Securely.

She glanced up. His eyes watched her with a profound sadness. He knew what she was doing. Their relationship had ended here so long ago. Today, she was saying goodbye.

Chapter 29

Valentin's mansion was silent when they returned. His brothers must have still been asleep. Without glancing his way, Evie went straight to her room. He was glad she did. There was nothing more to say.

He didn't bother returning to Cannes for their things. He'd have Alain grab their stuff from the hotel later. Instead, he headed to his father's wine cellar. He didn't want wine. He wished to be as far away from Evie, and anything that reminded him of her, as possible. He kept sensing her perfume in the house, and the tropical notes messed with his head. He needed to escape, to forget her for the rest of the day. Forgetting her for longer was impossible.

He knew that he'd remember her for the rest of his life. He could see himself on his deathbed, old and frail. She'd be the woman he'd think of as he drew his last breath, the one he'd always regret losing. She had imprinted herself on every cell of his body, and he'd miss her until the last of his days.

He didn't care about the Vegas investment.

He'd pull out of his partnership with Hayes.

The idea of moving forward with it now rang hollow and bleak. He didn't want to be somewhere as close to her as Nevada. Hayes could pursue the venture on his own.

Jackson no longer cared for any part of it. All he wanted was Evie. Someone he could never have.

Evie shut the bedroom door tightly behind herself and reached for her phone. Pain clawed at her. She couldn't breathe. Her ribs were closing in on her lungs, and any attempt at a full inhale hurt. Desperately fighting a fresh round of tears, she video called Joy. Her sister could always make her feel calmer.

Joy answered the phone lying against the bright-green cushions of her couch. The buttons on her hot-pink pajamas looked misaligned. A rainfall of loose tendrils escaped from the haphazard knot on top of her head, implying that she hadn't changed that bun in a while. She wore her blue light glasses again, and she peered through the treated lenses at Evie. "Holy crap you look awful! What happened?"

"It's over." It hurt to even say the words.

Joy sat up. "What's over?"

"Jackson and I… he told me he loved me. I told him I couldn't love him back. That I didn't even want to try."

Joy's face scrunched in confusion. "Why would you do that? He's the love of your life! I have never seen you be even remotely as happy with anyone else. You guys practically glow in each other's company."

Evie fought the tears. "That was a long time ago. Things are different now."

"Different how?" Joy didn't sound convinced.

"Our breakup shattered me the last time." She couldn't put herself through that again.

"So you decided to preemptively end it now and be sad and alone forever and not even give him a chance? What are you, stupid? What's wrong with you?"

Taken aback by her sister's reaction, Evie gripped her phone tighter. "Why are you insulting me?"

Joy's face softened. "I'm not insulting you. I'm being real with you. Give me a reason for why you broke it off and I'll tell you if it's stupid."

"How supportive of you."

"Girl, you want me to take care of you in your old age while you're all bitter and alone like Miss Havisham?"

"I hate that book," Evie ground out.

Joy raised a brow. "Don't be that book."

Her sister made a great point, but uncertainty still pulled at her. "How can I know that we won't end in disaster again?"

"You can't know that. You have to take the leap anyway. Is that your reason for breaking it off? Fear?" Joy leaned in closer to the screen. "I told you. It's stupid."

"It's not stupid," Evie bit out.

Joy rolled her eyes. "Oh, I'm sorry. You're right. Break it off with the only man who's ever made you happy. Come home, marry someone vanilla, and live a nice beige life until you meet your nice beige end."

"Joy!"

Her sister released a dramatic sigh. "Evie, I love you. Give him a chance. Trust him—no, I take that back. Trust yourself. What does your heart and gut tell you?"

Evie didn't have to think long. "That I love him."

"Well, duh."

"I don't want anyone else but him," Evie confessed.

"Thennnn… what's the problem?"

She tried to make her sister understand. "I can't survive another break-up with him."

Joy narrowed her eyes. "Am I wrong, or didn't you just break up with him?"

"Yes. But that's different. This is on my terms."

"And your terms mean being miserable?" When Evie didn't respond, Joy's tone tempered. "Listen, I can't tell you what to do. But if you're scared… talk to him. Maybe you two can take it really, realllllly slow until you feel more comfortable. Maybe you can be friends for a bit? Don't break both of your hearts because you're too scared to even have a conversation."

"I don't want to take it slow. I want what we used to have."

"Isn't that what he wants too?"

Evie's heartbeat sped up. Joy was right. It was. He had offered her exactly what she'd wanted and dreamed of, and she threw it back in his face and ran. What in the world was she doing? "I'll call you back."

"You better! And I'll want every single detail."

He couldn't even escape her in the wine cellar. His brain was playing tricks on him, making him hear her footfall when she was nowhere near him. She was probably in her room, most likely packing. He doubted she'd want to stay longer now that she'd said goodbye.

When she appeared at the bottom of the steps, he assumed it was wishful thinking. A trick of the light. Yet the image didn't waver. She looked solid, real. She had changed from her party dress into a plain white robe.

Her face was still swollen, her eyes puffy and red. They had spent a sleepless night in the Monte Carlo hotel room, the sounds of her sobs echoing the sorrow inside of him. His own tears had stained his pillow as he mourned the future that had never been within his grasp. Now she stood on the opposite side of the wine cellar, looking as uncertain as he felt.

He froze as he watched her, anticipating her next move. Her teeth worried her lip as she lingered near the steps, one hand gripping the banister. Her fingers released the carved wood. She took a deep breath and ran toward him. Her body collided with his as her hands wound around his neck. Before his brain could compute the implications, she rose on her tiptoes and kissed him.

He hadn't anticipated it. His whole body froze at the contact. Was it a dream? Was she real? Her tongue slipped inside his mouth.

She was real.

"God," he groaned, as his arms locked around her and he kissed her back.

"I need you. I want you," she sobbed against his mouth.

As he grasped the tie to her robe, his trembling hands struggled to loosen it. "Did you triple knot this?"

She laughed, reaching down to help. As their fingers tangled, realization of what they were about to do chilled him. She had made her wishes clear last night. She wanted nothing to do with him, wanted nothing to come of them. He couldn't keep making love to her knowing that she'd take off for the States in three days and he'd never see or touch or talk to her again. It was too hard. He let go of her robe belt. "I can't do this. What even is this?"

"I'm not ready to say goodbye."

His aching brain protested as he shook his head. "I'm not going to drag this out for three more days. You're either in or you're out. I won't go through limbo only to plunge into hell."

She sniffled against the tears that swelled. Her fingers rubbed at her eyes. "I'm scared. I'm a coward and I'm scared."

"I'm terrified too."

"I thought I could work you out of my system these past two weeks."

"Lifetimes won't be enough to work you out of mine."

"I'm sorry. I'm so sorry."

He wiped the tears from her cheeks. "For what?"

"For what I said last night. For wanting to run. I don't want to run."

She tilted up her face, hope edging out trepidation in her red-rimmed eyes. He brought his forehead down to hers, unable to stop stroking the velvet softness of her cheek.

She wasn't running.

They weren't done.

She hadn't told him she loved him, and maybe she no longer did, but he didn't care. He'd do everything in his power to make sure she didn't regret her decision.

"Now can you figure out the rope tie?" she murmured, a dimple popping up in her cheek.

"I'll untie it with my teeth if I have to," he growled, ripping at the loosened knot. He slid her robe down and watched it pool on the ground. Her skin glowed in the muted light of the cellar.

"You're so beautiful," he whispered, drawing a finger down her neck to the dip in her shoulder. Transfixed by the moment, by the sight of her in front of him, by the gentle rise and fall of her breasts as she watched him, he knew he'd regained something rare and precious. Goosebumps rose across her skin.

"Cold? We can go upstairs—"

"No." She shook her head. "Just… *happy*."

He had to swallow twice before he could trust his voice not to crack. Even then, it caught as he spoke. "I'm happy too."

"Why am I the only one naked?"

He glanced down at last night's shirt and suit pants he still wore. He had no idea where he'd left the bow tie or suit jacket. "Good question."

The buttons pinged across the marble floor as he tore his shirt open. Evie gasped in delight. Her cool hands traced his ribcage before slipping to his belt, finding the buckle. "It's like opening up a Christmas gift," she said, glancing up at him with glowing eyes.

He swooped down to catch her smile with his mouth. A large part of him still didn't believe this was real, that she was here in front of him. He briefly contemplated pinching himself just to make sure he wasn't dreaming. But then her cool hands released his ready erection, and he knew this was real.

She stroked him once, twice—

He pulled her to the nearest surface he could find. The sturdy, solid wood side table was lined with wine glasses of all shapes and colors. With one swoop of his elbow, he shoved the array to the ground. They shattered against the floor, shards scattering. She gasped. Good. He reveled in surprising her.

"Oof," she said, rubbing at her calf.

"Shit. You hurt?"

"No, but I felt some of the glass against my leg."

He hadn't anticipated that. He had wanted to lift her to the table and take her right there, but he didn't want either one of them cut by the glass.

"That didn't go how I envisioned it," he said, rueful.

She laughed. He could listen to the sound of her laughter on repeat. "It was really sexy though, the way you swiped all the glasses off."

"We better take this upstairs."

"Did we wake your brothers?"

He paused and listened. No footsteps above them. "Don't think so."

Before she could respond, he scooped her up in his arms and hurried up the stairs, out of the cellar, and to his room. Once inside, he laid her against the linens of his bed. She belonged here.

"You sure you didn't get nicked?" he asked, skimming his hand down her calf.

"Positive. You?"

"Got thick skin."

"You have thick other parts too," she murmured, curling her hands around him.

He skimmed his mouth along her jaw, sank his teeth into her lower lip. He could kiss her forever and never get tired of the taste and texture of her, of the sounds she made low in her throat when she wanted more.

Her fingernails traced along his skin to tug impatiently at his hair. "Hurry."

He pulled back, waited for her to lift her lashes, to look at him. Her gaze was soft as it refocused on him, mirroring the wonder in his. He entered her slowly, reveling in the emotions that suffused her features.

When he was fully seated, she wrapped her legs higher around him and moaned softly into his ear. "More."

He took her slowly, wishing to catalog every gasp, every stroke, every moment. She felt like home. Like happiness. Like peace. The only life he had ever wanted, the only future, was here in his arms.

I love you. I love you. His jaw hurt from keeping the words locked tightly inside. She had heard them once, and she ran. She wasn't ready to hear them again. He showed her instead, making love to her with all the hope coursing through his body.

He knew she was close, her muscles clasping around him as her gasps grew louder. She tensed under him, mouth gasping for air as she came. Her orgasm triggered his, and he exploded in a blinding release that left him lightheaded, in awe of the emotions only Evie could elicit. His limbs went numb from the pleasure, pins and needles coursing as he readjusted their position so she lay curled into him.

She nuzzled closer under his chin, her voice a breathy whisper. "I don't think I want to move ever again."

He squeezed his eyes against the sudden realization. "We didn't use protection."

He braced himself for her panic and anger, but instead she exhaled, relaxing into his body. "It's okay. I trust you."

He peered down at her. "You're not panicking?"

Her eyes were earnest as they met his. "No."

I love you. He set his molars firmly together to keep the declaration inside. "Me neither," he offered instead.

She kissed him gently on the lips before snuggling closer. Sleep claimed him.

Chapter 30

The incessant ringing of Jackson's phone jerked Evie awake. Prostrate on his stomach, he didn't seem to hear it. Exhaustion from the sleepless night had pulled them both under. As soon as she'd pressed herself up against him, every muscle in his body had relaxed. He had slept instantly, and she quickly followed.

I'll silence his phone, give him a few more minutes of sleep.

As she climbed out of bed and padded across the room to his phone, he stirred. His voice sounded sleep-slurred as he tried to track her movements. "What is it?"

Evie glanced down at the name reflected on his screen. "Noémie is calling you." She retraced her steps back to the bed to hand him the phone.

"Hey, Noémie," he said in a sleep-deepened voice. He sat up. "What? That's ridiculous—where the fuck is she?"

Dread flooded her. She sat next to him on the bed. "What is it?"

He looked grim as he responded, "Georgia is accusing me of assault."

"What?!"

"She said I assaulted her at the Zohra Cannes party."

"You didn't! You were with me the entire time!"

"I know that. She knows that. No one else does."

"That's insane!"

"I need to call my attorney," Jackson sighed. "Noémie, I'll call you later. Where's Richard? No. Tell him no statements. I refuse to implicate Evie in any of this."

Dismay gathered in the pit of Evie's stomach like lead sinkers. She held a profound belief in the need to believe women, but Georgia was clearly lying. She and Jackson had been inseparable at Zohra for the brief moment they were there. They had left soon after they'd arrived. Although they had snuck out the back way, the security guard stationed at the back entrance had seen them leave.

Jackson pulled up the text messages that began to beep into his phone.

Article after article from Noémie:

JACKSON AUCLAIR, SON OF VALENTIN AUCLAIR AND OWNER OF SEX CLUB CHAIN ZOHRA, ACCUSED OF SEXUAL ASSAULT BY CLUB MEMBER

GEORGIA CARLTON'S HUSBAND BREAKS SILENCE ON ALLEGED ASSAULT AGAINST PREGNANT WIFE BY SEX CLUB OWNER JACKSON AUCLAIR

A BREAKDOWN OF ALLEGATIONS AGAINST SEX CLUB CHAIN FOUNDER JACKSON AUCLAIR

QUESTIONS SWIRL AROUND SEX CLUB OWNER JACKSON AUCLAIR'S WHEREABOUTS AMID SHOCKING ASSAULT ALLEGATIONS

WHAT TO KNOW ABOUT JACKSON AUCLAIR SEX CLUB OWNER ACCUSED OF ASSAULT BY PREGNANT WOMAN

Evie scanned the headlines with him. "You didn't do this. You were with me the entire time. I'm a witness! The security guard saw us leave. You have cameras covering every angle of the outside of that building. You can prove that we were there only briefly—and that we came and left together!"

"Out of the question. No one can know you were at Zohra. I won't drag your reputation through the mud. It will destroy your career."

"This is a serious accusation. And I can prove that it's false!"

"Do you want people to know you were at a sex club with me?"

Tears filled her eyes. "We have to do something! You didn't do anything. You were with me."

Jackson stood from the bed to grab fresh clothes. "I promised you that you'd be safe and protected with me at Zohra. I won't break my promise. I have to call my lawyers and grab Nate. I'll see you later." He was already dialing.

Evie dressed in her room before returning to Jackson's, but he was no longer there. She assumed he was with his brothers somewhere in the house.

Evie needed to stop these malicious and false accusations. She had to speak to Georgia, woman to woman. Maybe she could make her see reason. She didn't have a phone number for Georgia, but maybe Noémie did. Reaching for her phone, she dialed.

Noémie picked up on the first ring. Evie didn't have time for pleasantries. "I need a phone number or address for Georgia."

"That's not a good idea," came the quick response.

"I have to talk to her."

"That won't accomplish anything. She blew a fuse."

"But Jackson didn't do anything! We were barely at the party."

"Anyone who'd accuse Jackson of that is unhinged. Stay far away from her."

"Just give me her phone number. That's all I need. Let me at least call her."

"Jackson would kill me."

"We can't let this continue. Please, Noémie?"

Silence stretched as Noémie considered. "You promise you won't go seek her out?"

"I promise. I just want to talk to her. I can't let Jackson be accused of something he didn't do."

Noémie released a long breath. "I'll text it to you. But be careful, Evie. That woman is demented and has all the money at her disposal. A bad combination."

As soon as Noémie texted her Georgia's cell phone number, Evie called her. She hoped reasoning with Georgia would help, because Jackson was right—she couldn't be a witness. Her young adult books would stop selling. She wouldn't be able to pay Joy's medical school bills. Her parents' reputation would be in tatters. The entire family would be destroyed were it to come out that she was at a sex club party making love with the sex club owner. She couldn't do that to her family. They depended on her and on the sales of her books. She couldn't chance it.

But she could talk to Georgia. Woman to woman.

Georgia didn't pick up.

Darn it. Evie sent a short text asking for a few minutes to speak instead.

"What's going on?" Her dad's voice echoed through the home.

She hurried toward the sound. Both sets of parents, and Alain, looked bewildered as she met them in the foyer.

"What's happening, Evie?" asked her mom. "It's insanity outside. There are camera crews and photographers and they've pretty much blocked the entire road. We barely made it inside."

"A lot's happening. I don't even know where to begin," said Evie.

"I'm booking you all a flight back to the States." Evie spun around at Jackson's statement. He strode toward them from the library, his face set. His brothers followed behind him.

Evie shook her head. "I'm not leaving you."

He stopped in front of her, his fingers curling around her shoulders. "You can't be around this. I'm not dragging you into the muck with me."

"I don't care. I stay."

"It's not a good idea, Evie," said Hayes. "Go back to California. Far away from all this."

Nate jumped in. "If this runs over, it will affect you. Better to have you as far away from here as possible."

"What are we missing?" asked Rose, crossing her arms. "One of you better begin explaining right now."

Evie couldn't find the right words. Jackson ripped the bandage off quick. "Today, you'll find out that I've been accused of assault."

"That can't be true!"

"That's absurd!"

"You wouldn't do that!"

"That's a false allegation!"

A sense of relief at their parents' reactions flooded Evie. Their outraged responses spoke volumes. She half expected the Icefalls to accept, and believe, the accusation. Yet they proved her otherwise. Maybe they weren't so terrible after all.

"What are you saying? Who accused you?" asked Leonard.

"A Zohra member. I didn't do it."

"Of course you didn't," said Lisa.

"But she did go to the press. That's why all the commotion outside," Jackson explained.

"What can we do?" asked Rose.

"We've gotten to know you a bit the last two weeks. We know you couldn't have done this. Tell us what we can do to help and we'll do it," added Michael.

"Nate?" Lisa turned to her lawyer son. "Do you have advice?"

Before Nate could respond, Evie spoke up. "I'm a witness to Jackson not doing anything. We were together the entire time."

"I'm not involving you in this," Jackson declared. "End of discussion."

"No end of discussion. Whether you like it or not, I am involved. And I won't sit back and let her do this to you."

"You want to blow up your career?"

Yes. Yes, I would. The realization hit her instantly, as clear as morning. She'd sacrifice her career—heck, she'd sacrifice her life—for him. "If that's what it takes, yes."

Jackson shook his head. "You worked too hard to be where you are. We'll find another way."

"I feel like we are missing a huge puzzle piece here. Tell us what happened exactly," said Rose.

Evie hesitated.

Ten years ago, Jackson had wanted to tell her parents

everything. That they were in love, married, expecting a baby. Evie had flat-out refused, terrified of their possible reaction. She had cared too much about what people thought of her then. It had almost cost her Jackson. She'd never make that mistake again.

She had kept a gigantic part of her life—a marriage, a miscarriage—hidden from her family. It was time to tell her parents, and the Icefalls, everything.

Her hand shook as she waved the group over to the cream couches that faced each other by the windows. Alain must have recognized the sensitivity of the topic. He took the moment to slip out toward the kitchen. Jackson's brothers joined his retreat.

The words didn't come easy, but she told their parents everything one word at a time. She started at the beginning—how she and Jackson had met ten years ago, had gotten married and pregnant, how the car accident near Monaco had caused her to have a miscarriage, how she and Jackson hadn't seen each other since their divorce. She skipped over the sex tape that led to their two-week deal. Instead, she told them how their reconnecting made them realize that they still had feelings for one another. She even told them about last night—how she was at Zohra with Jackson for the Cannes party, but how they were together the entire time until he got a call about his father having a heart attack, which luckily turned out to be a panic attack, but Valentin's emergency had caused them to leave early and race to the hospital.

Jackson sat silently next to her as she spoke, his palm warm and reassuring on her knee. He knew that she was the one that had to get the words out, and he didn't interrupt.

Their parents looked shell-shocked when she finished. Leonard opened his mouth, then closed it.

"Oh, Evie," her mom sighed. "You two went through so much together, and we didn't know." Her voice remained soft as she continued. "Why didn't you tell us any of this earlier?"

"I've always been terrified of setting a bad example, of being less than the daughter you wanted me to be."

Her mom moved from the couch across from her to sit on Evie's other side. She pulled her into a hug. "We put so much pressure on you. We are so sorry. You went through so much, and you suffered it all alone."

"We love you no matter what," added her dad. "I'm sorry that we failed to make that clear to you." He glanced at Jackson. "What can we do to help you get the truth out there?"

"I don't think there's anything to do. I'm not placing your daughter at Zohra. I've already spoken to the club staff. No one is to speak one word of her presence there. As far as anyone knows, there are no witnesses."

Evie grasped his knee. "No. Don't do this. You're sacrificing your whole future."

"It's my call," he said. "Now, if everyone will excuse me, I have another phone call to make."

Evie didn't know where everyone went after that. Leonard mumbled something about calling a buddy in PR in case he might have advice. Her parents and Lisa moved to the other side of the room, where they had a lengthy conversation in hushed tones. She didn't pay much attention, distracted by the gathering text messages from Noémie on her phone. She escaped to her room to call her.

"Did you reach her?" Noémie asked.

"No. I called and sent a text."

"Richard just called me. Jackson is going to hold a press conference at Zohra Cannes in a few hours. He's going to say that he's innocent. That Georgia's allegations are false."

"No one will believe him."

"He told the staff that he'll not only fire anyone who says they saw you with him, he'll ensure that they'll never work again. He's serious about it."

"He'll be destroyed by Georgia's accusations."

"It gets worse. Sebastian Carlton is suing Jackson and Zohra. He's going to try and take every penny and dime."

"He knows that his wife is lying! They're both horrible people. This will ruin Jackson."

"Did you read the articles? That woman goes into pretty graphic detail."

"Why would I read lies?"

"She includes a play by play. Says it happened just after midnight, he lured her to a private room, she tried to leave…"

Evie's fingers tightened on her phone. *Midnight? They were nowhere near Zohra at midnight.* "Oh my God," Evie breathed out in relief. "She included a time?"

"Yes. And she posted a very detailed story to all her social media accounts."

"Did she mention midnight there too?"

"Several times."

"Noémie, can you get me a good translator to meet me at Zohra Cannes?"

"Absolutely. I'll call you back in ten."

Jackson worked too damn hard in life to lose it all now.

She reached for her phone again. She had a few calls to make. The first, to her sister. Joy deserved to know she might need to get a job or take out a student loan to pay her tuition. The other calls were to her agent and her editor. Shit was about to hit the fan, and they needed to know. Maybe they would have some sort of contingency in place. In the very least, she owed it to them to warn them.

Evie wouldn't let the Carltons win without a fight.

Chapter 31

The press conference was about to start. Jackson felt strangely numb. He had worked hard to get where he did, and just like that, one stupid affair years ago had ended it all. He got his comeuppance. He accepted it. If he had never slept with Georgia all those years ago, she'd never have lied about the assault.

Evie should be on a flight back to California by now. He had asked Alain to take her and her parents to the airport before he headed to Cannes. At least he had been able to protect her. She would remain unscathed by the accusations against him.

Surprisingly, his mom and Leonard had refused to leave. They went with him and his brothers to Cannes—Hayes took them in Valentin's other car, driving behind Jackson, Nate, and Oliver caravan-style. They now sat with Valentin in Richard's office as reporters gathered in the atrium.

Jackson had refused to let Valentin join him at first. The man had just had a panic attack; he needed to rest. But there was no stopping his father. When Jackson arrived at Zohra with his brothers, mom, and Leonard, Valentin was already waiting for them inside.

The buzz from the gaggle of reporters grew louder. He'd need to step out there soon and provide his own account of what happened. The whole situation seemed surreal. Just that morning, he had held Evie in his arms. Now, a cold and lonely future loomed ahead of him.

When he was sixteen, Valentin had taken him to visit San Francisco for summer break. They had booked a tour of Alcatraz Prison, a former maximum security federal penitentiary located on a small island just over a mile from San Francisco. Jackson and his dad had walked along the empty jail cells listening to an audio guide. He remembered the story that one inmate had narrated, speaking of New Year's celebrations out in San Francisco. Lying in his cell, he would hear laughter and music from the yacht club just across the water—everything he ever wanted was so close to him, but forever out of reach. That's how Jackson felt now.

Evie and the life he'd planned with her was once within his grasp. Now, it was no longer a reality. This scandal would always follow him. Accusations of assault by a pregnant woman, even without proof, were impossible to shake. He wouldn't besmirch Evie with the cloud of suspicion that would continue to linger around him. At least they had spent these last two weeks together. He'd always remember them. It would be the last time he'd been happy and whole.

She deserved better than him anyway. His bad judgment had almost derailed her future. He'd never let that happen again. As he stepped out into the atrium, the reporters quieted. He crossed to the tangle of microphones that the various news outlets had set up against one side of the atrium. Daylight streamed from the skylights above, a stark contrast to the gloom that settled inside of him. At least he had a chance to speak the truth. It was all that was left to do.

"Wait!"

He recognized Evie's voice, but what the hell was she doing here? She, and her parents, were on their way back to the States. He turned to see Evie hurry toward him from behind a marble column. Richard walked alongside her. The traitor must have let her in through the back. Her parents followed, but they stopped when they saw the reporters and the cameras gathered inside. Evie kept walking, accompanied by some woman he didn't know.

"What are you doing here?" he demanded as she joined him at the microphones.

"I'm going to tell everyone what really happened last night. This is Louise. She'll help translate."

Evie turned and faced the press. "Hi, everyone," she said, terrified. A thorough introvert, she didn't like public speaking and certainly wasn't used to it in her career. But this was important. She had to get the words out.

Her vocal chords shook slightly as she continued. "I'm Evelyn Campbell, author of the Alvin Alby book series." She paused while Louise translated. A deep breath helped center her. As she began to speak again, her voice steadied. "I'm here to assure you that the accusations against Jackson Auclair are false. I know that they are false because I was with him at the Zohra event last night. I was with him the entire time." She paused for Louise to translate before continuing.

"I read the articles that have been written about what happened, and I listened to Georgia's account on her social media channels. Georgia Carlton is lying. And I can prove it. She said the assault happened after midnight. Well, what Georgia never realized, because no one did, is that Jackson wasn't at Zohra after midnight. He left Zohra before nine o'clock yesterday. There are cameras set along the outside perimeter of Zohra to protect its members. They'll show you that Jackson and I left before nine p.m.

"His dad was hospitalized in Monte Carlo, so that's where Jackson and I went. The hospital attendants can confirm that we arrived at ten. I was with Jackson the entire time.

"Jackson and I were together the entire night. I was with him at Zohra, we were upstairs in a private room, and we left from that room down the back stairs to his car. We then drove to Monte Carlo to be with his father.

"The reason I'm here today is to clear Jackson's name, and to share my disgust with Georgia Carlton's lies. Sexual assault happens every sixty-eight seconds in America. I can't even fathom the number when you count the entire world. I don't have the exact figures for France, I'm sorry. I did try to look, but I do know that cases of sexual abuse are growing significantly from year to year here as well.

"The problem is real, but Georgia Carlton was never assaulted by Jackson Auclair. Her false accusations are hurting every single victim here in France, in the United States, and in the world.

"I've asked the manager of Zohra Cannes to share footage with you of me leaving with Jackson four hours before Georgia said he'd assaulted her.

"Jackson and I remained in Monte Carlo until the following morning. Our hotel can provide you with proof of that.

"I'll take your questions next, but I wanted to say one more thing, this one to everyone who buys my books. It's the truth I want everyone to know. You see, Jackson and I were married a long time ago. I never shared that with anyone before, because we were so young when it happened. My parents just found out a few hours ago, so it's a secret that I've held close to my heart for many years. If you stop buying my books for your children and grandchildren, I understand. I was scared of others' opinions for so long—I was focused on my reputation for so long—and I've let that fear destroy too much. I won't do that again. Jackson is a good person, and I'm proud to stand by his side during these false accusations.

"Jackson Auclair's club has more rules around consent and safety than even most nightclubs do. He cares about the safety of Zohra members.

"He never assaulted Georgia. His only mistake was sleeping with her once—years ago—after he and I got divorced, but I guess we're all allowed a few errors in judgment."

The chuckle that worked its way through the group caught Evie off-guard, but she continued.

"I also want to add that it's outrageous that Sebastian Carlton is capitalizing on his wife's lies to sue an innocent man. If I were someone doing business with Sebastian, I'd reconsider. If he's lying about this, what else is he lying about?

"Now you have the facts. You can get copies of the security footage from Richard. Do you have any questions? For me or Jackson?"

They had a lot of questions. They volleyed them at her like tennis players on crack. Evie and Jackson answered them all, taking turns to elaborate further.

Evie was mid-sentence when a sudden ripple ran through the crowd of reporters as they reached for their phones. A few exchanged glances. Several raised their hands.

Evie nodded to a female journalist to her right. "Yes?"

"Is it true that Valentin Auclair and his girlfriend are expecting a baby?"

"Ummm…" Evie hesitated.

"That would be for my father to answer," said Jackson.

"Luckily, he is here to answer that question," came Valentin's voice. He joined them at the microphones. "Yes. It is true. I'm expecting a baby with my girlfriend. And, you heard it here first, I'm going to propose to her tonight."

The questions exploded.

Evie and Jackson stepped back as Valentin worked the crowd.

What seemed like decades later, the press conference ended. The reporters gathered their equipment and left, leaving a deafening silence in their wake.

Evie went directly to Valentin and hugged his solid frame. "You always come to our rescue, Valentin. You didn't have to tell them that though. I can only imagine the chaos that'll follow you now that they know about the baby and impending engagement."

"I called my publicist earlier today. Told her to leak it. Now, that's catnip to these tabloids. A fake accusation from a miffed ex-lover? A brief flash of spice, but it burns out quickly without proof. Your statement today and the security footage from Zohra and the hotel would have shut that story down quickly enough. I just helped speed it along a bit." Valentin glanced at Evie's parents, who hovered close. "You must be the Campbells. We finally meet! It's never boring with these kids, is it?" He went to greet his son's former in-laws.

Evie turned to Jackson. She tugged on his tie. "And I heard about your threat. You can't fire Richard or Noémie. They did a lot to help clear your name."

"Deal. But you realize that you just threw away your entire writing career for me?"

"I don't care about my writing career. I don't care what people think or say. I love you. I've loved you the last ten years, and I refuse to wait a minute longer pretending otherwise."

He kissed her passionately in front of their gathering family. One of his brothers—she wasn't sure which one—whistled.

"I love you," he said against her lips.

"I love you. Always have, always will. Besides, I have a great idea for a romance novel. My agent and publisher are already negotiating the advance. If Alvin Alby is shunned by my readers, which by the way I don't think he will be, I already have a series in mind for my more adult audience. Ones who can appreciate a little passion in an author."

Chapter 32

Richard insisted that everyone stay for lunch at Zohra. Although most of the staff had the day off, the chef was in the kitchen testing new recipes and he commanded that everyone sample his concoctions. Evie, curious about the food Jackson had been raving about, accepted the invitation on everyone's behalf.

"I should actually get going," said Valentin. "I don't want to leave Daniele alone too long. But I look forward to seeing you all again soon."

As everyone else settled around the table, Evie's dad squeezed her shoulder. "I'm so proud of you, Evie, for being honest with us today. I know it took a lot of courage."

"Thanks, Dad."

"You've inspired me to be honest too, Evie," said her mom.

Evie frowned. "Honest about what?"

"I've been nervous to tell you… to tell anyone… but I can't do it anymore. I can't just be a pastor's wife."

Her dad looked like he had misheard. "Rose?"

Evie's mom turned to him. "I love you, honey, you know that. And I love our life together, and our community. But I've been a pastor's wife for so long… it's become an identity for me. I'm not sure I want only that identity. I want more."

"Mom, what are you saying?"

Rose glanced at Lisa, who seemed to hold her breath. Rose closed her eyes. "I want to be an influencer." She spat the words out so quickly, Evie needed an additional moment to process them.

"What's an influencer?" asked Leonard.

"A social media influencer. Like on Instagram," clarified Lisa. "Rose and I have been talking. We have run into a similar wall. We're both home all the time. Cooking, doing laundry. Is that all we get out of life now that all our kids are grown? I want to go back to work."

"What work?" Leonard asked. "You haven't had a job since before Jackson was born."

"I was in marketing before Jackson was born. And I was great at it." She hissed the last sentence at her husband. Modulating her tone, she looked at Evie. "You inspired me too. I want to be honest too. Your mom is going to be an Instagram sensation, and I'm going to be her manager."

"I'm not sure what you two are saying," tried Michael.

Evie's mom searched for her phone. She leaned into the middle of the table to show her screen to the group. "Look. This is my account. Before I came to France, I had two hundred followers. Our church friends. Now I'm at seven thousand! With Lisa's help. It seems there's a market for women our age who have a taste for beautiful, but more conservative, clothes. Everyone's been loving our photos and videos from France. I've even had brands reach out to me. Lisa's screening them first, of course."

"You want to be an Instagram influencer," said Michael, as though he wasn't sure he had heard correctly.

"Not want to be. I am one now. And with Lisa's

marketing acumen, I think we can get to a hundred thousand followers by the end of summer."

"Maybe even sooner," said Lisa.

"Wow! Mom! That's so exciting," said Evie. "I'm very happy for you. It's rare to find a calling. I'm glad that this trip helped. And I'm happy for you too, Lisa. Getting that many followers in two weeks takes skill."

The mothers beamed.

The fathers didn't look so certain.

Finally, her dad smiled. "I'm proud of you, love. I guess I'll have to get an Instagram account now to follow you."

"Do you think any of your parishioners would mind?" asked Rose.

Michael glanced at Evie. "Let's take a page from our daughter's book and not care about what people think so much."

Rose fell into Michael's arms and kissed him on the lips. "Thank you."

He whispered something in her ear that made her blush, and the two kept their arms around each other.

"I guess your new activity comes at a good time, Lisa," said Leonard. "These last two weeks, in talking with Michael… I decided I want to go back to school. Divinity School. I'm going to take a few online courses first, to see if I like it, but it's something I've been wanting to do for years now. And, Michael, I appreciate your support and advice during this trip. I'm going to do it."

"I think that's a marvelous idea," said Lisa. "You've been talking about it for years. I'm glad that you're finally taking the leap."

"I quit my job!" announced Nate. "Being an attorney is not something I want to do for the rest of my life."

Everyone turned to Nate.

"What are you going to do instead?" demanded Leonard.

"I don't know, but I'll figure it out."

"Jackson and I are opening up a nightclub in Vegas," said Hayes.

Oliver reached for his glass of wine. "What a bad time to not have any secrets of my own to dramatically announce."

Chapter 33

They returned to Valentin's mansion after lunch. Exhausted and coming off a tidal wave of adrenaline and cortisol, all Evie wanted to do was lie around the pool and sip champagne. Everyone had the same idea in mind, and they spent a relaxing afternoon at the pool once she and Jackson had swept up the shards of glass in the cellar. Thankfully, no one had questioned how an entire collection of drinkware had fallen off a sturdy-looking table.

By the evening, Valentin's announcement had swept the tabloids like an unexpected snowstorm. A few hit pieces covering Georgia and Sebastian Carlton's shady business practices started to pop up as well, driven by the online backlash at her false accusations. Evie suspected that more thorough articles investigating the Carltons would soon be published as well. They seemed like the kind of people with a lot to hide, and reporters were eager to ferret out their secrets. She chose to not dive too deeply into the coverage. She only had a few days left in France, and she intended to make the most of them.

Not that she'd be saying goodbye to Jackson. He had bought a flight back to California with her. He'd stay with her while he and Hayes officially launched Arlo in Las Vegas. Joy had been enthused at the news. She had already reserved a weekend to drive down to Manhattan Beach from the Bay Area and reunite with her favorite (and only) ex-brother-in-law.

Jackson had disappeared a few hours ago, and Evie hadn't seen him since. As everyone dispersed to their respective rooms for the evening, she approached his door.

"Whatcha up to?" he asked, coming behind her and locking his arms around her waist.

She relaxed against him. "Looking for you. Where'd you come from?"

"I was scouting out something."

"Yeah? What were you scouting out?" she asked, tilting her head to grant him better access to the sensitive spot beneath her ear.

"I'm keeping it a surprise."

She craned her neck to glance at him. "For how long?"

"Mmmm… another few minutes. I'm waiting for Leonard to finally retire to his room."

Evie froze, listening for footsteps. Sure enough, she heard Jackson's stepfather's tread retreat as he headed up the stairs.

Jackson cocked his head for a moment and then pushed her in front of him through his bedroom to the outside.

"Where are we going?" she whispered.

"To the flower garden. I want to make love to you under the stars."

"What if someone sees us out the window?"

"I turned off the outdoor lights, and there's no moon tonight. The perfect opportunity."

He wasn't kidding. The yard was pitch-black. More

familiar with the surroundings than she was, Jackson led the way, holding her hand securely in his.

As they moved further through the garden, Evie's eyes adjusted to the nightfall. She could clearly make out the surprise—a midnight picnic. He had arranged soft-looking blankets on a flat wedge of land amid the flowerboxes and set out iced champagne and strawberries.

Evie sank onto the layers of cashmere and wool and glanced up at the sky. The evening breeze rustled the blossoms around them, surrounding them in a cool fragrance of spring flowers as he joined her. The moonless night revealed a riot of stars high above them. "It's so beautiful out here." Her gaze found his. "I think I'm still in shock," she admitted.

"Same. It's not every day one gets falsely accused by an ex-lover, then exonerated by an ex-wife."

She leaned in and kissed him. "Don't get used to it."

"Never…" he promised, reaching to strip her clothes.

Late the next morning, Evie let Jackson sleep in while she had her espresso by the pool and caught up with Noémie, with whom she had formed a surprisingly close friendship. Noémie had gathered several updates about the Carltons, which Evie couldn't wait to share with Jackson. Realizing the time, Evie promised Noémie that she'd call her back and went to wake up Jackson, but he was no longer in their bed. She found him brushing his teeth in his bathroom.

"Georgia is about to be arrested," she announced.

Jackson spat out a mouthful of paste. "I've called in every favor I had here and in the States to ensure she and Carlton are investigated and prosecuted to the fullest extent of the law, but that was fast. How'd you hear?"

Evie held up her phone. "Noémie. The police spoke with Tilly already. The guy who started the fire at Zohra Paris? Georgia found him at a bar. He told the police *she* is the one that dared him to set the fire. Don't ask me how he agreed. She somehow flirted or seduced him into it."

"I should have known."

"One of the Nice hotel employees confessed that Georgia offered him a small fortune for destroying the camera footage of her—and the room key entry log. Unbelievable. No wonder the cameras and log didn't catch her."

"How does Noémie know all this already?"

"She said she has friends in many places."

"That, I can believe."

"When the police questioned the Carltons, Noémie said that they turned on each other fast, and both ended up confessing. They probably would have never traced Georgia back to my push at the restaurant if Sebastian hadn't told the cops about it—and Georgia fessed up. She had a buddy of hers hire those hookers that she sent to your room. And she hit Tilly on that scooter. When the cops asked her about it, she told them that a tiny scooter like that couldn't have seriously injured Tilly, so it was all in good fun. Can you believe it? Also, the guys who threatened Tilly were Sebastian's pals. And, Georgia paid those kids to steal my purse. Not that I'll get it back. She doesn't even know who they are. She's the one behind all the license issues you've had too. But that's not the worst part."

"What's the worst part?" Jackson asked, setting down his toothbrush.

"Georgia Carlton was born Bethany Lee. In college, Bethany was suspected of setting fire to her boyfriend's dorm room after they had an argument. No one died, but her boyfriend had been seriously hurt—she disappeared soon after that, but her recent accusations thrust her into the spotlight, and someone recognized her. That's the upcoming arrest."

"You're joking."

"Nope. Dead serious. Don't know what she was thinking. Maybe she thought her new nose and new name and fortune would keep her out of past trouble. She was wrong."

"Fuck. I let a criminal join Zohra. She was one of the first members to join, our background checks were crap then. She wouldn't have gotten in now."

"I'm glad she'll be held accountable. Noémie said she has a history of violent behavior and acting out against exes. It seemed to calm down after she married Sebastian, but guess it didn't stay that way."

"Did Sebastian know?"

"I'm going to guess so. Sebastian is a bastard. He apparently wanted to make a quick buck off the lawsuit so he encouraged her. What terrible people. He knew what his wife was up to, and all he did was find a way to make money off it." Seeing his frozen expression, she frowned. "What? Aren't you excited? They both confessed and will be held accountable."

"You and Tilly could have been seriously hurt in all this."

"But we weren't! I really hope the courts mandate therapy for her."

Jackson smirked. "There's not enough therapy in the world. They'll soon be investigated for financial and tax fraud also. I've made sure of it."

Evie smiled. "Good."

"Are you ready to go? We should head out soon. I want to beat the traffic."

She leaned in and pressed a brief kiss to his minty lips. "I'm ready."

As Jackson led her out of the house, Evie couldn't believe she was willingly returning to the site of their accident—the place she had always dreaded and avoided. They made a stop to purchase several packets of local wildflower seeds. The flowers she had seen grow on that hill had given her a jolt of hope, and she wished to make the entire hill bloom with them.

When they approached the familiar curve, Evie tensed, anticipating the familiar stab of pain, but the sharp desolation never came. Her tension ebbed as Jackson pulled over in the by-now-usual spot. Being here today with him, knowing that she could finally let go of the guilt and fear, had seeded a tendril of hope within her too. She and Jackson had wondrously found one another again, and she didn't want to fear this place any longer. She wished to acknowledge the tragedy that took place on this road, to honor the baby they'd lost and the ten years they'd lived without each other by planting the wildflowers.

"You okay?" asked Jackson, tightening his hold on her hand.

"I think so."

They exited the vehicle and approached the mountainside together. When they couldn't get any closer, Jackson tore open a seed packet and handed it to her, then opened another for himself. Together, they sprinkled the seeds across the slope.

It felt startlingly freeing to be back, to be able to mark this twist of road in this way. When they'd drive it next, the wildflowers would be bursting like nature's fireworks, replacing dread with beauty. Just like her reconnection with Jackson had replaced pain with wonder.

Having emptied the contents of all their packets, Evie and Jackson returned to their car.

"I'm glad we did this," she said, tearing her eyes away from the hill to look at Jackson.

His voice was thick when he responded. "Me too."

Chapter 34

Later that night, Jackson picked up his watch from the nightstand to glance at the time. Evie, who lay naked and relaxed against his side, looked at it too.

"It's midnight," he said, setting the watch down. "Our two-week contract has officially ended."

Her eyes danced. "Time flew. What in the world do we do now?"

He couldn't help but tuck her even closer to his body. This was where she belonged. He'd never let her go again. "I have another contract in mind," he said, keeping his tone light.

"Yeah?" She beamed. "So do I."

"Mmm… we should probably negotiate the terms. Since my contract involves forever."

"So does mine."

"Mine involves a diamond ring."

Evie sat up, her face suddenly sad and serious.

Panic rose through him at the change in her demeanor. He sat up too. "Are we not talking about the same thing?"

"You're proposing."

"Yes."

She didn't look exultant. The corners of her lips drooped like that of a Persian cat. "Good. I thought so. Of course I'll marry you again. It's just… I want my ring."

The fear fled. She was worried about a ring? That was infinitely fixable. "The stores are closed for the night, but we can get you any ring you want first thing tomorrow morning."

She shook her head. "No, I want *my* ring. My old ring, the one you gave me ten years ago." She released a heart-wrenching sigh. "I miss that ring so much, I regret ever throwing it at you."

His fingers soothed her back. "It was a little cheap thing. It was barely even a diamond."

"I love that ring. I wish I still had it. I know it's silly to be upset about it now. What's done is done. I can never get it back. It just… feels wrong to replace it…"

"Well then," he said, grinning, "I have some great news for you. I still have it. In my house in Charleston."

Her eyes rounded. "How do you have it? You kept it this whole time?"

"I did. I couldn't part with it, as much as I'd tried."

Evie fell flat against him, her mouth finding his. "I love you so much, Jackson."

"I love you too. You can have the ring as soon as we're back stateside."

Epilogue

Evie and Jackson were married two months later in Coronado, with her father officiating. Valentin and Daniele flew in for the wedding.

Because Jackson and Hayes wanted to be near the site of their new nightclub as it underwent construction, she and Jackson decided to temporarily move to Henderson, a suburb near Las Vegas, into a house a few doors down from Hayes.

Their daughter, Elodie Valentine Auclair, was born a year later, two months before Arlo officially opened on the Las Vegas Strip. The nightclub became a global sensation overnight, establishing the Auclair-Icefall Hospitality Group. Hayes and Jackson were already mapping out a plan to expand into other areas of Vegas as well as into New York City.

The popularity of Evie's Alvin Alby series never dwindled. In fact, the books began to fly off the shelves at breakneck speed even before her press conference concluded. The books' success—and Evie's newfound name recognition—led to a bidding war for the rights to turn the books into a movie series. Evie had also branched out into adult fiction. Her first romance novel was not coming out until spring, but the buzz around it had already started.

Her mom reached 500,000 followers on Instagram and counting. She and Lisa also launched their own YouTube channel. Her dad continued to support his wife, even making an appearance or two in her Insta stories.

Leonard enrolled in a full-time master of divinity program. He moved to the East Coast temporarily to pursue it. Lisa relocated along with him, but she flew back to California often. They had kept their Coronado house, and both sets of parents made frequent trips to Nevada to see their granddaughter.

Valentin and Daniele had a healthy baby boy they named Zacharie. They were all currently on a flight to Nevada for a visit. Evie couldn't wait to see them. She and Jackson had been delighted to learn that they'd stay for a few weeks. They could sightsee around Nevada before she and Jackson officially moved.

As much as she loved their home in Henderson, she was growing tired of the desert heat. She certainly didn't want to spend another pregnancy in it.

To her infinite surprise, four weeks ago, Evie had learned that she was pregnant again. Jackson nearly fell off his chair when she'd told him. Neither one had expected another kid so soon, but Elodie was an easy baby and they welcomed the challenge of adding to their family.

Now that Arlo had grown more established, she and Jackson bought a house in San Diego. Close enough to their parents in Coronado for babysitting, but just far enough away for some privacy. Evie wanted to make the move in the next three months. They seemed to be on schedule.

Neither she nor Jackson much thought about the Carltons. Last Evie heard, they were both now being sued by Tilly and by Sebastian's business partners.

That morning, Jackson had taken Elodie with him while she worked against a writing deadline.

Sitting at the air-conditioned café, Evie felt him before she saw him. *Guess he still has that effect.* Pausing her typing, she lifted her head and watched her husband walk in with Elodie strapped to his front. The baby gurgled and cooed at seeing her.

She shut her computer as they approached.

"Should we head out to the airport? Did they land early?" she asked.

"Not for a couple more hours." Jackson leaned down and brushed her lips with his. "But I thought maybe you and I could make the most of those hours while the baby naps."

She slipped her hand through his. "A difficult offer to resist, Monsieur Auclair."

About the Author

Anya London resides in California. When she's not writing, she enjoys running, hiking, reading, and traveling. She weaves experiences from her travels into her novels. Please contact her at:

https://www.anya-london.com/.

www.ingramcontent.com/pod-product-compliance
Lightning Source LLC
Chambersburg PA
CBHW060430310726
48977CB00001B/123